Praise for
Dangerous Desires

"These are fun, fast-paced reads with just the right amount of tension and romance. Larger-than-life heroes finally find their matches in strong, sassy heroines that love them not for what they are, but for who they are. All three authors captivate and entertain."
—*Romantic Times*

Dangerous Desires

KATHIE DeNOSKY
KRISTI GOLD
LAURA WRIGHT

*M&B™ and M&B™ with the Rose Device
are trademarks of the publisher.
Harlequin Mills & Boon Limited, Eton House,
18-24 Paradise Road,
Richmond, Surrey TW9 1SR*

DANGEROUS DESIRES © by Harlequin Books S.A. 2007

(This anthology was published in the USA as *Taken by Storm*)

The publisher acknowledges the copyright holder of the individual works as follows:

Whirlwind © Kathie DeNosky 2005
Upsurge © Kristi Goldberg 2005
Wildfire © Laura Wright 2005

ISBN: 978 0 263 85837 2

009-0607

*Printed and bound in Spain
by Litografia Rosés S.A., Barcelona*

CONTENTS

Calms appear, when Storms are past;
Love will have his Hour at last...
—John Dryden

WHIRLWIND
Kathie DeNosky

* * *

There are some things you learn
best in calm, and some in storm.
—Willa Cather

I embraced the challenge of writing this novella and learned all that I could about storm chasers and meteorologists. This story blends fact, fiction and a few creative liberties. And although I know more about weather and atmospheric changes now than I ever did, by no means am I an expert on storm chasing or meteorology.

This novella is dedicated to the brave souls who chase these monsters of nature for scientific and photographic purposes. Countless lives have been saved through their heroic efforts to collect research for improving early warning systems.

And a special thanks to talented authors and very dear friends Kristi Gold and Laura Wright for joining me in this anthology.
Let's do it again soon.

CHAPTER ONE

"KACIE, you're not going to like what I'm about to say."

Concentrating on the weather maps and latest forecasts pinned to the bulletin board behind her desk, Kacie Davidson shook her head. "Then don't say it and we'll get along just fine, Darryl."

He hesitated a moment, then added quietly, "I'm not chasing this year."

Kacie whipped her head around so fast the end of her ponytail slapped the side of her cheek. The maps and forecasts forgotten, she stared at the man nervously shifting from one foot to the other in her office doorway. Darryl Newmar looked ready to run at the slightest indication she might try changing his mind.

"You'd better be joking."

Even before he slowly shook his head, his apologetic expression answered her question.

Angered by the fact that he'd waited until they were only three days away from going out into the field to conduct their research, Kacie didn't even try to hide the irritation in her voice. "We've been planning this for the past five months and this is just coming up now?" Her movements jerky, she turned to tidy the stacks of papers on her cluttered desk. If she didn't keep her hands busy, she wasn't entirely certain she wouldn't reach out and strangle him for waiting until the eleventh hour to spring this on her. "When did you make your decision?"

Suddenly taking an inordinate interest in the front of his tie-dyed T-shirt, he seemed to have trouble looking her in the eye. "Last night. But I've been thinking about it for a few days now."

Abandoning the stack of papers, she propped her fists on her hips. "And may I ask what brought you to this conclusion and why you waited to tell me?"

"I wanted to be sure." Finally raising his brown-eyed gaze to meet hers, he raked a hand through his thick copper-red hair. "You have to understand, Kacie. Since our surrogate had the baby last week, Artie and I have both been taking a look at our priorities and making a few adjustments. I'm giving up my position here at the Institute and storm chasing in favor of the meteorologist job at Channel Thirteen." He shrugged one slender shoulder. "Artie's hired another paralegal and will be cutting back on his caseload at the law firm."

Kacie's anger began to cool. She could understand Darryl and his life partner's decision to devote more time to their new daughter. If she had a child, she'd feel the same way. But having her chase partner quit at the last minute was really putting her in a bind.

For the past four years, she and Darryl had been chasing storms across Kansas, Oklahoma and the Texas Panhandle to gather important data they hoped would one day lead to earlier detection of the devastating twisters that tore through Tornado Alley each spring. But their boss at the Institute of Weather and Climate Analysis had a real problem with storm chasers going out alone and especially if they were female.

As the last of her irritation receded, she slumped into

her desk chair. "Have you told Hennessy about your decision?"

Darryl shook his head. "I wanted to let you know, first. I figured I owed you that much."

Kacie sighed heavily. "I just wish you'd given me a little more warning about all this—like when you first started thinking about it."

They remained silent for several uncomfortable moments before he spoke again. "If you're able to find another partner by tomorrow morning, we can all go in and face the old man with the news at the same time I turn in my resignation."

A knot began to form in the pit of Kacie's stomach. She knew Darryl had waited to tell her because he'd dreaded her reaction. But by putting off his announcement, he'd all but destroyed her chances of chasing this season.

They both knew the chances were slim that she'd find anyone, or that their boss would approve her choice, on such short notice. Fergus Hennessy was old-school from the top of his bald head to the bottom of his worn-out loafers when it came to women doing fieldwork. The man simply didn't believe the fairer sex, as he called them, had any business racing across the countryside chasing storms. And his procrastination in approving any kind of change to the status quo was legendary. A snail crawled faster than old Gus made decisions.

"Have you heard of anyone here at the Institute in need of a partner?" Kacie asked hopefully. Her only hope would be finding a co-worker who had already been approved by Gus for scientific storm chasing.

When Darryl sadly shook his head, the knot in her stomach tightened.

"Everyone is pretty much set to go."

"What about Finney? I thought I heard him mention that his partner is still recovering from knee surgery."

"He's pairing up with Warren." Darryl looked thoroughly miserable when he added, "I'm really sorry about this, Kacie. I know how important it is for you to carry on Mark's work."

At the mention of her late fiancé's name, a pang of sadness swept through her. Mark Livingston wasn't supposed to have died. He'd been a brilliant young meteorologist destined to discover Mother Nature's violent secrets and use what he learned to save lives. The fact that his own life had been cut short while trying to find a way to save others had been the ultimate irony, and so unfair.

Taking a deep breath to chase away her disappointment and regret, she nodded. "That's why I'm chasing this season, with or without a partner."

"You know Hennessy won't let you do that." Clearly alarmed by the determination in her voice, Darryl took a couple of steps toward her. "He hasn't let anyone go out alone since—"

"Since Mark's death." She glanced at the picture of her and the young man she'd once loved with all her heart, sitting on top of the dingy gray file cabinet. "He's the reason I have to go. I have to make sure that Mark didn't die in vain. He devoted his entire career to finding ways to give people more time to seek shelter, and the scientific data we gather is essential to doing that. I'm going to finish what he started and find a more accurate way to predict which storms are likely to produce tornadoes, even if it kills me."

Darryl quickly closed the gap between them then, firmly gripping her shoulders, forced her to look up at him. "Promise me you won't go if you can't find a partner." When she remained silent, he gave her a little shake. "Dammit, Kacie, give me your word that you won't go if you can't find someone else with the right qualifications to be your partner."

She studied his grave expression. "You're not going to give this up, are you?"

"No way." Taking a deep breath, his voice grew gentle. "Mark was my friend, too, Kacie. I loved him like a brother and there isn't a day goes by that I don't miss him. But we can't put our lives on hold to finish what he started. You and I both know he'd be the first one to tell us that."

"But—"

"It's been four years, honey. It's time to let him go and move on with your life." He smiled. "Now, promise me you won't go out alone."

She gazed up at Darryl's deceptively youthful features for several strained seconds. There was no denying his deep concern or that she'd given up her own research to carry on Mark's. But as long as she continued to pursue Mark's theories and collect storm data, it was as if he wasn't really gone. And after four years, she wasn't sure she even knew how to start living again.

Crossing her fingers, she smiled. "You have my word that I won't do anything stupid."

A STORM WAS BREWING. There wasn't a cloud in the bright blue sky or any other indication that bad weather was on the way, but there was a storm coming just the same. Josh Garrett knew it as surely as he knew his own name. It was too damned hot, too deathly still for mid-May in the Texas Panhandle.

Standing on his front porch, he rolled up the sleeves of his chambray shirt as he gazed out at the southwestern horizon. The heavy, ominous feeling in the air was a harbinger of danger that only a fool would ignore. A fool like he'd been six years ago. The day all hell had broken loose.

As he stared out across the vast expanse of Broken Bow land, a plume of dust in the distance caught his attention. Pulling the wide brim of his Resistol down to shade his eyes, he watched an SUV speeding along the dirt road toward the ranch entrance. Unless he missed his guess, that would be the storm-chasing team from the Institute of Weather and Climate Analysis.

For the past few years, they'd shown up around the same time each spring, usually just ahead of a big storm; always asking to use his private roads to chase violent weather across the prairie. And year after year, he gladly granted them access to every inch of the Broken Bow Ranch in the hope that one day they'd find a way to improve early-warning systems.

When the SUV bumped its way down the dirt lane, then came to a stop in front of the ranch house, Josh waited until the choking cloud of dust the vehicle had kicked up settled before he descended the steps to greet the pair. But to his dismay there was only one occupant in the SUV.

What was the female member of the team doing without her partner?

Kacie Davidson flashed him a smile that robbed him of breath as she got out of the Jeep and closed the driver's door. "Hello, Mr. Garrett."

He swallowed hard, but couldn't seem to get his vocal cords to work. What the hell had gotten into him? Had it been so long since he'd been around a woman that he couldn't even exchange a polite greeting with one?

"Where's—" Josh searched his memory but, for the life of him, he couldn't remember her partner's name "—your sidekick?"

"He decided to stay home this year."

Josh frowned. "Will someone else be joining you?"

"No, it's just me." Looking a bit uncertain, she said, "I suppose you know why I'm here."

He nodded. "Mother Nature's gearing up for another big one."

"Unfortunately, that's the way it looks." As she glanced at the southwestern sky, she tucked her delicate hands into the hip pockets of her well-worn jeans, inadvertently drawing his attention to her shapely backside. "There's a low-pressure system moving this way from the west and the jet stream is pulling moist air up from the Gulf. From all indications, when they meet it's going to produce some really nasty weather that's likely to spawn several tornadoes." Turning back, she looked almost apologetic when she added, "And unless the jet stream changes directions, which would be nothing short of a miracle at this time of year, I'm afraid this area is going to be in the direct line of fire."

Josh forced his attention off her cute little rump and back to what she'd said. He wasn't surprised, nor was he at all happy with what he'd heard. Having a sizable blow headed toward the Broken Bow Ranch was bad enough. It brought back memories of another spring when he'd lost everything that made life worth living. And just knowing that the beautiful scientist would be by herself—a woman alone, racing across his property chasing a Texas twister—was enough to give him an instant ulcer.

Why in the name of Sam Hill would what's-his-name stay home in Albuquerque while his girlfriend chased tornadoes around the Texas Panhandle? Didn't the man care that Kacie might be in danger? And why the hell could Josh remember her name, but not her male partner's?

His gut clenched. It didn't matter what the man's name was, Josh didn't approve of him sending Kacie out alone to chase dangerous weather all over hell's half-acre.

But as irritated at the man as Josh was, God only knew it wasn't his place to condemn another. Not when he'd failed his own woman.

As he stood there trying to find a way to talk Kacie out of conducting her research alone, his housekeeper, Earl Crawshaw chose that moment to walk out onto the porch. "Are you gonna stand there lollygaggin' like a moon-eyed calf or are you gonna ask this little gal in for a bite to eat?" Giving their guest a toothless grin, Earl added, "I got manners, even if Joshua here, don't."

Josh cringed at the use of his given name. The only two people who ever dared call him Joshua had been his mother and in recent years, Earl. And the only reason Josh let the old man get away with it was out of respect for Earl's seventy-plus years.

"Ms. Davidson—"

"Please call me Kacie."

Her smile did strange things to his insides and Josh had to clear his throat to finish the introductions. "Kacie, this is Earl Crawshaw, the orneriest old coot this side of the Mississippi."

"It's nice to meet you, Mr. Crawshaw." Giving Earl a smile that Josh was sure would send the old man into cardiac arrest, she shook her head. "Thank you for the lunch invitation, but please don't worry about me. I'll be fine." Her pretty blue eyes twinkled when she added,

"I have a bag of corn chips and a cooler of soft drinks in my truck."

Josh watched Earl's smile slip and his left eye begin to twitch—a sure sign he was gearing up for one of his lengthy commentaries on the eating habits of the younger generation. To save them all the discomfort of having to listen to it, Josh placed his hand to Kacie's back and hurried her toward the steps.

"What are you doing?" she asked, clearly alarmed by his actions.

"Believe me, you don't want to get Earl started. Once he gets going there's no stopping him," Josh said, careful to keep his voice low. He hustled her up the steps and past the old man. "Just eat a couple of bites and it will spare us both a lot of grief," he added under his breath.

"Was it the mention of the corn chips or soft drinks?" she whispered.

Josh laughed as he opened the front door, then stepped back for her to enter the foyer. "Both."

Following her into the house, he gulped in some much needed air as he hung his hat on a hook beside the door. When she'd preceded him up the steps, he'd noticed the gentle sway of her shapely hips and how a small worn place in the seat of her jeans gave him a glimpse of the creamy skin where her cute little bottom met the top of her long, slender leg.

He swallowed around the cotton coating his throat. Since when did the sight of a little female skin and the edge of a pair of red panties leave him feeling like the air had been sucked from the room?

By no stretch of the imagination would he be considered a player. But he hadn't exactly been a monk since his wife died, either. He tried to think back. When was the last time he'd had sex? Had it been six months or a year?

Well, hell. It had been so long, he couldn't remember the last time he'd been with a woman. No wonder he was ogling Kacie as if he'd like to make her his next meal. A man of thirty-four had needs and he'd apparently been neglecting his.

But he shrugged it off and focused his gaze on her dark ponytail as they crossed the unfurnished great room of his big two-story house. Physical relief was just one of many things he hadn't paid much attention to over the past six years.

Once they entered the kitchen, Josh remembered enough of his manners to hold the chair for Kacie, then seated himself on the opposite side of the table. As he watched her reach for the glass of iced tea in front of her, he wondered for the second time why old what's-his-name would stay at home while his pretty girlfriend placed herself in the path of a potentially deadly storm system.

"Eat up," Earl said, breaking into Josh's disturbing thoughts. The old man plunked heaping plates full of chicken-fried steak with red-eye gravy, fried potato wedges and sourdough biscuits in front of them. "There's plenty more where that came from."

When Earl moved away to take a pie from the oven, Josh asked, "How long do you think it will be before the storm hits?"

"Probably late tonight or early tomorrow morning." She took a sip of the cold tea then, placing the glass on the table, shook her head. "And I'm afraid that won't be the end of it. There's another front behind this one and another one behind that."

He cut off a piece of steak and put it into his mouth,

but the normally mouthwatering beef had no taste—he might as well have been chewing on one of his own boots. "In other words, we're going to be hammered by storms for the next week."

"It looks like it." She poked at the potatoes on her plate with her fork. "I haven't seen this kind of back-to-back activity for quite some time."

The more Josh heard, the less he liked it. Kacie's description of the storm systems sounded a lot like the dangerous weather they'd experienced the year his wife had been killed.

His stomach churning like a cement mixer, he gave up all pretense of eating and sat back in his chair. "And you're going to be right in the middle of the action doing your research?"

"That's the plan."

"Alone?"

"Darryl didn't make the decision to stop chasing until a few days before we were scheduled to leave and I couldn't find another partner." She gave Josh a smile that sent a streak of awareness zinging from the top of his head to the soles of his size-fourteen boots. "I know that he's the one you've dealt with in the past about the use of your roads, but I was hoping you'd give me the same access."

Josh was between a rock and a hard place. His gut told him to point out that it was too dangerous for her to be out chasing storms by herself, deny her the use of his property and send her back to Albuquerque where she'd be relatively safe from the violent weather. Unfortunately, he knew beyond a shadow of doubt that his refusal wouldn't stop her. She'd just stick to the public roads or find another, less concerned rancher to grant her request. Either way, she'd still be out there alone.

Taking a deep breath, he came to a decision that he was sure she wouldn't like and one that he wasn't altogether certain he was comfortable with. But that couldn't be helped. There was no way in hell he was going to let Kacie Davidson chase storms alone.

"I'll grant you the use of my roads…"

"Thank you."

"…on one condition."

Her hopeful expression turned guarded as she sliced a piece of steak and started to take a bite. "Condition?"

He nodded. "You have to agree to take me with you as your chase partner."

CHAPTER TWO

WITH A PIECE of steak halfway to her mouth, Kacie froze. She couldn't believe what she was hearing. The sexy-as-sin rancher was insisting that she had to take him with her before he'd let her use his roads?

"Excuse me?"

"Before I grant you access to my property you have to agree to take me along as your storm-chasing partner," he repeated calmly.

The delicious meal forgotten, she slowly lowered her fork to her plate as she studied his determined expression. She'd always encouraged Darryl to deal with Josh Garrett for several reasons. Darryl was outgoing and possessed the gift of gab. She and her co-workers at the IWCA had even joked that if he set his mind to it, Darryl could carry on a conversation with a marble statue and get it to respond.

But the real, most relevant reason that Kacie had insisted on Darryl making the arrangements to use the private roads crisscrossing Garrett's vast acreage had nothing to do with his negotiating skills and everything to do with her comfort zone. Josh Garrett was more raw virility than any man had a right to be and had always made her feel edgy and unsettled in his presence.

In fact, when she'd discovered that Darryl wasn't going to accompany her this season, she'd seriously debated limiting her chases to the public highways, rather than ask permission to use the Broken Bow's roads. But the truth of the matter was, the ranch covered such a vast area—stretching into the corners of three different counties—that it would seriously hamper her efforts if she were unable to take the shortcuts across the property.

"Could I ask your reasons for this new stipulation, Mr. Garrett?"

"The name's Josh."

"Okay…Josh." Saying his name sent a little quiver of awareness skipping through her. She did her best to ignore it.

First and foremost on her mind was the fact that Josh had never before withheld his permission for her and Darryl to conduct their research on the ranch. Of course, that had been when she was working on behalf of the IWCA and part of an official team. But as far as she knew Josh was unaware that she was acting on her own and presently on leave from the Institute. In fact, not even Darryl knew what she was up to.

"Is there a reason why you want to accompany me while I conduct my research?"

When his hazel eyes met hers, a tingling sensation skipped over every nerve in her body and she had to concentrate on what he was saying. "I can't, in good conscience, let you go alone." He shook his head. "It's too dangerous."

Kacie frowned as she fought the irritation building inside her. It was the same old tune, just a different singer. Only this time, instead of her boss and Darryl trying to hamper her effort to carry out her plan, it was Josh Garrett.

Why did men think that women needed their

presence to be safe, no matter what the situation? She was a trained scientist, used to dealing with the dangers that went along with collecting data in the field. What did he think he could do that she couldn't?

Gritting her teeth, she forced a smile. "Let me assure you…Josh, I'll be perfectly fine on my own. I'm a seasoned storm chaser with four years of fieldwork under my belt. And I've never been one to take unnecessary chances."

His smile was just as determined. "That may be, but it won't hurt to have an extra pair of eyes watching for wind shifts. And I'm sure it would make it easier to have help loading and unloading your equipment."

"Joshua's got a point there, gal," the housekeeper said as he walked over to place a dessert plate with a slice of scrumptious-looking peach pie in front of her. His expression thoughtful, he added, "And he could drive while you…" The old man stopped, then giving her a sheepish grin, he shrugged. "While you do, whatever it is you do."

Kacie took a deep breath as she continued to stare at Josh. She couldn't dispute the fact that having a partner made chasing a lot easier. But why did her only volunteer have to be a sexy Texas rancher who should be arrested for the way he filled out his Wranglers?

From the top of his wide-brimmed, black cowboy hat to the soles of his big, booted feet, Josh Garrett was—as one of the IWCA college interns would say—sex on a stick and then some.

Well over six feet tall, he had impossibly wide shoulders, narrow hips and a commanding presence that was as much a part of him as his thick, straight brown hair and striking hazel eyes. And unless she missed her guess, the man didn't have a clue how attractive he was or the effect he had on women.

Kacie's heart suddenly skipped a beat. Since Mark's passing, she hadn't spent much time noticing the attributes of other men. It had been much easier to immerse herself in work and cling to the memory of the man she'd loved rather than face the prospect of once again entering the dating scene and all the hassles that went along with it. But staring at Josh, Kacie realized that, for the first time in four long years, she was not only noticing a man's attributes, she was appreciating them.

Not at all comfortable with her newfound insight, she had to find a way to dissuade him. "Once we get started, a chase could take us all the way up into Oklahoma. You might be away from the ranch for a day or two at a time."

He shook his head. "Not a problem. I have hired men to take care of the stock."

"At times, chasing can be extremely boring."

"I think I can handle it."

His confident grin caused her pulse to race. She had no doubt he could handle just about anything he set his mind to. Thoughts of what that might be sent a tingling sensation throughout her entire body.

"And you're sure you want to do this?" she asked, already knowing the answer.

"Sure do, Kacie." His smile, as he nodded his head, made her feel warm all over, and the sound of her name on his deep baritone caused an interesting flutter in the pit of her stomach.

Unsettled by her reaction and knowing it was futile to debate the issue any further, she nodded as she rose to her feet. She needed to put some distance between them in order to regain her perspective and come to terms with the fact that she'd be spending a lot of time in the close confines of her new truck with one of the sexiest men she'd ever met.

"All right, Josh. I'll take you along. But when you're bored half out of your mind, don't blame me." Turning to Earl, she smiled. "Thank you for lunch, Mr. Crawshaw. It was delicious."

"What's your hurry, gal?" Earl frowned. "You ain't even touched your pie."

"I'm positively stuffed," she lied, edging toward the door. But at Earl's crestfallen look, she added, "If you'll save it for me, I'm sure I'll have room for it when I return this afternoon."

The old gentleman's wrinkled face split into a wide, toothless grin as he reached for the dessert plate. "I'll do that, gal."

"Where are you headed now?" Josh asked, following her across the empty great room.

A tiny shiver slid through her when his arm brushed hers as he reached around her to open the front door. "I…need to find a motel room, then check the latest forecast and the Doppler to track the front moving this way."

When they stepped out onto the porch, he put on the hat he'd retrieved from a hook by the door. "There's no reason for you to stay in a motel." He made a motion over his shoulder with his thumb. "I have an extra bed upstairs and you'll have your own private bathroom."

Kacie tried to pull her scattered thoughts into some semblance of order. With Josh standing so close, it wasn't easy. "That's very nice of you. But I wouldn't think to impose. I'd have to bring my laptop in and tie up your phone lines—possibly for several hours—when I connect to the IWCA and National Weather Service networks and—"

His hand on her shoulder stopped her nervous babbling and sent a streak of heat straight to her mid-section. "Look, Kacie." He pointed to a satellite dish attached to the roof of the house. "I have a high-speed internet connection and a brand-new computer. You can leave your laptop in the truck and it will be ready to go when we take off. Besides, the nearest motel is down in Pampa. That's twenty-five miles away. It would be easier if you're already here when it's time to go out to monitor the storm, instead of having to come back for me."

What he said made sense and would save time. But as practical as his suggestion was, she wasn't sure it would be in her best interest to take him up on the offer.

For one thing, they were really no more than acquaintances. And for another, in less than an hour of being in Josh's presence, she'd been reminded several times that she wasn't just a scientist who chased storms and studied weather patterns. She was a living, breathing woman who hadn't felt the warmth of a man's touch in a very long time. And the apparent awakening of her comatose libido after years of dormancy was going to take some getting used to.

Before she could find a graceful way to decline his invitation without telling him that he could be a serious threat to her peace of mind, he smiled. "Besides, while we're waiting for the front to get here, you're going to have to give me a crash course in storm chasing and what you need me to do."

Hold me like I haven't been held in four years.

Her heart stalled and she had to struggle to draw her next breath. Where had that come from? And what on earth was wrong with her?

More than a little unsettled by it all, Kacie didn't even

think to protest when Josh guided her down the steps and over to her SUV. "Just tell me what you'll need to take inside and I'll carry it for you," he said, sounding so damned reasonable she wanted to scream.

"I...um..." Why couldn't she get her thoughts collected?

When his arm touched hers as he reached to open the SUV's rear door, Kacie knew exactly why she was so distracted. She was on sensory overload. The feel of his solid muscles where he'd lightly brushed her arm, the sight of the sinew flexing beneath the tanned skin of his forearm as he pulled out her small suitcase, and his clean masculine scent sent her pulse into overdrive and made drawing her next breath all but impossible.

"Are you all right?" he asked, concern marring his handsome face.

No.

"I'm fine. Why wouldn't I be?"

He stared at her a moment before his mouth turned up in a wide grin. "No reason that I can think of. No reason at all."

AN HOUR LATER, the hair at the nape of Josh's neck stood straight up as he watched the ominous mass of colors displayed on his computer screen. "Is that what's coming at us?"

"I'm afraid so." Kacie keyed in another command, switching from Doppler radar to a satellite image of the cloud cover. "It appears that the first front is going to produce some severe thunderstorms. But I'm not as concerned about it as the one that's developing behind it. From all indications the second storm system is building into a supercell."

Josh frowned as he pulled up a chair and sat down

beside her to stare at the monitor. He didn't have to be a meteorologist to know they were talking about some serious weather.

"How much time do we have between the first storm and the big one?"

"It's hard to tell." Bringing up another screen with several sets of numbers, she sighed. "I can narrow it down to within a day, but Darryl was the one with an uncanny ability to project a storm's arrival time within a couple of hours."

At the mention of her partner's name, Josh's curiosity got the better of him. "I know it's none of my business, but why did he decide to stay home this year? I would think this is the kind of weather activity that a storm chaser would want to be right in the middle of."

She shrugged one slender shoulder. "After the baby was born, he said his priorities changed. In order to be home with her every night, he resigned his position at the Institute to take a meteorologist job at one of the television stations in Albuquerque."

Josh couldn't believe what he was hearing. "And you'd rather be chasing all over hell's half-acre than staying home with your daughter?"

"My daughter? I don't—" She stared at him a moment, then laughed so hard that tears gathered in her eyes. "You thought Darryl and I are a couple?"

"I assume by your reaction that you're not." Josh had been damned near certain that she and her geeky partner had something going between them. After all, the man had always called her "honey" and wasn't at all hesitant about putting his arm around her. Finding out they were only colleagues wasn't the least bit disappointing.

"We never have been involved." Wiping her eyes,

she shook her head. "Darryl is gay. He's been in a committed relationship with his partner, Artie, since they were in college."

Grinning, Josh shook his head. "I missed that one."

"By a mile," she said, returning his grin.

Before he could stop himself, he asked, "What about you? Is there someone waiting for you back in Albuquerque?"

Her easy smile faded and when her sky-blue gaze met his, he could have kicked himself for bringing up an obviously painful subject. But just when he thought she might take a strip off his hide for being so damned nosy, she slowly shook her head. "There used to be."

Josh knew he should let the matter drop, back off and leave her alone. But the shadows in the depths of her azure eyes reflected a sadness that he knew firsthand.

Without hesitation, he put his arm around her. "How long has it been since you lost him, darlin'?"

She was silent for so long that he didn't think she'd answer him. "It was four years ago last month. Mark worked at the IWCA. He'd chase storms and collect data, then bring his findings back to the lab for me to analyze. He was Darryl's first chase partner. But Darryl was tied up in the lab that day and couldn't get away, so Mark decided to go out alone to take readings on a pulse storm."

"Pulse?"

Nodding, she explained, "It's a thunderstorm that only has a single life cycle, instead of the stages that a more severe storm has. They usually last less than an hour, then dissipate. As a rule, they don't develop into anything because they don't have the cyclic winds to produce a tornado."

"But this one did." Having lost his wife to one of the

deadly storms, Josh knew what Kacie must have gone through.

"It was only an F1, and with Mark's experience it shouldn't have been a threat," she explained. "We'll never know for sure what happened, but he either underestimated how close it was or it was a freak accident." Josh felt a slight tremor run through her before she finished. "The coroner's inquest determined that he suffered head trauma and a broken neck from flying debris."

"I'm sorry, Kacie."

Pulling her to him, he held her close for several minutes, offering her his comfort and silent understanding. But the feel of her soft body against his and her sweet feminine scent soon had awareness coursing through his veins at an alarming rate.

She must have felt the same magnetic pull because she raised her head from his shoulder to give him a questioning look. "Josh?"

Tucking a strand of silky brown hair that had escaped her ponytail behind her ear, he touched her porcelain cheek with his fingertip. "I want to kiss you, Kacie."

As she stared at him, he thought he saw a spark of desire flicker in her wide blue eyes. But just as quickly as it appeared it was gone, leaving him to wonder if he'd only imagined it.

He almost groaned out loud when her attention dropped to his mouth a moment before her tongue darted out to moisten her perfect coral lips. "Kissing probably wouldn't be a good idea."

"Probably not."

"But if it had been, I think I would have liked it," she murmured.

Taking her admission as an invitation, Josh effortlessly lifted her from the desk chair to settle her on his lap. "Let's find out."

Slowly lowering his head, he gave her the chance to call a halt to the kiss. But to his satisfaction, from the first touch, Kacie's mouth was soft and yielding beneath his and very receptive to his exploration.

As he traced her lips with his tongue, nothing would have pleased him more than to taste her sweetness, to test the limits of her response to him. But not wanting to take more than she was willing to give, he did his best to keep things light and friendly.

However, when she raised her arms to circle his shoulders, then leaned into him, Josh's good intentions went right out the window along with his good sense.

Holding her close, he abandoned the casual approach and deepened the kiss to acquaint himself with her tender inner recesses and the sweetness that was uniquely Kacie. Her sigh of acceptance encouraged him, and boldly stroking her tongue with his, he coaxed her into exploring him as well. But with her first tentative touch, fire streaked through his veins and robbed him of the ability to breathe.

Her soft body pressed to the hard contours of his sent hungry heat to the pit of his belly and tightened his groin with a need that left him dizzy. Her small breasts were crushed to his chest, the pebbled tips scoring his skin through the layers of their clothing, assuring him that Kacie was feeling the same magnetic pull.

But an obtrusive wail suddenly invaded the room and effectively brought the kiss to an abrupt and less than satisfying end. At least for Josh.

"What the hell is that?" he growled.

When the alarm on her portable NOAA weather-alert unit went off, Kacie felt as if she'd been doused with ice water. What in God's name had she been thinking? She was here to carry on Mark's work, not make out with the Broken Bow's sexy owner. It appeared that when her libido decided to wake up, it did so with a vengeance.

Embarrassed by her uncharacteristic actions, she quickly reached down to unclip the handheld unit from the waistband of her jeans. Then, unable to meet Josh's curious eyes, she concentrated on listening to the broadcast from the National Weather Service. A severe thunderstorm watch was being issued for the area from afternoon well into the evening. The information wasn't anything she didn't already know, but giving it her full attention was much easier than looking at Josh.

"I need to take a look at the latest Doppler and satellite images." She started to stand up, but his arm around her waist held her firmly in place.

"Kacie, look at me."

"I really need—"

Before she could finish telling him she needed to track the storm system and check the height of the approaching clouds, he placed his index finger under her chin and forced her to face him. "What's the verdict?"

"Verdict?" She couldn't for the life of her figure out what he was talking about.

His slow smile sent tingles racing throughout her body. "You said if me kissing you had been a good idea, you thought you'd like it." He slowly brushed the pad of his thumb over her lower lip. The friction sent a wave of heat straight to her lower belly. "Did you like it, Kacie?"

Her heart skipped several beats. She couldn't in good conscience tell him anything but the truth. "Yes, Josh. I liked it very much. But it won't be happening again."

When he raised one dark brow, she added, "I can't afford the distraction."

Giving her a smile that curled her toes inside her worn tennis shoes, he softly kissed her cheek and whispered close to her ear, "Oh, I'm going to kiss you again, darlin'. And when I do, I promise you that your research will be the last thing on your mind."

Kacie swallowed hard as she gazed into Josh's intense hazel eyes. She had no doubt that he'd do exactly what he'd said. And that was the problem. If he could make her forget what she was doing in just a couple of hours, what would happen in the next few days?

If she had any sense, she'd collect her weather charts, pack up the few items of equipment she'd unloaded from her truck and race back to the safety of her lab at the Institute of Weather and Climate Analysis. But the alarm on her weather-alert unit going off a second time reminded her of the reason she'd come to the Broken Bow Ranch and the job she had to do.

After listening to the latest weather broadcast, when she moved to stand this time, Josh let her go. To keep from looking at him, she busied herself stacking data charts and weather maps while she waited for the latest Doppler and satellite images to come up on the computer screen.

"What do you need me to do?" he asked, rising to his feet.

As she analyzed the latest information from the National Weather Service and IWCA Web sites, she motioned toward the door. "While I figure out which direction this thing is going, I'd suggest that you get ready to hit the road because we have a storm to chase."

CHAPTER THREE

JOSH GLANCED at Kacie, sitting in the passenger seat beside him as he drove her SUV down State Route 70 toward Pampa. He wasn't sure whether she was giving her full attention to the charts on her lap because of the approaching storm or because she wanted to avoid talking to him.

He suspected it was the latter. And if he was right, he was certain he knew why. That kiss had shaken her. For that matter, it had done a real number on him, too.

When he'd taken her in his arms, he'd only meant to offer her comfort, to let her know that he understood the pain she'd suffered from losing a loved one. But he hadn't expected the feel of her soft body against his and her sweet feminine scent to be quite so powerful, so compelling.

In the six years since Marianne's death, he'd kissed several women, but none of them had stirred his blood the way Kacie had or caused him to want them as quickly as he wanted her. His body tightened at the thought and his jeans suddenly felt a couple of sizes too small in the stride.

"When you get to the Roberts County line, pull over. We'll watch the dryline from there," Kacie said, bringing him back to the matter at hand. She scanned the horizon. "That's where I think we'll intercept the activity."

"Dryline?" He'd given Kacie's team access to his land for the past few years, but this was the first time he'd been privy to the weather jargon and technical terms used by a meteorologist.

She nodded. "It's the boundary that separates moist Gulf air from the east and the dry desert air from the west. During the spring storm season it usually runs from north to south and severe storms often develop on the eastern side of it."

Fascinated, Josh peered through the windshield at the white, puffy clouds rising in the distance. As the cloud bank drew closer, he could see that the bottom was growing ominously dark while the tall tops looked like heads of cauliflower.

"Those are tower clouds, aren't they?"

"Yes, and they're the best indication of a severe storm developing." She pushed the record button on the dash-mounted camcorder a moment before she added, "I'd estimate the tops of these clouds are around thirty thousand feet and growing."

The closer the system got, the more activity Josh could see within the angry-looking mass coming at them. From the base of the storm to the top, the clouds were twisted and appeared to be moving in a spiral.

"That's a tornado in the making," he said, thinking out loud.

"From the rotation of the updraft, I'd say that's exactly what it is." She pointed to a side road up ahead. "That looks like a good place to pull over. I'll take a few readings, then we can watch the direction it goes. Hopefully, it will come straight at us."

As he steered her truck to the side of the road and

killed the engine, the wailing sound of the weather radio clipped to Kacie's belt once again sounded the alarm and raised the hair on the back of Josh's neck. He wasn't surprised to hear the broadcaster announce that a tornado warning had been issued. Hell, the damned thing was forming right before his eyes. It was the tone of the alarm that had him feeling as edgy as a green-broke colt in a field full of rattlesnakes. It brought back memories of another time when severe weather had threatened the Panhandle and taken the life of the woman he'd loved.

"Josh?"

"What?"

"Are you all right?" Kacie asked, placing her hand on his forearm.

A streak of heat raced up his arm and spread throughout his chest. "Couldn't be better," he lied.

She frowned as she continued to stare at him. "Are you sure?"

Nodding, he decided a change of subject was in order. He didn't particularly want to explain the events of that fateful day and his role in Marianne's death. "What do you need me to do besides drive and watch the clouds?"

"How good are you at taking pictures?"

He grinned. "If all I have to do is point and shoot, I guess I'm about as good as the next man."

"Good." She handed him a digital camera with a built-in zoom lens, then pointed to a button on the side. "Press this for close-ups. It's self-focusing, so all you'll have to do is keep the camera steady as you take the shot."

"Anything else?"

"Could you please hand me the hygrometer? I'd like

to take a measurement on the relative humidity and dew point."

Staring at an array of handheld instruments attached to the top of the dash, Josh took a chance and handed her a small unit that looked a lot like a walkie-talkie with a digital screen on the front instead of a speaker. "Is this what you wanted?"

"That's it." Her smile sent the heat in his chest straight to the region south of his belt buckle.

As he watched, Kacie got out of the Jeep and walked several yards away to hold the instrument skyward. Even though the approaching storm was still a couple of miles away it made Josh uneasy having her out of the truck.

When she returned, he breathed a little easier. But instead of getting back into the Jeep, she stood between the opened passenger door and the seat to write a set of numbers on one of her charts.

"There's a lot of moisture in the atmosphere," she said, handing the hygrometer back to him.

Chuckling, he attached the instrument back to the top of the dash. "I could have told you that. The air's too heavy and thick for there not to be a lot of water in it." He stared out the windshield at the darkening sky. "It's the perfect recipe for a Texas twister."

"There's a little more to the equation than that," she said dryly. "But it is a good indicator." She pointed to a tan rectangular case on the dash beside the hygrometer. "If you'll hand me the anemometer, I'll get the wind speed and direction and we'll be ready to go."

Her smile did strange things to his insides and, without another word, he did as she requested, then waited until she got back into the SUV to scribble more numbers on her chart before asking, "What now?"

"Now we drive toward the clouds and hopefully get the opportunity to take more measurements just before the storm hits."

Josh waited while she checked the Doppler image on her laptop, then consulted the figures she'd written on her chart. He didn't like the idea of heading directly into the storm when common sense told him they should turn tail and run like hell. But he wisely kept his mouth shut. As long as he was behind the wheel, he had control of how close they got and when to call a halt to the chase. And although Kacie might not agree, he wasn't going to take any unnecessary chances.

"Damn!"

"What?"

She pointed to the darkening sky. "The system is turning east."

He wasn't the least bit unhappy that the storm was moving away from them. But he hated the disappointment in Kacie's voice and the expression on her pretty face. He also knew that her research depended on them getting close enough to gather the data she needed. It was the reason she'd come to the Panhandle, and without it there was no reason for her to stick around. And that was something he definitely wanted her to do.

Starting the Jeep, he put it into gear and steered it back out onto the highway. "There's a road about a half mile from here that runs due east. I doubt that we'll get close enough for you to take more measurements, but there's a ridge where you can take pictures of the storm and observe its movement as it crosses the valley." From a safe distance, he added silently as he turned onto the dirt road.

"Thank you," she said, smiling. "That's better than nothing."

Kacie appreciated Josh's willingness to help, even if his swerving to miss the potholes pitting the dusty lane scared her witless. "SUVs are known to turn over easily at high speeds," she said, reaching out to grip the dash when he narrowly missed a hole big enough to bury a half-grown calf in.

His ear-to-ear grin caused her pulse to race. "Where's your sense of adventure, darlin'?"

She couldn't help but laugh at the absurdity of his teasing question. "I tend to pursue tamer activities."

"Yeah, right." His rich laughter wrapped around her like a warm blanket. "And I'm the king of England."

"It's nice to meet you, Your Highness," she said, holding on for dear life.

But as they raced after the storm, her smile faded when the rapid rotation at the updraft base claimed her full attention. It was the area where a tornado was most likely to drop and as she watched, a ropelike funnel suddenly protruded from the clouds and began snaking its way down to hover over the green fields up ahead.

"Damn," Josh muttered, bringing the Jeep to a sliding halt at the top of a ridge. "I've seen tornadoes aloft and on the ground, but this is the first time I've actually seen one forming."

Quickly checking to make sure the video recorder was still on and positioned correctly, Kacie grabbed her 35-mm camera and, throwing the passenger door open, vaulted from the truck. They were too far west of the vortex to take any significant readings, but the unob-structed view was perfect for taking pictures of the storm's development for later analysis.

"Take some shots with the digital camera," she called to Josh as she began snapping pictures as fast as she could. "Hopefully, you'll get what I miss."

Unfortunately, she'd no sooner issued the instructions than the funnel vanished completely.

"Where did it go?" Josh asked, walking up to stand beside her.

"It'll be back." She pointed to the "wall cloud" in the center of the updraft. "See how it's expanding and contracting?"

"It looks like it's breathing."

She nodded. "It's building strength for an even stronger showing."

She'd no sooner gotten the words out than a large, white cone developed in the center of the massive wall and descended to the ground below. A debris cloud immediately formed at the bottom of the tornado as it ripped up everything in its path.

She started to remind Josh to take pictures, but the look of frustration on his handsome face and the stream of vehement curses coming from his mouth stopped her. "What's wrong?"

He pointed to a small town in the distance. It was in the direct path of the vortex. "Unless it turns, the twister is going to hit Bealville and there isn't a damned thing we can do to warn the people."

Her heart felt as if it came up in her throat as she watched. "Yes, there is."

The tornado was still several miles south of the town. After hurriedly unclipping her cell phone from the waistband of her jeans, she used the speed dial to call the National Weather Service office in Amarillo. Identifying herself, Kacie quickly gave the coordinates of the vortex and stressed that an immediate warning needed to be issued for the tiny town of Bealville.

The photos she'd planned on taking forgotten, she gripped the cell phone and helplessly watched as the tornado bore down on the town with deadly accuracy. "Turn, damn you, turn."

Kacie was vaguely aware of Josh putting his arm around her shoulders and drawing her to his side to shield her from the rain that had started falling. As they silently watched, the storm hit the southern outskirts of the town and immediately tore into several structures. When the debris cloud at the base of the tornado darkened and grew larger, her heart pounded and her stomach twisted so hard that she thought she might be sick.

She could only imagine the havoc it was creating, and the terror. She prayed that the buildings it destroyed were empty and that no lives would be lost. But with such little time for the townspeople to seek shelter, the likelihood of someone being gravely injured was extremely high.

Fortunately, just before the twister reached the center of town, it lifted and as quickly as it had formed, the vortex was sucked up into the wall cloud. Weak with relief that the storm had spared at least part of the town, yet sickened by the powerlessness she'd felt at being unable to do more to warn the people, she sagged against Josh.

"In all the years that I've been chasing, this is the first time I've actually seen a tornado hit something."

"Really?" He sounded surprised.

Nodding, she drew strength from his solid presence. "Since a lot of our research is visual, the best place to observe a storm's development is out in the open, rural areas where there's very little to obstruct our view."

"And very little for a tornado to destroy."

"Exactly. I've seen the aftermath of it having torn through a town, but I've never been an eyewitness to a direct hit." She took a deep breath to steady her nerves. "I just wish there had been more time to get the warning issued."

He kissed the top of her head as they walked back to her truck. "You did all that anyone could have done, darlin'."

His strong arm wrapped around her, holding her securely to his side made her feel safer than she had in years. "I just hope it was enough to keep everyone from being badly injured."

"We'll go down there and see if anyone's hurt and if there's something we can do to help." He brushed his lips over her forehead with a featherlight kiss. "And don't worry, Kacie. One day you will find a way to detect these things earlier."

She appreciated Josh's confidence in her, but scientists had been trying for hundreds of years to predict Mother Nature's tantrums. And although great strides had been made in understanding the atmosphere and how the violent storms developed, there was still a long way to go in perfecting the accuracy of detection.

When they drove into Bealville a short time later, Kacie was relieved to see that as bad as it had looked from the ridge, the damage from the tornado could have been much worse. The roofs of several buildings had been peeled away to reveal the rafters, and an empty boxcar, sitting on a side track, had been pushed over. But other than a large building that looked like it might have been some kind of storage facility being totally destroyed and a few mobile homes being pushed off their foundations, the town had been spared.

"From the amount of damage, I'd say this was an F1 or F2 tornado," she murmured as Josh drove her SUV toward the part of town that had been hit the hardest.

But as they drew closer to the point where the tornado had dissipated, her breath caught and a chill raced up her spine. Across the street from the flattened warehouse sat a school that had been minutes away from dismissing for the day.

Suddenly chilled to the bone, she couldn't seem to stop her teeth from chattering. "W-what would have happened if the v-vortex hadn't lifted? A-all those c-children would have—"

"Don't think about it, Kacie." As his much larger hand covered hers, his voice was gentle but with an underlying firmness that told her it would be useless to argue. "You've had enough storm chasing for one day. We're going back to the Broken Bow."

His presumptuous attitude grated on her already frayed nerves. "No, we're not. There's still a possibility of another cell—"

"I'm not giving you a choice, darlin'." He shook his head as he turned the Jeep onto a highway headed west. "It's not like this is your last chance to do research. You said yourself there's another storm system a day or two behind this one. By the time it gets here, you'll be rested and have everything back in perspective." He grinned. "Besides, as attractive as you are in that wet T-shirt, we need to change clothes before you catch pneumonia and I embarrass the hell out of myself."

Checking the pale pink knit, Kacie gasped at how much the wet fabric revealed. She had no doubt that Josh could see the size, shape and color of her puckered nipples through her thin shirt and lacy bra.

"Maybe you're right," she said, folding her arms over her breasts. "I am pretty chilled."

"I can tell."

"A gentleman wouldn't notice."

"Oh, he'd notice." Josh's deep chuckle sent a wave of goose bumps shimmering over her skin. "He just wouldn't say anything about it."

"So you're telling me you're not a gentleman?"

"I can be as much of a gentleman as the next guy."

His sexy grin heated her all the way to her soul and had her wondering if it wouldn't be in her best interest to give up chasing this season, in favor of hiding away in the lab.

"But there are certain things that will make even the most refined man forget his manners. The sight of a beautiful woman in a wet T-shirt is one of them, darlin'."

Josh thought she was beautiful? How long had it been since she'd had a man tell her that he found her attractive?

Kacie's body tingled with an awareness that she hadn't felt in years and she couldn't have found her voice if her life depended on it. Now she was certain that the wisest thing she could do would be to pack up, bid the sexy rancher farewell and beat a hasty retreat back to Albuquerque as fast as her new SUV could get her there.

But even as the thought materialized, she abandoned it completely. As much of a distraction as Josh posed to her research, she had nothing left to go back to. At least not until her leave of absence from the IWCA was up at the end of June.

When her boss had denied her request to do field-work without a partner, she'd taken a stand and made a choice. She'd traded in her aging Chevy for the Jeep and invested every dime of her savings in scanners, cameras and a variety of digital weather instruments to measure everything from dew points to wind speed.

No, there was no turning back now. She had too much at stake.

Kacie glanced over at Josh as he steered the SUV onto the lane leading up to his ranch house. As tempting as he was, she'd just have to try harder to resist the sexy Texas rancher.

She took a deep breath. Her research and reputation weren't the only things dependent on her keeping her head. Her peace of mind was on the line as well.

CHAPTER FOUR

SEATED ON the porch swing, Josh propped his legs on the rail in front of him, then crossing his booted feet, leaned back to listen to the rhythmic sound of water dripping from the leaves of the live oak trees closest to the house. The rain had stopped a little over an hour ago, but instead of cooling things off, the air had only grown more heavy and thick, making the temperature seem several degrees higher.

As he stared out into the moonless night, he lifted the longneck bottle in his hand to take a swig of cold beer. The feeling that something more ominous was headed their way wasn't just a premonition anymore, it was a promise.

When the back-door screen creaked, he looked up to find Kacie stepping out onto the porch. "Done for the night?" he asked.

Nodding, she walked to the edge of the steps and stared out at the dark. "The second system has temporarily stalled over southeastern New Mexico. Nothing left to do now but wait to see what tomorrow brings."

When she walked over to sit on the swing beside him, he asked, "Would you like something to drink?"

"No, thanks. I just thought I'd get a breath of fresh air before I turn in for the night."

They sat in silence for several minutes before he

asked, "Any chance of this second storm missing us or blowing itself out before it gets here?" He already knew the answer, but he liked listening to her soft voice.

She shook her head. "Unfortunately, it looks like the smaller system behind this one is going to catch up. If that happens, the larger one will feed on it and we'll be looking at a supercell." There was a reluctance in her voice when she added, "And if my calculations are correct, it's going to gain even more strength as it comes up through the Panhandle and hits this moist air."

Deciding he didn't want to discuss something they couldn't do anything about, he asked, "Is your room okay?"

"Yes, thank you. Your home is...beautiful." He could tell from her hesitation that she was curious about the majority of the rooms being completely devoid of furniture, so it came as no small surprise when she asked, "How long have you lived here?"

"About five and a half years."

He laughed out loud when she whipped her head around to stare at him openmouthed. "I take it that decorating hasn't been a high priority?"

"When I first built this place I didn't care what it looked like or how comfortable it was. It was just somewhere to eat, sleep and take a shower." He lifted the longneck and took the last swallow of his beer. "Later, I was too busy culling the herds and starting a new cattle-breeding program to give it much thought."

"Then why did you—" She shook her head. "Never mind."

"Why did I build such a big house?"

"I'm sorry. I didn't mean to pry. It's none of my business."

When she started to rise to her feet, he set the empty

bottle on a small table beside the swing, then caught her hand in his. "It's no big secret. When our house was destroyed by a tornado, I took the insurance money, handed it to a contractor friend of mine and told him I didn't care what size or style, just build me a house."

"Our?"

"My wife and I. We had a house about five miles from here."

He hadn't talked to anyone much about what happened the day Marianne died. At first, it had been too painful. Then, as time went on and the wound of losing his wife healed, it seemed to make people uncomfortable when he talked about it. But having lost someone herself to one of the deadly storms, Josh knew that Kacie would understand.

"When I found her that day, she was floating facedown in a pond about a hundred yards from what was left of the house."

Kacie gasped. "Oh, Josh, I'm so sorry."

He took a deep breath. "I'm not sure if she was inside the house or if she'd been trying to get to the storm cellar when the twister came through."

She gave his hand a gentle squeeze. "You weren't home?"

He shook his head. Time had dulled the pain of his loss, but he still struggled with the guilt of having failed the woman he'd loved. "She asked me to stay home that day, because the forecast called for the possibility of severe weather. But I thought hauling a trailerful of cattle to the stockyards in Amarillo was more important than staying home with a woman who was afraid of a little thunder and lightning."

Disengaging their hands, Kacie gave him a sympathetic hug. "You can't beat yourself up over it, Josh. The

Texas Panhandle is a huge area and the probability of a tornado hitting the exact spot where your home was located had to be a one-in-a-million chance. There was a bigger possibility of it not hitting anything at all."

"I know that's the logical way to look at it." Wrapping his arms around her, he rested his cheek against her silky hair. "But I can't help but wonder if I had done what she wanted that day if it would have made a difference in the outcome."

"I asked myself the same thing when Mark died. I've always wondered if I'd tried to talk him out of going…if—" She stopped to lean back and look at him. "But that's something we'll never know."

As he continued to stare into the bluest eyes he'd ever seen, Josh slowly lowered his head to kiss her satiny cheek. "I'm sorry he died, Kacie. But I'm glad you weren't with him. You might have been lost, too."

He felt a slight tremor course through her a moment before she asked, "Wh-what is this, Josh?"

"I don't know, darlin'." He wasn't going to insult the intelligence of either one of them by pretending that he didn't know what she was referring to. The chemistry between them was undeniable. Kissing his way to the delicate shell of her ear, he added, "All I know is whenever I touch you I want more."

Before she could call him a boneheaded jackass and tell him to leave her the hell alone, he gave in to the need to once again taste the sweetness of her soft lips and lowered his mouth to hers. To his satisfaction, instead of pushing him away, Kacie tightened her arms around him and pressed closer.

When she parted for him, then did a little exploring of her own, her passionate response sent blood surging through his veins and aroused him in ways he could have never imagined. He wanted her with a hunger that was staggering and he knew for certain they were walking a fine line. It wouldn't take much for either of them to throw caution to the wind, cross that line and spend the rest of the night getting to know each other in every sense of the word.

He should stop now before things got out of hand, but instead of breaking the kiss and setting her away from him, Josh moved his hand from her back, down her side, to caress her slender, blue-jean-clad thigh. The thought of the small rip he'd noticed in the denim that afternoon—the one where her sweet little rear met the top of her leg—caused him to groan.

Raising his head, he decided that if they handed out awards for stupidity, he'd be in line for the top honor. Kacie hadn't come to the Broken Bow to be seduced and, as much as he'd like to deny it at that moment, he was a gentleman. Pressing her for more than she was ready to give just wasn't his style.

He closed his eyes and took a deep breath. He was about to go against everything his body was telling him to do, but he couldn't in good conscience take advantage of the situation. "Darlin', I hate to cut the evening short, but there's something that needs my attention."

She looked soft, sweet and more than a little bewildered. "Is it something I can help you with?"

Josh broke out in a sweat at the thought of what she could do to help his current situation. "Yes, as a matter of fact, there is." Groaning, he shook his head to help clear it, then gave her a quick kiss and set her away from him before he had the chance to change his mind. "You can go on upstairs and turn in, while I go freeze my butt off in a cold shower."

STARTLED BY an anguished cry, it took a moment for Kacie to realize that the sounds that had awakened her had been her own. She'd been dreaming about the tornado she and Josh had seen the afternoon before. But in her dream, instead of watching the destructive power of nature's fury from a distance, they'd been running from it.

Sitting up, she pushed her hair away from her face with a trembling hand and looked around the dark bedroom. Her heart pounded hard against her ribs and she had to take several deep breaths to calm herself.

She'd never been one to believe in premonitions or prophetic dreams, but the nightmare had been so vivid, so real. She and Josh had been running to escape the tempest, but it was as if they were moving in slow motion; held back by some unseen force.

Without warning, the bedroom door suddenly crashed back against the wall and Josh came charging into the room like some kind of avenging warrior. With his body backlit by the light from the hall, he looked extremely imposing.

"Kacie, are you all right?"

Her heart stopped, then took off in overdrive as much from the shock of his unexpected entrance as from the sight of his perfectly sculpted male body. Wearing nothing but a pair of white cotton briefs, he looked like an outraged Greek god come down from Olympus to right the wrongs of the world.

"I was doing just fine until you scared the living daylights out of me," she lied, pulling the sheet up to her chin.

Walking over to the night table, he switched on the bedside lamp, then turned to look down at her. His formidable frown clearly stated that he didn't believe her.

"If that's true, then why were you calling my name? And why do you look like you're scared half to death?"

Her cheeks heated with embarrassment. She'd cried out his name? Not good. Not good at all.

"I...had a nightmare."

His deep scowl was instantly replaced with a look of understanding. "About the storm?"

"Yes."

Before she could stop him, Josh sat down on the side of the bed and gathered her to him. "It's all right, Kacie. You're safe here. I promise I won't let anything happen to you."

"I know."

It was absolute insanity, but she'd felt safer in the past several hours than she'd felt in her entire life. And there wasn't a doubt in her mind that Josh would move heaven and earth if he had to, in order to keep her safe.

"Would you like to talk about it?" The gentle, under-standing tone of his voice brought tears to her eyes.

"I'd rather not." She couldn't stop a chill from coursing through her and, without a second thought, Kacie wrapped her arms around his waist and laid her head on his shoulder. "It was too real."

They sat in silence for several minutes before the effects of the dream were replaced with an entirely different kind of tension. Josh's clean masculine scent and the feel of his firm muscles surrounding her with their gentle strength sent a wave of heat from the top of her head all the way to her toes. It felt good to be held by a man, to experience the contrast of his hard maleness pressed to her much softer feminine form.

He tenderly stroked her hair with one hand while he used the other to lightly massage the tension across her shoulders. "You feel good."

"So do you," she whispered, enjoying the feel of his warm, bare skin beneath her palms and against her cheek.

She heard his sharp intake of breath a moment before he leaned back to look down at her. The heat in his hazel eyes stole her breath. He was going to kiss her again and she wasn't going to do a thing to stop him.

Her pulse sped up and her stomach fluttered with anticipation when he started to lower his head. She wanted the warmth of his kiss, and although it could spell disaster for her, she wanted the heat of his touch.

At first he nibbled and coaxed then, tracing her lips with his tongue, he teased her with the promise of a deeper, more satisfying caress. In silent invitation, she parted for him, but instead of deepening the kiss, he continued his tender torment.

Raising her arms, she encircled his neck and tangled her fingers in the hair at the nape of his neck. "Josh, please...kiss me."

His deep chuckle caused her body to tingle to life. "I thought that's what I was doing, darlin'."

"What you're doing...is driving me crazy," she said, unable to stop a frustrated whimper from escaping.

"And how am I doing that?"

"I want you to kiss me, Josh. Really kiss me."

He continued to nibble and tease. "Is it all you can think about?"

"Y-yes." He was driving her wild and he wanted her to think?

"That's all I needed to hear, darlin'," he said, settling his mouth over hers.

Kacie fleetingly remembered him telling her that when he kissed her again, it would be the only thing on her mind. And he'd been right. Earlier, on the porch and now, nothing else seemed to matter.

But when he deepened the kiss, she ceased thinking at all and surrendered herself to the way Josh was making her feel. Her heart raced and every nerve in her body sparked to life when he slipped inside to explore her with a tenderness that left her breathless. His taste, the gentle stroking of his tongue on hers, sent a honeyed warmth flowing through her veins and caused a delicious heaviness to settle in the pit of her belly.

As he coaxed her into exploring him as well, he moved his hands from her back to her sides, then up to the underside of her breasts. Her nipples tightened as she anticipated his touch, but when his large hands covered her, nothing could have prepared her for the exquisite sensations he created with his gentle caress. She felt as if liquid fire raced from every part of her body to form a spiraling coil of need deep inside when he tested her weight and size. But as he grazed the tight nubs through the fabric of her gown, tiny sparkles of light flashed behind her closed eyes and she couldn't stop a moan of sheer pleasure from escaping her lips.

An answering groan rumbled up from deep in his chest a moment before Josh broke the kiss. Shaking his head, he rested his forehand against hers. "I can't believe I'm going to say this. But I think I'd better mosey on back to my own room while I still can, darlin'."

"That would…probably be best," she agreed even as she tightened her arms around him. The feel of his thumbs still chafing her sensitive nipples made rational thought all but impossible and the very last thing she wanted him to do was stop.

"I like holding you."

She traced the ridge of heavy muscles across his wide shoulders. "And I like you holding me," she admitted.

He continued to tease her as he kissed her eyes, her cheeks and the tip of her nose. "Tell me to stop. Tell me to go back to my own room and leave you alone."

"I'm...not sure that I can," she said honestly. "Or that I want to."

"Then we're in real trouble here, darlin'." Unbuttoning the front of her thin cotton gown, he slipped his hand inside to touch her so tenderly it brought tears to her eyes.

"Why do you...say that?" she asked, wondering if that sultry feminine voice was really hers.

"Because I'm not sure I have the strength to be noble and walk away this time." Every cell in her being tingled to life at the feel of his callused palm cupping her, his thumb grazing her puckered flesh as he spoke.

Is that what she wanted? Did she want Josh to go back to his room and leave her with such an incredible longing that she ached from it?

"You're right." Closing her eyes, she shivered from the wave of desire sweeping through every part of her. "We're in big trouble because I don't want you to be a gentleman."

She heard his sharp intake of breath a moment before he asked, "What do you want, Kacie?"

That was a good question. What did she want?

Never in all of her twenty-eight years had she been prone to spontaneity. Even the first time that she and Mark had made love, they'd planned it right down to the last detail as if they were conducting some kind of scientific experiment.

But in Josh's arms she felt liberated and impulsive.

For the first time in her life, she felt free to experience the thrill and excitement of newfound passion. And she wanted to make love with him.

Leaning back to look into his heated gaze, she knew that what she was about to do was impetuous and completely out of character for her. But she didn't care. If she didn't make love with Josh now, she was sure that she'd be out of her mind by morning.

"I want you, Josh."

He took a deep breath and she could tell by the darkening of his hazel eyes that he wanted her just as badly. "Are you sure?"

"Yes."

His slow, sexy smile caused a quivering sensation deep in her belly as he removed his hand from inside her gown then giving her a quick kiss, rose to his feet. "I'll be back in just a minute."

As Kacie watched Josh leave the room, she tried not to think. For just one night, she didn't want to be a scientist, didn't want to analyze their coming together or think about the possible consequences. Tonight, she simply wanted to be a woman being loved by a caring, compassionate man.

When Josh returned, she watched him place a small foil packet on the nightstand, then pinning her with his smoldering gaze, he hooked his thumbs in the waistband of his briefs and slowly slid them from his narrow hips.

Kacie's eyes widened and her heart skipped several beats at the sight of his magnificent body. Josh was impressively built and the perfect specimen of a man in his prime. The muscles of his wide shoulders, chest and thighs were well defined from years of ranch work, his flanks flat and lean. A light sprinkling of dark brown hair covered his heavily padded pectoral muscles, then arrowed down his rippled stomach to his proud, full erection.

Her breath caught when he smiled, then reached out to remove her gown. Raising her arms for him, she suddenly wished she'd asked him to turn off the lamp. But when he whisked the light garment away and tossed it on the floor with his briefs, the appreciative look in his eyes helped dispel the last of her inhibitions.

"You're perfect," he said, sounding slightly winded.

Lying back against the pillows, she smiled. "I was thinking the same thing about you."

He chuckled as he stretched out on the bed beside her. "I'm not so sure about looking perfect, but you can damn well bet that I'm going to do everything in my power to make this perfect for you."

When he gathered her into his arms, Kacie shivered with excitement. His vow to bring her pleasure and the feel of his hard, male flesh pressed intimately to her thigh sent a river of hungry desire flowing through her veins and made finding her voice all but impossible. But she discovered that words were unnecessary when Josh captured her lips with the promise of things to come.

Never breaking the kiss, he turned her to her side as he moved his hand from her shoulders to the small of her back. His touch, the enchanting contrast of his callused palm on her much smoother skin made her feel more feminine, more desired than she'd ever dreamed possible. When he slipped his hand beneath the waistband of her panties to cup her bottom, a need deeper than anything she'd ever experienced caused her to tremble against him.

As he slid the scrap of silk away, her body hummed from the sensations he was creating deep inside of her and she didn't think twice about moving to help him divest her of the last barrier between them. But when he pulled her close, heat streaked to every part of her and she moaned from the intensity of it.

An answering groan rumbled up from deep in his chest and she felt him shudder a moment before he broke the kiss, then eased her to her back. Staring down at her, he shook his head. "Darlin', I'd like to go slow, but I'm not real sure that's going to be an option. You feel too good and I want you too much."

His raspy voice and the hunger in his hazel eyes was evidence of the strain he was under and his admission only heightened the answering need building deep within her. "I don't want you to slow down." Sliding her hands the length of his broad back, she reveled in their differences—the contrast of woman to man. Testing the firmness of his tightly muscled buttocks, she smiled at his sharp intake of breath. "I want you to make love to me now, Josh."

The heat in his eyes seared her as, without a word, he rolled to his back and reached for the foil packet on the bedside table. Arranging their protection, he gathered her to him once again then, nudging her knees apart, rose above her.

Her pulse pounded in her ears as she watched him guide himself to her then slowly, surely join their bodies. Tiny volts of electric current skipped over every inch of her as she took him in. Closing her eyes, she savored the exquisite stretching as their bodies became one. She'd never before considered herself a sexual being, but in Josh's arms it was as if a part of her she hadn't known existed blossomed to life.

When he slowly began to move within her, a spiral of tension deep in her lower stomach began to tighten and quickly grew to a delicious ache. Kacie fought to prolong the connection between them, to savor the feelings of being one with this incredible man even as her body urged her to find the satisfaction she knew awaited.

Apparently sensing her readiness, Josh cradled her close and, kissing her, deepened his strokes and urged her toward the precipice. Without warning, the coil of tension inside of her womb suddenly began to unwind, sending waves of pleasure through every cell of her being. Shivering from the force of it, she was only vaguely aware of Josh growling her name a moment before he thrust into her a final time and found his own release from the captivating storm.

As they slowly floated back to reality, Kacie fleetingly wondered what she'd done. She'd never been one for meaningless encounters or one-night stands. In fact, she'd only been with one other man and they'd been engaged for a couple of months before they made love. What was there about Josh that had her abandoning propriety and a lifetime of inhibitions for a few incredible moments in his arms?

But her instincts told her that what they'd just shared was neither meaningless nor the only time they'd be together. As incredible as it seemed, intuition told her that their coming together was just the beginning of something that neither of them could deny or be able to resist.

"Are you all right?" he asked as he rolled to her side and held her close.

Snuggling into the warmth of his embrace, she nodded. "That…you were incredible."

He shook his head as he tightened his arms around her and kissed the top of her head. "We were both too hot for each other, darlin'. I promise the next time we make love, I'll take my time and bring you all the pleasure you deserve."

Kacie's heart skipped a beat and she gave up trying to analyze what was happening between them or what it would mean to her in the light of day. His husky promise and the feel of his strong arms holding her as if he'd found a precious treasure were all the assurance she needed to know that whatever was happening between them, Josh felt it, too. And as she drifted off to sleep, she felt more secure, more cherished than she'd felt in her entire life.

CHAPTER FIVE

THE NEXT MORNING, as he stood in front of his bathroom mirror, Josh muttered a graphic expletive when the razor he held bit into his skin for the second time. If he didn't pay attention to what he was doing, he'd end up looking like he'd tangled with a wildcat from all the shaving nicks along his jaw and chin. But after one of the most amazing nights of his life, it was pretty damned hard to think of anything but what he and Kacie had shared. And what he intended for them to share again.

Rinsing the remnants of the shaving cream from his cheeks, he stared at himself in the mirror for several long seconds. What the hell was happening to him?

Since Marianne's death, he'd been with a few women for the physical release that a man needed after a long stretch of celibacy. But none of them had left him feeling more hungry for her after their encounter than he'd felt before.

As he pulled the towel from around his waist and tossed it into the hamper, he shook his head as he walked into his bedroom to pull on his clothes. What was there about Kacie that was different? After making love to her, why did he still want her with a passion that was staggering? And why, instead of feeling guilty for living, did he feel he'd been given a second chance at life?

He stopped dead in his tracks. Had he finally come

to terms with the role he'd played in Marianne's tragic death? Was he finally ready to put the past behind and move on?

Sitting on the side of the bed to pull on his boots, he decided there were no easy answers. Only time would tell him what he needed to know. And until he figured it all out, there was no sense dwelling on what it all meant. Besides, he decided as he rose to his feet, the longer he sat around thinking about it, the less time he'd have to spend with Kacie.

When he entered the kitchen a few minutes later, Josh forgot all about his disturbing introspection as he listened to Kacie and Earl debating the benefits of eating a big breakfast. Earl insisted that steak, eggs and hash browns was a far better way to start the day than the whole-grain muffin and strawberries Kacie was nibbling on.

"I tell ya, gal, that ain't enough to keep a gnat alive," Earl complained. "You need to eat somethin' that'll stick to your ribs."

Looking up, Kacie gave Josh a shy smile that damn near knocked him to his knees. "Good morning."

"Morning," he said, surprised that he could get his vocal cords to work. "Did you sleep well last night?"

"Yes, I did." When her gaze locked with his there was a glow in the azure depths that sent his blood pressure skyward. "How about you? How did you sleep?"

"I had a fantastic night," he answered, wishing he could take her back upstairs. He'd like nothing better than to spend the day rediscovering just how amazing their lovemaking had been.

She stared at him for several seconds before she turned her attention back to Earl. "I'm sorry, Mr. Crawshaw. What were you saying?"

The old man fell silent as he looked from one to the other. Then, to Josh's discomfort, Earl threw back his head and cackled like an old hen. "Well, if that don't beat ever'thing I ever seen, I'll eat my hat and give you fifteen minutes to draw a crowd to watch me. It's about time you—"

"Earl," Josh warned, cutting him off. "You're about two shakes of a calf's tail away from getting yourself fired."

"You can't fire me." Earl laughed even harder. "If you'll remember, Joshua, I quit three times last week."

Looking thoroughly confused, Kacie frowned. "Did I miss something?"

"No." Wishing he could reach out and throttle the old geezer, Josh settled on giving him a warning scowl. "Most of the time Earl is harmless. But when he forgets to take his medication, he's been known to hallucinate and say some pretty bizarre things."

It didn't surprise Josh in the least when Earl ignored him. "Don't let Joshua fool you, gal. The only medicine I take is for my rheumatism." Earl wiped his eyes on his apron as he limped over to the stove to dish up a plate full of steak and eggs. Setting it on the table at Josh's usual place, he laughed like a damned hyena when he added, "And me and this here young buck both know that I see things a whole lot clearer than most folks. He just don't like hearin' me tell him about it."

If Josh held out any hope that Earl hadn't noticed the attraction between himself and Kacie, it had just dissipated like mist in the wind. "How does the radar look this morning?" he asked, hoping to divert the conversation into safer territory. "Has that front start moving again?"

"By my calculations, it should get here sometime late

this afternoon or early evening," she said, nodding. He barely managed to keep from groaning out loud when she paused to lick strawberry juice from her fingertips. "We should start seeing the first of the feeder bands by midafternoon."

"Feeder bands?" Earl poured himself a cup of coffee and sat down beside Josh. "Ain't those part of a hurricane?"

"Well, yes. But the term actually refers to any line of low-level clouds that move ahead or behind a thunderstorm or hurricane," Kacie explained. "Eventually they're consumed by or *feed* into the main body of a storm, making it even bigger and stronger."

Taking a sip of his coffee, Josh asked, "What time do you think we should leave here to find a safe place to observe this thing?"

"I'd say an hour or so after lunch." When she stood up, he and Earl rose to their feet, causing her to look at them like they'd lost their minds. "Is something wrong?"

Josh smiled and shook his head. "We may not use them all that often, but Texas men do have manners."

She laughed. "I guess it's been so long since I was treated like anything but one of the guys, I've forgotten that some men are gentlemen." Placing her plate and coffee mug in the dishwasher, she turned one of her killer smiles his way. "Josh, would you mind if I use the phone in your office to make a few calls? I'd like to double-check my figures with my colleagues at the IWCA and National Weather Service."

"Go right ahead." As long as she kept smiling at him that way, she could do just about anything she damned well pleased and it would be fine with him.

"Thank you."

When Josh stood there enjoying the slight sway of her hips as Kacie walked from the room, he failed to notice that Earl had returned to his seat. Earl's snicker alerted him to the fact that the old fart was sitting there grinning like a toothless jackass.

"What's wrong with you?" he asked irritably.

Earl chuckled. "Ain't nothin' wrong. I'm thinkin' ever'thing's looked pretty right for the first time in years."

Sinking into his chair, Josh narrowed his eyes and glared at his longtime friend. "You have something you want to say, Earl?"

Earl's expression turned serious. "Well, now that you mention it, I reckon I do." He pointed toward the hall. "After what happened to Marianne, I kinda wondered if you'd ever find yourself another woman."

Suddenly losing his appetite, Josh pushed his untouched plate away from him. He wasn't going to deny the attraction between himself and Kacie. But he wasn't quite ready to discuss it with anyone, either.

"Earl, we've been friends for a lot of years."

"Yep. And me and your daddy and mama, God rest their souls, were best friends before you were more than a twinkle in your mama's eye."

Josh nodded. "There's not a lot you don't know about me. But this is one area—"

"Now, don't go gettin' your nose outta joint, Joshua." Earl gave him an understanding smile. "I ain't wantin' to know your business. All I'm sayin' is that it's nice to see you and that little gal makin' eyes at one 'nother." He gave Josh a toothless grin. "Gives me hope that I'll live to see a couple of younguns runnin' around here one of these days."

Josh laughed out loud. "If I did settle down with

another woman and have a couple of kids, it would just give you one more thing to complain about."

"A man's gotta have somethin' to occupy his time, don't he?" Laughing, the old man got to his feet. "Now git. We're both burnin' daylight and I got chores to do."

As he grabbed his hat and walked down to the bunkhouse to let his men know what needed to be done for the day, Josh thought about what his old friend had said. When he'd married Marianne, he'd fully expected them to have a family together. But was that what he wanted now? Was he ready to once again reach for the dream of having a wife and family?

Most people would think he'd lost his mind if he told them that since Kacie's arrival on the ranch a little less than twenty-four hours ago, she had him thinking that's exactly what he'd like to do. But he wasn't most people.

Josh came from a long line of men who knew what they wanted the minute they saw it. His grandmother and grandfather had married within seventy-two hours of meeting. And his mother and father had only known each other a week before they made a trip down the aisle. Both marriages had been very happy and had stood the test of time.

Of course, he and Marianne had been the exception to the Garrett legacy. They'd dated for a couple of years before they got married. And although he'd loved her and had had no doubts that their marriage would have lasted, Josh had always wondered why he hadn't known she was the woman for him from the moment he laid eyes on her.

He certainly hadn't had that problem with Kacie. The minute she'd stepped out of her Jeep—

Stopping dead in his tracks, Josh felt as if the air had suddenly been sucked from the atmosphere. He'd felt an instant connection with her unlike anything he'd felt with any other woman, including his late wife. But that didn't mean Kacie was his soul mate, did it?

"You're losing it, Garrett," he muttered, shaking off the disquieting thought.

But as he continued on to the bunkhouse, Josh had to admit that he'd felt more alive in the past twenty-four hours than he'd felt in years. And whether it was the Garrett legacy or something else, he couldn't deny that he felt like he'd finally found the other half of himself each time he took Kacie into his arms.

WHILE JOSH DROVE Kacie's truck along the roads due west of the Broken Bow ranch house, she checked the forecast chart in her lap. To most people the green, purple, red and blue pencil marks probably looked as if she'd been doodling while talking on the phone. But the lines and numbers told her a story. And it was enough to send a chill down the spine of even the most seasoned meteorologists.

"Those are the early predecessors to the main event, aren't they?"

Kacie glanced up from the chart to see a band of small cumulus clouds drifting toward them. "Yes, but we still have a couple of hours before the main body of the storm gets here. I don't expect to see any real activity until later in the afternoon." Pausing, she shook her head. "Of course, this is Texas and sometimes the exception to the rule."

"I've heard some of the weathermen on TV call it West Texas magic," he said, turning the SUV onto a sideroad with barbed-wire fences on both sides as far as the eye could see.

Kacie nodded. "We never have figured out how it

comes about, but storms in West Texas often produce
tornadoes when meteorological conditions aren't
present to support them." Looking around, she pointed
to a parking area beside a series of holding pens that she
assumed were used for cattle. "We can pull off here and
wait for the next NWS update."

Parking where she'd indicated, Josh leaned over to
look at the papers spread across her lap. "How big of
an area do you expect this thing to cover?"

"When I talked to the office in Amarillo this morning,
they concurred with my forecast of a relatively high
risk for severe storms in a one-hundred-mile range."
She traced a line around the area on one of the maps
with her fingertip. "This is where parts of the supercell
are expected to become tornadic. There's a strong jet
stream overhead, a good amount of surface moisture and
a weather disturbance moving in."

He nodded. "In other words, a witch's brew of atmospheric conditions."

"That's a good way to put it."

She wondered what he was thinking. Neither of them
had mentioned what happened the night before, but she
knew it had been foremost on both of their minds.

For her, their coming together had been much more
than an awakening from a long period of mourning or
simply being caught up in the passion of the moment.
As crazy as it sounded, in the circle of Josh's arms she'd
felt as if she'd found what she'd been searching for all
of her life. Not even Mark had made her feel as complete
as Josh did. And it didn't seem to matter that they'd only
known each other for a day. Their lovemaking had been
a natural union of both body and soul and the inherent
rightness of it was unlike anything she'd ever experienced.

"Darlin', did you hear what I said?"

Startled back to the present by his question, Kacie's cheeks grew warm as much from thoughts of their lovemaking as from being caught daydreaming. "Sorry. I had something on my mind."

"So do I." His smile told her that he had a good idea what she'd been thinking about and that it hadn't been far from his mind, either. "Do you have any idea how amazing you are, Kacie?"

Unable to find her voice, she shook her head.

"When we get back to the ranch this evening, we need to talk."

Her heart skipped several beats as she continued to stare at him. The tenderness in his voice and passion in the depths of his eyes held a promise that stole her breath.

"Yes, we do," she finally managed, amazed at the sultry quality of her own voice.

When he reached out to cup her cheek with his callused palm, her eyes drifted shut as she savored the feel of his gentle touch. Unfortunately, the moment was short-lived when the shrill alarm on her weather-alert unit intruded.

Opening her eyes, she switched off the offensive sound and listened to the latest weather advisory. A tornado watch was being issued for the entire Texas and Oklahoma panhandles, as well as a large section of southwestern Kansas.

Kacie immediately refreshed the browser on her laptop and brought up the latest Doppler image. A long, jagged green line—running over a hundred miles from southwest to northeast—had become quite prominent.

"That's the dryline. As things develop, we'll be able to narrow down the area where a tornado is most likely to form. Then we'll know where and when to start our chase."

Josh nodded. "It looks nasty."

When she switched to the satellite screen, it showed small clouds developing on the northern end of the line. "I'm afraid this thing is developing faster than any of us anticipated." Taking her instruments from the dash, she got out of the Jeep and took several readings. When she got back in the truck, Kacie shook her head as she jotted numbers on the charts. "The dew point and southerly surface winds are increasing and the barometric pressure is taking a nosedive."

"What do you want to do? Sit here and wait or try to intercept it?" Josh's expression was grim and she could tell that he wasn't happy with either option.

"We can drive a few miles to the southwest and take more readings, but I don't think we'll have to go far." She checked the Doppler and a chill raced through her when she noticed the bright yellow ring circling an even brighter spot of red. The radar had detected rotation in the clouds—the signature of tornadic activity. "From the direction it's moving and the increased wind speeds, I'd say we'll have a visual on it within the next twenty minutes or so."

As if on cue, the weather alert sounded again with a tornado warning for three counties and included most of Josh's ranch.

Josh listened to the broadcast and felt like ice water flowed through his veins. "It's going to come right through here, isn't it?"

He watched Kacie busily rifle through her charts, then check the road map. "Unless these readings and the radar are completely off—which is highly unlikely—it's going to pass close by. And it's not going to be long before it gets here. The best I can tell it's only about fifteen or twenty miles from us now."

His gut twisted so hard it robbed him of breath as he started the Jeep and steered it back onto the road. Assisting Kacie with her storm chasing had by no means made him an expert, but even he could tell from looking at the radar that the system moving toward them was three times the size of the one that had hit Bealville. And the fact that they were on the same part of the ranch where Marianne had been killed only added to his trepidation.

"This looks like a good place to pull over," Kacie said when they reached the top of a small hill.

Although the sky was hazy from the high humidity, he could see clouds rising up in the distance like an angry giant awakened from a deep sleep. "More measurements?" he asked, bringing the Jeep to a halt.

"And pictures." She positioned the camcorder on the dash and turned it on, then handed him the digital camera he'd used the day before. "There's a tripod in the cargo area. Why don't you set it up and get the camera mounted while I check the Doppler one more time."

When he got out of the SUV and set up the equipment as Kacie requested, he made sure to stay well back of the barbed-wire fence that ran along the side of the road. There was no sense adding the danger of electrocution, should lightning strike and turn the fence into a high-voltage power line.

"So this is where we wait to see which direction it goes?" he asked, walking over to stand beside her. She looked so damned desirable, standing there looking out over his land, that it was all he could do to keep from taking her in his arms and kissing her senseless.

Nodding, she held the anemometer at arm's length.
"We could go out and try to intercept it, but if it stays
on the course it's traveling, we won't have to. It's going
to come within a mile of us."

With her chase experience, that probably sounded
like a safe distance, but as far as he was concerned a
couple of miles between them and the storm was cutting
it too close.

As they continued to watch the darkening sky, Josh
realized he hadn't been on this part of his ranch in five
years—not since he'd finished tearing down what was
left of the house he'd shared with Marianne. He wanted
to make damn sure he had their route of escape plotted
on the outside chance the storm changed directions.
Satisfied that he had a plan of action and grateful that
his men had kept the roads in good shape, he began
taking the pictures Kacie wanted.

"These clouds are about twice as high as yesterday's," he said, clicking off several shots.

She nodded as she pointed to the storm bank. "See
how they've flattened out on top with only an occasional overshooting cloud?"

"It's look like an anvil."

"An anvil filled with ice crystals. I'd say hail is falling
on the other side of the wall."

While Kacie walked back to the Jeep to check the
Doppler, Josh marveled at the way the anvil stretched
out for miles and miles. He hated to think of the damage
the hailstones were doing to the crops of his neighbors
to the west.

"Look at that large area of organized rotation," she
said when she returned.

Through the zoom lens, he watched the swirling
motion in the center of the wall cloud suddenly take

shape into a conelike funnel. A dull white, it resembled the tornado from *The Wizard of Oz* as it snaked its way to the ground. Wispy bits of clouds began to dance around it and, awed by the sight, Josh stopped taking pictures to watch the immense power of nature at its ferocious best.

"This is going to be an F3 or above. See how those vortices are gathering into the main cone?" She raised the anemometer when the wind began to gust. Checking the measurement, she shook her head. "I don't like this."

"What?" Something about the tone of her voice warned him that he wasn't going to like what she had to say.

"The wind is starting to shift."

Josh stared at the growing vortex while Kacie recorded the data on her charts. Still about a mile away, the once white tornado was turning an ugly, charcoal-gray and a dome of dust and debris had formed at the base as it tore across the green fields. No longer cone-shaped, it had fattened into a massive, ugly monster that had no sympathy and would show no mercy for anyone or anything in its path.

When it became clear that it was headed directly toward them, he began folding up the tripod with the camera still attached. "It's turning toward us."

Looking up from the chart, she gasped. "Oh, dear Lord! It's picking up speed."

"Get in the truck. Now!"

Josh had no sooner gotten the words out than the wind picked up considerably. Grabbing Kacie by the arm, he tugged her along as they made a mad dash for the SUV. When they reached the Jeep, he threw open the driver's door and tossed the tripod into the back. He shoved Kacie across the seat and slid in behind the steering wheel.

"We're not going to make it, Josh." The panic in her voice twisted his insides.

"The hell we aren't," he said, starting the Jeep and throwing it into gear.

He'd lost Marianne to one of the violent storms, but he'd be damned if he'd lose Kacie. As long as he had breath left in his body, he'd do whatever it took to get them out of this. And if that meant going back to a place that he'd vowed never to visit again, then that's what he'd do.

CHAPTER SIX

KACIE HAD BARELY latched her seat belt when Josh spun gravel and fishtailed her Jeep back onto the road. The strong, inflow jet winds feeding into the twister's circulation buffeted the SUV and nearly forced them into the ditch several times as they sped along the narrow dirt lane. While he fought to keep from wrecking the vehicle, she glanced into the side mirror on the passenger door.

Her heart pounded and her palms grew clammy. The tornado was gaining on them and, just like in her dream, the wind was impeding their escape, holding them back in their race for their lives.

When Josh veered off the road and crashed through a fence to cut across a pasture, she was glad that she'd had the foresight to buy a four-wheel drive. It made their cross-country flight possible. She just prayed that it made it successful as well.

"Hold on," he shouted as they crashed through another barbed-wire fence. He reached down and released the catch on her seat belt. "There's a storm cellar just up ahead. It's probably partially flooded since no one's used it in years, but it's our only hope. I'm going to get as close to it as I can and once I stop the truck, I want you to run like hell for it. You got that?"

Her vocal cords paralyzed with fear, she nodded as

she checked the side mirror once more. She immediately wished she hadn't. It only confirmed her worst fear. The tornado was gaining on them and it would be nothing short of a miracle if they reached the storm shelter before her truck was sucked up in the humongous vortex.

When Josh stomped on the brake and brought the Jeep to a sliding halt, Kacie did as he said. She jumped from the truck and ran as hard as she could toward the metal door in the side of a small grass-covered mound. The wind tore at her clothes and the roar was deafening as she struggled to stay on her feet. Small pieces of debris stung her skin, but she barely noticed. Nothing mattered but reaching the safety of the shelter. Thankfully, Josh got to the door a split second before she did and, using his greater strength, managed to lever it open.

Normally, venturing into a dark, musty space where she'd be unable to see what kind of crawly things were lurking would have given her pause, but Kacie didn't hesitate when she ran down the steps into the tomblike cellar. About halfway down the stairs, her breath caught at the cold water swirling around her ankles, but she didn't stop until she reached the shelter's floor.

She heard Josh follow her down the steps, stopping only long enough to pull the metal door shut. In complete darkness and standing in waist-deep water, her relief was so great that they'd made it to safety, tears filled her eyes and her knees threatened to buckle.

But just when she thought she'd collapse into the stagnant water, Josh wrapped his strong arms around her and pulled her to his chest. "I didn't think we were going to make it," she said, sagging against him.

"We're safe now, darlin'."

His heart pounded hard beneath her ear and his

breathing sounded labored, but the fearsome sounds coming from outside quickly drowned out everything else and caused her to burrow deeper into his embrace. It sounded like a freight train rumbling over the top of the mound. Kacie clung to Josh and trembled from thoughts of how close they'd come to being a statistic.

Aware that Kacie was close to losing what little control she had on her frayed nerves, Josh brought his hands up to cup her cheeks and tilt her face to his. He not only wanted to make her forget that they'd just stared death in the face, he desperately needed to assure himself that they'd actually survived the encounter.

As his lips moved over hers, a shudder ran through him and he sent a silent prayer of thanks heavenward. Whether it had been divine intervention, stubborn determination or sheer dumb luck, he wasn't going to question how he'd managed to get them to safety. All that mattered was that the woman he loved was in his arms and he hadn't let her down.

The realization that he loved Kacie had him slowly easing his mouth from hers. Considering the Garrett legacy, he wasn't really surprised. But he wasn't entirely certain what he was going to do about it, either. She chased tornadoes for a living and their mad dash for shelter had just proved how dangerous that could be. He wouldn't ask her to change careers, but he wasn't sure he'd be able to accept it and run the risk of losing her the way he'd lost Marianne.

When she shivered against him, he decided there was plenty of time to figure it all out later. Right now, he needed to get them out of the flooded cellar, back to the ranch house and into something warm and dry.

"It's moved on, Kacie. Let's get out of here."

"G-good idea," she said through chattering teeth.

Even though the outside temperature had been pushing ninety when the storm moved through, the water in the cellar had been kept frigid from a lack of sunshine to warm it. Coupled with the fact that Kacie was coming down from a fear-induced adrenaline rush, he knew she had to be chilled to the bone.

Taking her by the hand, Josh felt his way along the concrete wall in search of the opening to the stairs. When he found it, he led her up the stone steps and pushed the door back.

"Oh…d-dear G-God!"

"What?" Turning to look over his shoulder, he found her pointing to the step he was standing on.

"S-snake."

Not at all surprised to see the garter snake curled up by his boot, Josh shook his head. "You can't blame him for crawling in here to escape the tornado, darlin'." He wisely refrained from telling her that they'd probably shared the shelter with more repulsive critters than one little green snake.

When he led her the rest of the way up the steps, he put his arm around her shoulders to protect her from the rain as they stood surveying the landscape. His chest tightened and he had to take a deep breath to force air into his lungs. The last time he'd stood in that very spot looking at the destruction left by a tornado, the scene had been a lot different. This time, there wasn't a pile of splintered lumber where his house and barns had once stood, nor was there any reason for him to search for a woman he'd left at home by herself.

"My…Jeep." Kacie pointed toward the SUV a good twenty yards from where he'd parked it. "It's not… wrecked."

To Josh's amazement the truck was still upright. It

was facing the opposite direction, but it appeared to be intact. Apparently, the twister had picked it up, turned it around, then set it down like a child moving a toy.

"You'll need a new paint job and there's a couple of dents you'll need to have repaired, but it looks drivable," he said when they walked over to the SUV.

He opened the passenger door and helped a still-shivering Kacie into the seat, then quickly walked around to get in behind the steering wheel. He had a feeling that her trembling was more from shock than from standing in the flooded storm cellar, and he needed to get her back to the ranch house.

"Hang in there. We'll be home just as fast as I can get us there."

Fifteen minutes later, Josh ushered Kacie into the house and straight upstairs to the master bathroom. Turning on the water, he stripped away their soggy clothes then, taking her with him, stepped into the shower. She hadn't said more than a handful of words since they'd come out of the storm shelter and her continued silence worried him.

"It's all right, Kacie," he said, picking up the soap from a built-in holder in the shower wall. "You're safe now."

Rubbing the bar into a rich lather, Josh replaced the soap in the holder. He slid his soapy hands over her back and around to her chest, his gaze catching hers as he cupped her breasts. The absolute trust he detected in her blue eyes caused his heart to thump hard against his ribs. Kacie had allowed him to take control of the situation when they were fleeing the tornado, and she was placing herself in his care now.

Gently rinsing the soap from her delicate skin, he

made a vow as he wrapped his arms around her and held her close—he would never let her down as long as he lived.

THE WARM SPRAY HELPED wash away the smudges of mud from her skin and warmed her body, but it was Josh's strength and reassuring presence that chased the chilling numbness from Kacie's soul. When they were standing in the flooded cellar, all she'd been able to think about was how much he'd come to mean to her in such a short time and how close she'd come to losing him.

It didn't matter that they'd really only known each other a little over twenty-four hours. Love was a force of nature that couldn't be measured in increments of time, nor could its power be held back.

Looking up at his handsome face, she started to tell him how she felt, but he lowered his head and the moment their lips met, she forgot anything she was about to say. The words could wait. Right now, she wanted to get lost in the feel of Josh's reassuring touch, to show him how much she loved him.

When she twined her arms around his neck and pressed herself to his slick, wet body she felt as if every nerve in her body sparkled to life. As his mouth moved over hers with such tenderness that it brought tears to her eyes, he ran his hands the length of her back to the curve of her bottom. Cupping her with his palms, he pulled her closer and the feel of his hard arousal, the need to once again be part of this wonderful man sent desire racing through her at the speed of light. She desperately wanted to feel all of him against her, feel their bodies joined in a reaffirming celebration of life.

Easing away from his kiss, Kacie sipped water

droplets from his collarbone as she trailed her fingers down his spine, then around to his lean flanks. His groan and the shudder that ran through him encouraged her and taking him in her hands, she gently caressed his strength and the heavy softness below.

One glance at him from beneath her lashes and she knew that he was experiencing the same burning need that had overtaken her. "Please, love me, Josh. Make me feel alive."

"It'll be my pleasure, Kacie." His kiss was so passionate it caused her knees to buckle and the world to spin dizzily around her. "And I'm going to make damned sure it's yours, too."

Before she knew what was happening, Josh ushered her out of the shower, then grabbing a fluffy towel from the towel bar, blotted the water from her skin with a reverence that left her breathless. Quickly toweling himself dry, he swept her into his arms and carried her into his bedroom.

He set her on her feet only long enough to pull back the colorful patchwork quilt then, picking her up again, gently placed her on the bed and stretched out beside her. His smile and the heat in his hazel eyes stole her breath and caused her to feel as if a thousand butterflies had been released in the pit of her stomach.

He drew her forward until their bodies met, and the touch of skin to skin sent pleasure rippling along every nerve in her body. His warm strength, his clean male scent and the sound of his steady heartbeat beneath her ear made her feel as if she'd finally come home. She'd never felt such peace and contentment as she experienced at that very moment. It was as if she was right where she belonged.

When Josh began to massage and caress her body, the

tension from their harrowing experience quickly drained away and the exquisite sensations of desire and passion overtook her. Everywhere he touched became an erogenous zone and, by the time he reached the juncture of her thighs, the desire coursing through her was so intense that Kacie wasn't sure how much more she could take. But when he parted her sensitive folds to stroke her intimately, heat and light flashed behind her closed eyes and she felt as if she'd go up in flames.

"Please."

"Not yet, Kacie. I'm just getting started."

Her eyes snapped open. "I don't think...I'll be able to stand it."

His tender expression made her insides feel as if they'd turned to warm pudding. "Last night I was too hot to love you the way you deserve to be loved."

She smiled. "I had no complaints."

"When you're back in Albuquerque in your lab, I want you to remember tonight." He brushed her lips with his and every cell in her being tingled to life when he cupped her breast in his large hand and teased the tight tip with his thumb. "I want you to remember me."

Kacie's chest tightened and she suddenly felt as if she couldn't breathe. He was talking as if this was their final night together. Had she mistaken his protectiveness and the undeniable chemistry between them for love?

When his mouth came down on hers there was a desperation, an urgency as his lips moved over hers. Unable to stop herself, she returned his kiss with the same passionate need. There was nothing soft or tender when his tongue sought and found entry to the inner recesses of her mouth. He demanded her response and she was powerless to deny him.

If all she could have with Josh was tonight, then she

was going to store up as many memories as she could. And she wanted him to remember her with the same degree of bittersweet longing that she would carry with her for the rest of her life.

Slowly sliding her hand along his lean, muscular side, she memorized every angle and plane, his latent strength and the feel of his firm male skin. But at the same time she committed his magnificent body to her memory, she intended to brand him with her touch as well. She wasn't going to be the only one who remembered this night and what they'd shared.

When she trailed her fingertips down his thigh then back up to encircle his engorged flesh, his hands on her body stilled and he shuddered against her. "Damn, darlin'. Are you trying to give me a heart attack?"

"No." She kissed his chest, letting her lips linger a moment over one flat nipple while she lightly stroked his hard arousal. "I'm just making sure this is a night *you'll* remember."

"There isn't a chance in hell that I'll ever forget, Kacie," he said through clenched teeth.

Seized by a compelling need to permanently imprint herself in his mind and on his heart, she drew on everything she'd ever heard or read about pleasuring a man. Nibbling kisses down his abdomen, she was going to leave the brand of her love on his very soul. And by the time she was finished, he was going to know just how much she loved him.

An unfamiliar feminine power that only the shedding of twenty-eight years of inhibitions could bring filled her as she leaned forward to kiss him intimately.

"Kacie—"

Josh felt like the top of his head was coming off when, without a word, Kacie deepened the caress and took him in her mouth. Clamping his back teeth together so hard he figured it would take surgery to get them apart, he closed his eyes as the flames in his lower belly burned out of control. No other woman, not even his late wife, had loved him with such unbridled passion.

His heart pounded in his chest like he'd run a marathon and, unable to take any more of her sensual assault, he reached down to stop her. "Darlin', a man has limits. And you've pushed mine into the danger zone."

Brushing her dark brown hair away from her face with a delicate hand, she gave him a look that sent his blood pressure skyrocketing. "Hand me the condom."

He wasn't sure when he'd lost control of the situation, but he wasn't going to complain about it. He was living every man's fantasy of having a woman love him with total and complete abandon.

When he gave her the foil packet, he watched as she tore it open, then gently rolled the latex in place. If he lived to be a thousand years old, he'd never forget how exciting and erotic Kacie had managed to make the simple act of arranging their protection.

"Come here," he said, reaching for her.

She surprised him by shaking her head as she straddled his hips. "I want you to remember this. I want you to remember *me*."

Before he could tell her that he'd go to his grave with her on his mind and in his heart, he watched her guide him to her, then slowly, completely, take him in. Rendered speechless, Josh didn't think he'd ever seen anything as sexy or amazing as Kacie. And it didn't matter that he'd only known her for a couple of days—he loved her more than life itself.

She gave him a smile that caused his heart to hammer against his ribs and slowly began to rock against him. He grasped her hips as the pressure in his lower body built to an almost painful state. He wanted to prolong their union, but the fire racing through his veins and the incredible friction of her body caressing his caused a red haze of need to cloud his mind to anything but finding the satisfaction they both sought.

The feel of her feminine muscles tightening around him signaled that she was close and wanting to insure her pleasure, he reached between them to touch her intimately. Her beautiful blue eyes widened a moment before she brokenly whispered his name, then gave in to the storm. Following her into the tempest, Josh pulled Kacie into his arms and held her close as he came with a force so intense he thought he might pass out from it.

As their bodies cooled, he hugged her tight. He wanted to tell her what he was feeling and how much he loved her, but he first had to decide if he could live with her choice of careers. Could he accept that her research might lead to another close call with a tornado?

They'd been lucky today. They'd been on a part of the ranch that had a shelter and he'd been able to lead her to it. But what about tomorrow or the next day or the next? Chances were that she'd eventually have another close encounter while she was out in the field. What would happen if he wasn't with her? Or, worse yet, what if there was no place to go? Could he live with the possibility that he might one day lose Kacie to one of the violent storms, the way he'd lost Marianne?

When Kacie snuggled close and her breathing signaled that she'd fallen asleep, Josh pulled the quilt over them and contented himself with the moment. He had several days to sort things out before she left. Right now, he was going to enjoy having her in his arms, in his bed and in his heart.

CHAPTER SEVEN

WHEN KACIE AWOKE the next morning, the darkness of night was just beginning to fade into the gray light of dawn. The sound of a gentle rain falling outside told her that unless conditions changed later in the afternoon hours, the next storm system wouldn't be moving through the Panhandle for a couple more days. And that made her choice a bit easier.

With a lack of severe weather to monitor, it would make her excuse for her sudden departure from the Broken Bow Ranch more credible. She certainly couldn't tell Josh the real reason she had to leave. Pride wouldn't allow her to tell a man who obviously wasn't looking for a lasting relationship that she'd fallen in love with him.

Turning her head, she looked over at him sleeping peacefully beside her. She clamped her lower lip between her teeth to keep it from trembling as she remembered his words from the night before. She'd thought her heart would break into a million pieces when he told her that he wanted her to remember him when she returned to Albuquerque. And that was the very reason she intended to pack up her equipment and leave as soon as possible. If she loved him this much after only two days, how would she feel after a couple of weeks of being with him in the close confines of her SUV every day and in his arms every night?

It would make leaving him that much more difficult, and God only knew it was going to be the hardest thing she'd ever done now. No, if she intended to save even a scrap of her dignity she had to go back home today.

Tears stung her eyes as she slowly eased from beneath his arm where it rested over her abdomen. Careful not to disturb him, Kacie slipped out of bed and grabbing a towel from the bathroom to cover herself, walked over to his side of the bed.

Leaning down, she lightly kissed his lean cheek. "Please…remember me, Josh," she whispered on a soft sob.

Then before she could change her mind, Kacie padded down the hall to the guest bedroom to take a quick shower and get dressed. She wanted to be packed and on the road before he woke up. She couldn't bear the thought of saying goodbye to the man she'd fallen hopelessly in love with.

WITH HIS EYES still closed, Josh rolled over to pull Kacie into his arms. But the bed beside him was empty. The only proof that the most incredible night of his life hadn't been a dream was the sweet scent of her lingering on his pillow.

Not wanting to waste one single minute that he could be with her, he tossed the covers back, sat up and swung his legs over the side of the bed. She was probably downstairs arguing with Earl about breakfast, he thought as he quickly showered and got dressed.

He was looking forward to a day without the worry of racing around the countryside chasing a storm. With a break in the weather, he wanted to show Kacie around the ranch and maybe see if she'd take a trip with him down to Amarillo to pick out some furniture for his empty house.

Walking into the kitchen, he stopped short when he found Earl sitting alone at the table. "Where's Kacie?"

His old friend looked at him through sad brown eyes. "She left. I tried to talk her out of it, but she wasn't havin' none of it." He ran a gnarled hand through his snow-white hair. "She looked like she'd been cryin'."

Josh felt like he'd taken a mule kick to the gut. "How long ago did she leave?"

"No more than five minutes." Earl shrugged. "You just missed her."

"I don't guess she told you what route she was taking?" he asked, walking over to grab a set of keys to one of the ranch trucks from a key rack by the back door.

"She didn't say for sure that she was goin' that way, but she asked if she could get to State Route 70 usin' that road you were on yesterday." Earl grinned. "I told her that it did."

"You lied to her?"

The old man took a sip of his coffee and shook his head. "Stallin' for time sounds better than lyin'."

Josh grinned for the first time since entering the kitchen. "Thanks, Earl. I owe you one."

"You owe me more than one," Earl called after him as he left the house.

Jogging over to one of the white trucks with the ranch logo painted on the side, Josh jumped in and gunning the engine, raced down the ranch road to find Kacie. Deciding to take a shortcut, he prayed that he'd be able to intercept her close to where they'd stopped to take pictures of the tornado yesterday.

The rain had turned the dirt lanes into slick, muddy

paths, but Josh wasn't about to let that slow him down. It suddenly didn't matter what she did for a living. He could live with her choice of careers a lot more than he could live without her.

WHEN A WHITE TRUCK SHOT out of one of the fields and came to a sliding stop in the road ahead of her, Kacie had to slam on the Jeep's brakes to avoid hitting it broadside. Her heart stopped, then took off doubletime when the driver got out and started walking through the rain toward her.

Josh looked wonderful to her. He also looked absolutely furious.

"What do you think you're doing?" he asked when he opened the driver's door of her Jeep. His voice was tight and controlled and she could tell that he was taking great pains to hold his obvious anger in check. "After last night, I would have thought you could at least stick around long enough to tell me goodbye."

"I thought it would be best…" She let her voice trail off. She wasn't sure she could finish without breaking down and making a complete fool of herself.

"Best to leave before we discuss what's happening between us and what we're going to do about it?" He reached inside, put the gearshift in Park and turned off the engine. "I don't think so."

"Josh, I really don't see the point—"

"I do."

Her throat tight with emotion, she took a deep breath. "I think you said all there was to say last night."

He stubbornly shook his head. "As I recall, there wasn't a lot of talking going on last night." Placing his hands on her shoulders, he turned her in the seat to face him. "Why are you leaving the ranch early, Kacie?"

Swallowing hard, she shook her head. "The longer I stay, the harder it will be for me to leave."

Josh put his index finger under her chin and tilted her head until their gazes met. "And why is that, darlin'?"

"Because I'm in love with you," she said before she could stop herself. She hadn't intended on blurting out her feelings, but once the words were out, there was no taking them back.

He shocked her when he let out a whoop, then wrapped his arms around her waist and pulled her from the SUV to swing her in a circle.

"Josh, have you lost your mind?" She circled his neck with her arms to steady herself. "What on earth are you doing?"

"I'm holding the woman I love more than life itself."

The world seemed to come to a screeching halt. "What did you say?"

When he set her on her feet, the intense emotion in his hazel eyes stole her breath. "I said I love you, Kacie Davidson."

Confused, she shook her head. "But last night, you talked like we wouldn't see each other again once I returned to Albuquerque."

"No, Kacie. I told you I wanted you to remember me and what we shared when you were back in your lab." His tender smile caused her insides to hum. "I just failed to add that I'd be making frequent trips to Albuquerque to be with you when you weren't working."

Tears of relief filled her eyes. "Is that what you really want, Josh? A long-distance relationship?"

"Not really. What I'd like is to have you say you'll marry me and live here with me on the Broken Bow." His demeanor turned serious. "But as much as it bothers me to think of you chasing tornadoes all over hell's half-acre, I know how important your work is to you and I won't ask you to give that up."

Loving him more than she ever dreamed possible, Kacie shook her head. "Storm chasing isn't what I normally do, darling."

He frowned. "If collecting wind speeds and humidity isn't your usual job, what is?"

"I'm a lab rat."

"A what?"

She laughed at his startled expression. "I'm a weather analyst. My job is to take the data collected from field research, break it down and find patterns that can be used for predicting and detecting severe weather. There's nothing in my job description that says I have to chase storms." She paused. "In fact, I don't even like fieldwork."

"Then why do you do it?" he asked, frowning.

"I made a promise the day Mark was buried to carry on his research and accomplish what he'd set out to do." Kacie took a deep breath and when she exhaled, it was as if she let go of the past once and for all. "I wasn't ready to face that I'd lost him and it was the only way I knew to keep at least a small part of him alive."

His smile was understanding. "And you're ready to let go of that now?"

"Yes. That was my past." Cupping his lean cheek with her hand, she returned his smile. "My future is here with you on the ranch."

"What about your career?" he asked, kissing the tip of her nose. "I don't want you giving that up unless it's what you really want to do."

"I'll check with the National Weather Service in Amarillo." She shrugged. "They've offered me a job in that office a couple of times. I'll just tell them to keep me in mind when the next position comes open."

"Are you sure?"

She didn't hesitate. "I've never been more certain of anything in my entire life."

He gave her a kiss that warmed her all the way to the depths of her soul. "I love you, Kacie."

"And I love you." Staring up at the man who owned her mind, body and soul, she had to ask, "Josh, why didn't you tell me last night that you love me?"

Explaining that Garrett men had a history of immediately knowing they loved a woman, he added, "But I wasn't sure you wouldn't think I was some kind of nutcase, telling you I love you after only a couple of days."

"If you're crazy, then I am, too," she said, laughing. The rain had stopped and, just like the sunshine emerging from the clouds, Josh's love lit the darkest corners of her soul.

"Let's go home, Kacie. We have a few things we need to do."

"And what would that be?"

"We have a wedding to plan and furniture to buy." His heart-stopping grin made her knees weak. "Right after I spend the rest of the morning making love to you."

As Kacie followed Josh back to the Broken Bow ranch house to start their new life, she marveled at the beautiful colors suddenly painting the sky up ahead. A double rainbow was a rare and precious gift. And, just like the love she and Josh had found, it promised a rebirth and renewed hope to all who believed in its power.

UPSURGE
Kristi Gold

* * *

The peace which others seek they find;
The heaviest storms not longest last;
Heaven grants even to the guiltiest mind
An amnesty for what is past...
—William Wordsworth

To Kathie and Laura for your friendship
and unflagging support. It's been a joy
weathering the storms with you.
And many thanks to hurricane survivors
Carol, Ellen, Elizabeth, Roxanne and Vicky
for your invaluable input.

CHAPTER ONE

FOR MUCH OF Marissa Klein's thirty-three years, the aqua-blue Florida cottage had been her summer sanctuary, feeding her fantasies as well as her soul. For five of those years, she'd only visited through reminiscent conversations with her dad, until he'd been unable to speak. But eight months ago, she'd left New Hampshire and made the house her permanent residence, a respite from the bitter northern winters and recollections of her father's final hours. And now she might be leaving it all behind.

The moment she stepped into the bright coral-colored living room, the significance of the decision she now faced hit her full force, as did the many memories. Special memories of a place where she'd spent hours as a motherless child in the company of her adored father. Her father's favorite black leather rocker, now cracked and peeling, sat catty-corner near the window overlooking the lush front lawn. And next to that, the glass-topped end table that had held his evening brandy.

Marissa could still imagine him sitting there, extolling the virtues of reading the classics while she listed the merits of modern literature. They'd argued often, but they'd always ended their debates with a good-natured hug and the realization that it was okay to disagree.

Yes, so many good memories and good times were tied to this house, even if she had spent recent days there alone.

"Who's your baby?"

Okay, almost alone.

Marissa immediately dropped her suitcase onto the carpeted floor, kicked the front door closed behind her and rubbed her throbbing temples. After enduring a four-hour layover and a jam-packed flight, there was nothing quite like being greeted by a parrot with a predilection for thievery and a penchant for nonstop chatter.

As she bypassed the massive gold cage, Marissa muttered, "Just a minute, Baby," on her way to the kitchen to drop off the bag of groceries. She was simply too tired to deal with the macaw at the moment, even if the bird had been her constant companion for three years and without her for the past five days. Right then, exchanging corporate attire for casual grunge was foremost on her mind.

On the way down the hall, Marissa kicked off her heels, shed her black blazer and slacks and, once in the bedroom, sailed her bra across the room like a slingshot. After dressing in khaki shorts and a navy tank top, she fell back on the bed, closed her eyes and kept company with her current dilemma—go or stay.

As always, you're too indecisive, Marissa...

Indecision had always been one of her faults, the inclination to weigh and measure ad nauseam before throwing herself into a situation. Maybe this time, she shouldn't beat it to death. After all, a career change would do her good. So would working outside her home, holding daily conversations with real live people, not just a parrot. She could have new experiences in an exciting city. Maybe even date again. That would definitely be new and different.

Baby's insistent squawking drove Marissa from her musings and off the bed to see about the bird. While gathering her hair into a ponytail atop her head to secure in a cloth band, she trudged back into the kitchen, stopped by the cage and peered inside. "You've got food and water. What else could you possibly need?"

The red-and-blue macaw stopped preening long enough to stare at Marissa blankly. "Yes, I'm talking to you," she told her. "And it looks like you've been well taken care of in my absence. Now I'm going to run next door and thank Jen and Greg for putting up with you."

Baby ruffled her feathers, blinked twice and then proclaimed, *"Greg's a hunk."*

Greg's a hunk? That had not been in Baby's verbal repertoire before Marissa left town. No doubt, her eighteen-year-old neighbor, Jen, had taught the parrot the phrase. Only one way to find out.

Marissa slid her sore feet into her favorite well-worn flip-flops, grabbed the groceries and left out the front door. Once outside, she stepped to her left and navigated the rock path leading to the beige stone house, an act so routine she could do it blindfolded. The fortress next door had been built in her five-year absence, and she hadn't been too happy when she'd returned to Ocean Vista to find that the owner had stripped the lot next door of almost every tree, from palms to loblolly pines to majestic live oaks. Regardless, she couldn't have asked for better neighbors than the divorced doctor and his gregarious daughter. Besides, her own trees were still intact, aged and stately and plentiful.

Pausing at the low hedge dividing the property line, Marissa savored the pungent scent of the sea coming off the nearby Gulf of Mexico, even welcomed the sticky dampness on her skin. Although she was too far from the beach to hear the emerald waves lapping on the shore or to witness the setting sun turning the sugar-white sand to orange-and-pink glitter, she could imagine the scene. And any time she wanted, she only had to travel the three miles to experience the ocean's tranquility. As far as pros and cons went, the atmosphere was definitely a plus compared to the urban chaos in Chicago, the place of her possible relocation. No sirens. No honking horns. No disgruntled drivers shouting obscenities. Nothing but peace and quiet.

Heading to the Westbrooks' backyard as she always did during visits, Marissa skirted the driveway, noting Jen's sedan wasn't in its usual spot behind her dad's SUV. Most likely the recent high-school graduate was out on a Friday-night date, either with girlfriends or the current guy of the month. Marissa reached the gate, and paused when she heard odd sounds coming from behind the privacy fence—creaking metal mixed with harsh breathing.

She shifted the grocery sack from one hip to the other and strained to listen. Surely Greg wasn't engaging in dirty dealings on the pool-deck chaise with his current girlfriend, Sophie—or Penny Peroxide, as Marissa fondly referred to her. Granted, his daughter was obviously gone, but sex in broad daylight?

She didn't even want to think about it, didn't want to consider the possibility. She needed to turn around and go back home. She should have called first. But when Greg muttered a loud oath and she heard no female response, her curiosity got the best of her.

Crouching down, Marissa peered through a widening

in the fence's wooden slats and almost laughed over her erroneous assumptions.

Dr. Westbrook was doing some pumping—with an exercise machine. He sat on the black bench and pulled two cords toward his bare chest, back and forth, his efforts showcasing every sinewy muscle in his chest and abs and highlighting the straining veins in his neck. He wore a pair of navy mesh sport shorts and cross-trainers, leaving his toned thighs and legs out in the open for Marissa's enjoyment, and she was definitely enjoying this.

With longish layered sun-bleached hair and dark pensive eyes, he looked more rock star than physician, minus the leather pants and piercings. His skin retained a bronze cast year-round, partly from his maternal grandmother's Cuban heritage and his routine run every afternoon. Atypical family doctor would best describe him. Atypical, and gorgeous, the man known as a "hottie" to his daughter's friends and most of the women in town. Rightfully so, especially at the moment.

Greg's a hunk....

Yes, Baby, he sure is.

While Greg continued to work off steam, Marissa heated up with his every move. But her legs were starting to cramp, so the spy game needed to end. Besides, she feared Jen might pull up and catch her ogling Dr. Dad through the crack in the fence like some peeping Thomasina.

After straightening her legs and her composure, Marissa stepped through the gate and smiled. "Hi, honey, I'm home."

Greg's gaze snapped to hers, a distinct look of surprise splashed across his face, either from her unexpected appearance or her use of the endearment. "When did you get back?" he asked, followed by a blatantly sensual smile that highlighted his dimples, the right one more prominent than the left. He actually looked happy to see her, and she was definitely happy to see him.

"I just got in a few minutes ago, as a matter of fact." She pointed to the complicated-looking contraption. "New toy?"

Greg rose from the bench, snatched a towel from the nearby chaise and rubbed it over the back of his neck. "Yeah. More convenient than going to the gym. I decided to try it out here on the patio while the weather's still good, before I roll it inside." He gestured toward the bag. "What do you have there?"

"Steaks. I thought we could have a barbecue. Unless you and Sophie already have plans." She held her breath and hoped.

He looked away. "Sophie won't be coming around anymore."

"Really?" Marissa tried to temper the delight in her voice but wasn't sure she'd succeeded. "What happened?" When Greg looked ill at ease, she added, "Sorry. That's none of my business."

"Let's just say the relationship was going downhill for the past few months and died a natural death," he said, no hint of remorse in his tone. "She wanted a commitment, and I didn't."

Once burned, and all that jazz, Marissa decided. Although she knew very few details about Greg's divorce, she did know it hadn't been pleasant, or at least that's what his daughter had intimated. "That's too bad," she said while thinking, *No, it's not.* In her limited exposure to dear Sophie, she'd found the twenty-some-thing woman to be overstated in the makeup department and underdeveloped in terms of her brain. And that was probably just plain and simple jealousy speaking.

Greg stepped forward, opened the bag and peeked inside. "What, no T-bones?"

She snatched the plastic sack from his grasp, bringing about his smile. "Consider yourself lucky I found anything at all. The store was a madhouse. Everyone must be stocking up for the weekend."

He frowned. "Not for the weekend, Marissa. For the possibility of a hurricane."

Marissa followed with her own frown. "Hurricane? I thought it was just a tropical storm."

"You haven't been watching the weather?"

Not to any extent. Unfortunately. "It's July. September is typically hurricane month."

"The season begins in June. You should know that."

She did, and she also knew better than to ignore the possibilities. "I was in interviews for the past two days and I basically fell into bed at night—"

"Alone?"

That deserved a good eye-rolling, which she gave him. "Yes, alone. I *was* propositioned though." There was no harm in letting him know she wasn't totally hopeless in the social department.

"Who propositioned you?" He looked and sounded seriously concerned.

"A salesman. Nice-looking guy. Very successful."

"But you didn't take him up on his offer." Now he sounded skeptical.

"No. I don't believe in sex for the sake of sex. Or going to bed with a man who has a wife and two kids." Something she'd learned from the company's personnel director following the tour of the offices.

Greg streaked the towel over his forehead. "Anyone

else try to get you into bed? Maybe a pilot or cab driver?"

She was a little baffled that he would care, and determined to avoid the topic, considering no one else had come on to her, a sad commentary on her life. "As I was saying, I heard about a tropical storm, but I didn't know it had been upgraded."

He forked his fingers through his hair. "Yeah. Yesterday afternoon. Right now it's tracking toward the Keys."

"And it's heading here?" Her voice held an edge of distress, probably because she felt more than a little distressed.

"They're not exactly sure yet, but it's possible." He nodded toward the back entrance. "Come inside and we'll watch the latest update."

Marissa followed him through the French doors opening to the sunroom then up the three steps that led into the main house. She automatically walked into the cook's dream kitchen while Greg stayed behind in the adjacent family room. She didn't want him to see her anxiety over the possibility of a destructive storm, but she was teetering on the edge of panic. She'd missed the hurricane season last year, and all other seasons before that. In days past, if a storm had threatened Ocean Vista during a planned visit, her father had simply rearranged their schedule while they prayed the house survived—and it had, for over thirty-five years, even through the rounds of storms that had gripped the Florida Panhandle on occasion. Some repairs had been required, but nothing too major up to this point.

"What's happening?" she called as she withdrew the steaks, prepackaged salad and baking potatoes from the grocery bag.

"Right now they're saying if it continues a westward track, it should hit somewhere else." Marissa experienced a strong sense of relief until Greg added, "But that's no guarantee."

She absolutely hated that anyone would have to suffer from nature's rage, but she couldn't help hoping the storm stayed on course. "What's this one called?"

"Eden."

Eden? That denoted paradise, not destruction. A very poor name choice, as far as she was concerned.

Marissa leaned through the opening to find Greg standing before the TV, his back to her. "Where's Jen?"

"In Europe."

That brought Marissa straight into the family room on the heels of her surprise. "Europe? When did that happen?"

"Two days ago," he said, while remaining focused on the TV. "She's backpacking with her mother."

Her mother was how Greg had always referred to his ex-wife, though he'd rarely mentioned her at all. Marissa had met Beverly Westbrook only once and that had been a very brief encounter. "Jen didn't say a thing about it before I left."

He dropped down onto the sofa and flipped through several channels. "She didn't tell me about it until the day after you left. She was afraid I might not let her go."

He sounded as if he wasn't too pleased. "How long will she be gone?" she asked.

"Ten more days."

Marissa did a mental countdown. "That means she'll only be home a couple of weeks before she leaves for college."

"I know. I was hoping to spend some time with her before then."

Deciding dinner could wait, Marissa took the sea-green chair adjacent to the matching couch. The first time she'd entered this room, she'd been taken aback by the gray-painted cement floors and stone walls. A hurricane-proof design with no insulation, Greg had told her. Very basic and somewhat sparse, but she'd grown to like the surroundings. In fact, she liked everything about the house, including the owner. Especially the owner.

She slipped off her flip-flops and curled her legs beneath her on the cushions. "Well, look at it this way. Georgia's not all that far from here. You can visit Jen at school, and she'll probably come home at least one weekend a month, or when she needs money, whichever comes first."

Greg didn't look as if he appreciated her attempt to lighten the mood. "You know how it is when kids go to school away from home. They get busy and don't bother with their parents after a while."

Marissa could argue that point—she'd always stayed close to her father, even when distance had separated them for a few years, before he'd needed her home for good. "You don't have to worry about that. Jen's definitely a daddy's girl." Just as Marissa had been with her own father. "Why else would she have chosen to stay with you after the divorce?"

"Because she'd just started high school. She didn't want to leave her friends."

"Jen's outgoing. She would have adjusted to a new school. She didn't want to leave you. She told me so."

"She probably thought I'd starve to death having to fend for myself."

He definitely hadn't starved in the four years since his divorce. In fact, he looked quite healthy. "Has she called you yet?"

He continued to hold the remote control in a death grip. "Yeah, when she got to London. But I won't hear from her again until Monday, if she can get through if the weather turns bad."

"At least she'll be out of harm's way if it does turn bad," she said. "And when she does call, find out where I can reach her. I'd like to read her the riot act."

His gaze zipped from the TV to her. "What did she do?"

"Nothing serious. It has to do with Baby."

The beginning of a smile played at the corners of his mouth. "Oh, yeah? I had to take care of that bird for the past few days and she looked fine to me."

Marissa got the distinct feeling he already knew about *that bird*'s newest expression. In fact, he'd probably already heard Baby say it. "Actually, it has to do with something Jen taught her. She can now say 'Greg's a hunk.' Do you know anything about that?"

He tossed aside the remote, sank back on the sofa and laughed. "I'll be damned. For two days I tried to get her to say it, but she never would. Guess she was just waiting for you to get home."

Marissa took a moment to mull that over. "Let me get this straight. You taught my parrot to say you're a hunk? Might I ask why?"

He shrugged. "I'm about to turn forty. I need my ego stroked."

"I can't even imagine that, Greg Westbrook," she said. "I'm sure plenty of women would like to stroke your ego. Among other things."

He leaned forward and draped his forearms on his knees. "You know any of these presumed women?"

Yes. She was one of them. "I'm sure you'll have no trouble finding them yourself, Doctor."

He nailed her with those deadly dark brown eyes. "Admit it, Marissa. Everyone needs a few strokes now and then, including you."

She lifted her chin. "I don't need to rely on anyone to stroke my ego."

He inclined his head and studied her a long moment. "Who said anything about your ego?"

On the wings of her sudden discomfort, Marissa practically flew out of the chair. "I'm going to fix dinner now."

She'd barely made it back into the kitchen before Greg appeared and leaned one hip against the counter to face her. Snatching up a potato, she began scrubbing it over the sink, dropping it twice while he just stood there watching her. "You need to start the grill," she said, without looking at him.

"In a minute. First, I want to know something."

Marissa suspected she knew what that *something* might be, and she was surprised he hadn't bothered to ask until now. "Yes, they offered me the job."

"That's not what I want to know."

She ripped a paper towel from the holder and draped it on the counter as a resting place for the potato. "Ask away."

"You've been here almost a year, and not once do I remember you going out with anyone."

She shrugged. "So?"

"You're an attractive woman. I'm surprised you haven't had any kind of relationship. Why is that?"

She turned and leaned back against the sink. "How

do you know I haven't been having a torrid affair with the pool boy?"

He sent her a crooked smile. "You don't have a pool."

Good point. "How do you know I haven't been carrying on with *your* pool boy?"

"Because I'm the pool boy, and believe me, I wouldn't have forgotten that."

A span of silence and a sudden spark of awareness filled the small space between them. For the past eight months, Marissa had effectively hidden her attraction to him, in deference to his former girlfriend and his daughter. Yet she wasn't sure how well she was masking that attraction at the moment, so she went back to scrubbing the second spud. "If I decide to move to Chicago, I'm sure I'll have a boost in my social life."

"I'm going to start the grill and grab a shower," he said, then left the room without even questioning whether she'd arrived at that decision. No *Congratulations, Marissa,* or *Have a nice life.* Nothing but his abrupt departure.

The truth was, Marissa still didn't know whether to take the job. If she accepted the position, then she would have to give up the freedom of owning her own marketing-research business, and working from home. But she would have more money than she'd ever had before. She would also have to sell the house and, in a way, say goodbye to her father once and for all. Worse, she would have to leave behind Greg and Jen, who had saved her from being a complete recluse.

But with the prospect of a hurricane hanging over her head, she had more to worry about at the moment— namely that if the storm changed course and made Ocean Vista its target, the decision to leave could very well be made for her.

SURROUNDED BY STARS and the string of patio lights, Greg watched Marissa sip her after-dinner wine while he struggled for something casual to say. That normally wasn't a problem. She'd been a great neighbor and a good friend, easy to talk to. She was also a fantastic-looking woman with sleek brown hair and deep blue eyes. And even though she wasn't his usual type—tall and narrow—he'd come to appreciate her small stature and liberal curves. She definitely filled out her clothes well, even though she was prone to wearing shapeless shirts and baggy shorts. But he'd seen her in a swimsuit, so he knew those curves existed. In fact, he'd memorized just about every one of them—with his eyes but unfortunately not with his hands.

He'd also grown accustomed to having her around, even if this was the first time he could recall having her all to himself since Jen had always been present during their frequent get-togethers. And now that he'd had this opportunity to spend some quality alone-time with her, what had he done? Acted like an ass.

During dinner, not once had he offered his congratulations over the job offer, not that he didn't wish her well. He just didn't like the thought of her leaving. Didn't like the possibility that she might move away now that he had come to terms with the truth—he wanted more from her than friendship. Little did she know, the demise of his and Sophie's relationship had been in part because of her. He'd begun to compare his former lover to his current neighbor in every respect, and Sophie had come up short. Still, he'd be a fool to consider taking his relationship with Marissa to another level, especially if she did decide to move. Foolish or not, he was considering it, and he'd be damned if he could stop it.

In an effort to make amends for his lack of courtesy, Greg settled back in his chair and asked, "When are you supposed to be in Chicago?"

She rimmed a fingertip around the base of her wine-glass. "I haven't given them an answer yet."

Good news. Great news, in fact. "When do they want to know?"

She looked up and leveled her blue eyes on him. "End of next week. It's a lot to consider, but it's a once-in-a-lifetime opportunity."

He didn't like the way that sounded, as if she'd begun to travel in the acceptance direction. "What about your business?"

"I only have two employees, and Susan wants to buy the business. I have several contracts already lined up and, with the connections I've made, she can step right in without any problem. Bill is willing to stay on with her if I decide to hand it over."

Time to bring out a few logical arguments, for selfish reasons. "But that means you'll be giving up some freedom. You won't be the boss anymore. Are you sure that's what you really want?" He sounded almost desperate to sway her. Maybe he was.

"Actually, I will be the boss," she said. "I'll be heading the market-research department."

Now he understood why she would want to make the move. He didn't like it, but he understood it. "What exactly will you be marketing?"

She took a quick sip of wine and set the glass down a little harder than necessary. "Mostly feminine products."

"What kind of feminine products?" he asked, although he already had his suspicions.

Marissa sported a schoolgirl blush as her hand fluttered to her ponytail. "Feminine hygiene products, if you must know."

He chuckled. "Don't look so mortified, Marissa. I have a teenage daughter, I've been married, and I'm a doctor. If you can't talk about this kind of thing with me, then I don't see how you can market the stuff."

"I'm not mortified." She rubbed her forehead before looking up at him again. "I don't have a problem going into a boardroom and discussing it with ten corporate moguls. It's just strange talking about it with you. Quite a switch from what we normally discuss."

He grinned. "We're usually talking to Jen about Jen."

"That's true." She clasped her hands in a white-knuckle grip on the table before her. "Anyway, the company is considering a new line of top-grade lubricants. They want me onboard before they begin the test marketing."

Man, he wasn't sure if he should even enter into a discussion of this nature, but he was more than curious. "Lubricants, as in postmenopausal-women kind of lubricants?"

She grabbed up a napkin and began twisting it with a vengeance. "As a matter of fact, no. These products will be geared to a younger age group. Late twenties to mid-thirties."

"I'm assuming your age group."

She balled up the napkin and tossed it at him. "Yes, my age group. And if you're fishing for my age, I don't mind telling you that I'm thirty-three. And a half."

In reality, Jen had already told him. He leaned forward until his hands were only an inch from hers.

"I'm of the opinion that if a man knows what he's doing during foreplay, bottled lubrication isn't necessary."

She gave him a serious scowl. "Remind me not to test it on you."

Man, that got his attention. He held up his hands, palms forward. "Hey, I didn't say I wasn't willing to try it. Got any samples?"

"No." She reached for her plate. "I'm going to clean up your kitchen then go home. I need to start preparing in case the storm does land here."

Damn, he'd driven her off with his blatant innuendo. He needed to be more subtle, take it more slowly. "I'll do this later," he said as he caught her wrist when she stood. "Sit down for a few more minutes. There's not much you can do tonight." In all honesty, he didn't want her to go yet. If he had his way, she'd spend the night.

When he released his hold on her, she dropped back down in the chair. "I can gather up my keepsakes. Store stuff in plastic, that sort of thing."

"Tomorrow morning, I'll board up your windows, just in case."

"Don't worry about me. You need to make sure you're ready."

If she knew exactly how ready he already was, she'd probably take off in a heartbeat. "My shutters are metal and remote controlled. I've got all the necessary supplies. All I have to do is get some meds from the clinic and move them into the safe room."

"You *are* prepared, aren't you?"

"I have to be. That's part of the job of being on an emergency-medical-response team. I've got to stay ready in case someone needs my services."

"And I hope this passes without anyone needing your services."

So did Greg. He'd seen it all when he'd headed up the trauma unit in Miami, from shootings to car wrecks to abused women and kids. The worst of the worst. But he'd grown accustomed to treating beach injuries and retirees since he'd established his clinic in Ocean Vista. He didn't welcome the prospect of caring for the seriously wounded from his own community, people he knew all too well, and so far he'd been fairly lucky in that regard. But if necessary, he would. "On the off chance that we do see some destruction from this storm, I'll need to secure the clinic in the morning. After that, I'm all yours."

Marissa tapped a fingertip against her chin. "You know something? I just realized I've never seen your safe room."

"You've never seen my bedroom, either, and that's where it is. Want to check it out now?"

Fortunately, she didn't slug him. "Maybe some other time. Right now, I need to go see *my* bedroom."

When she came to her feet, this time he didn't try to stop her. Instead, he stood, too. "I'll walk you home."

Greg's gaze immediately homed in on her breasts when she folded her arms beneath them. "I'm a big girl, Doctor. I can walk myself home."

He forced his eyes back to her face. "I insist, unless you have some reason you don't want me to escort you. Like maybe you have a pool boy waiting for you."

"Unfortunately, no one's waiting for me except the bird. And I'm sure she'll be reminding me all night that you're a hunk."

He rounded the table and stood before her, probably a little closer than necessary. "Hey, whatever works to convince you of that."

She patted his chest. "If it makes you feel any better, I'm convinced."

With that, she turned and left out the gate before he'd even had a chance to move. But move he did, intent on convincing her that they could be good together. But he would proceed with caution and not overwhelm her by coming on too strong. He could manage that without any problem—even if time could be running out before she was gone from his life.

CHAPTER TWO

THEY WALKED in silence down the path joining their properties, the tension as thick as curdled cream, as foggy as Marissa's thoughts. Never had she been so aware of Greg, every move of his athlete's gait, every rasp of his breath. Tonight something had changed in their relationship. A slight shift toward more than friendship, and that had her unsettled.

Once they reached the front porch, Marissa fished her keys from her pocket, reluctant to tell him goodbye, knowing the evening was about to end and she would again be alone. All too mindful of his presence behind her, she tried to unlock the door, and proved to be about as successful with managing the simple act as she had been with washing the potatoes. His arm came around her to assist, putting them in closer proximity, sending Marissa's heart on another marathon. He mastered the lock with a twist of his wrist and opened the door with a push of his palm.

When she faced him, he leaned over and brushed a soft kiss over her lips. "Good night. I'll see you in the morning."

"I'll be up early." If she even went to sleep after that surprise show of affection. He'd never kissed her before, even chastely. Not on the cheek. Especially not on the lips.

She stood in stunned silence, watching him walk away until without any warning, he turned abruptly, strode back to her and framed her face in his palms. Then his mouth met hers in a kiss that would surely curl her straight hair had it not been piled on her head. While the kiss continued, deeper and almost desperate, Greg pulled Marissa closer, tightening his hold, demonstrating his strength. A responding heat smoldered low in her belly and traveled much lower at a rapid pace. Still, as her thoughts spiraled out of control, she was coherent enough to realize she had finally gotten what she'd wanted for months—a kiss from her neighbor. Heck, she was making out with her neighbor on the front porch for anyone to see. Not that she really cared.

Just when she thought her legs might give way, Greg stepped back while Marissa braced against the wall to keep from collapsing. They stared at each other for a time before he turned and headed down the walkway without a word.

"Greg, wait a minute," Marissa called as soon as she had the presence of mind to speak.

He laced his hands behind his head and kept walking. "Go inside, Marissa."

"Don't you think we should—"

"I've got to go," he said, then disappeared into the darkness as if she'd dreamed the entire episode in living color.

Marissa touched her fingertips to her tender lips. No, it hadn't been a dream at all, and her body still carried flaming reminders of the effects of Greg's kiss. After stepping inside and closing the door behind her, she used the adjacent wall for support. She'd inherently known he would be a good kisser, but she hadn't thought he would be *that* good. She also hadn't expected him to run off, either. And that simply wouldn't do.

Jerking the door open, Marissa rushed onto the path, barely making it a yard or so before her flip-flop caught on a flagstone and nearly sent her tumbling to the ground. Balancing on one foot, then the other, she took off the shoes and slipped one on each hand like a pair of rubber-thong gloves.

When she reached the front door, she punched the bell twice with a shoe and still no one answered. Greg had probably gone to bed. He'd probably looked out the window, seen it was her and decided not to answer. Just when she thought she might as well give up and go home, the porch light snapped on and the door opened. And there he stood, one devastating doctor sporting a questioning look—and a bare chest. Now how was she supposed to think, much less speak, with him half-naked? Ridiculous. She'd seen him in swim trunks. She'd shamelessly studied every inch of him when he'd been working out earlier. She'd viewed him without his shirt more times than she could count. Still, she had always kept the urge to touch him reined in. Now the reins were about to snap.

"Mind telling me what that was all about?" she said, while fighting to maintain her gaze on his face, not on his pecs or that little dusting of hair below his ridged abs.

He propped an elbow on the door frame and leaned into it. "You've really been out of the dating loop so long that you didn't recognize a kiss?"

Frustrating man. Beautiful, frustrating man. "Very funny. I know what it was, I just don't know what it meant. And I don't appreciate you leaving without any kind of explanation."

He slicked a hand through his hair then trained his dark eyes on her. "What's there to explain, other than I wanted to do that all evening long? Hell, I've wanted to do it for several months, if the truth be known."

That was one truth she hadn't expected. "Why now? Why tonight?"

"It's the first time I've had the opportunity." He shifted his weight from one leg to the other. "And I ran off because if I hadn't, I would've backed you straight into your bedroom."

And she would have gladly let him. "Oh, really?"

"Yeah, really."

Marissa gaped for a few moments before she finally said, "Okay, then."

He hooked his thumbs in his pockets. "Is that all you have to say?"

Like a trained seal applauding for tourists, she slapped the heels of the flip-flops together. "I need to think. This is a lot to handle."

He rubbed a slow hand down his bare chest, pausing right above his navel. "By all means, go think. I'm going to think, too. All night, about you. About us, doing more than kissing."

His voice was so low, his words so compelling, that Marissa nearly suggested they do it tonight. But she had too much to consider to bound into bed with him, though she felt as if the soles of her bare feet had springs attached.

She waved one flip-flop in the direction of her cottage. "I'm going now. I'll see you in the morning."

Marissa spun around and left before she changed her mind. Before she let carnal need railroad her common sense. In the middle of the path, she tipped her face up and studied the stars. A host of stars unencumbered by even one hazy cloud. Maybe the storm wasn't heading this way after all, but she had a big one brewing inside her soul.

Greg's timing sucked. He'd effectively thrown a solid wrench into her decision making. She could stay and explore a relationship with him that held no guarantees, or take a job that ensured she would get ahead. Alone.

Years ago, she'd been on the fast track in her career and she'd had a fiancé—a man who hadn't been able to accept her decision to care for her father after he'd become ill. She'd given up a lot to do that very thing, yet she had few regrets. After all, her dad had unselfishly cared for her all by himself since the day she was born. Until recently, she hadn't discarded the dream of having children of her own, and a life partner. Unfortunately, she'd had no prospects for several years. Until now.

But after she seriously considered it, Greg hadn't offered anything beyond sex. He hadn't said he cared for her, only that he wanted her. As good as it felt to be wanted, Marissa wanted more. And unless he gave her a better reason to stay, she would have to regard her future in terms of her career.

Too much to think about, and too little time, Marissa decided as she continued toward home. Tomorrow, as soon as the weatherman lifted any serious threats, she would weigh all her options. However, in her mental list of pros and cons, she'd already added a big pro to staying in Ocean Vista—Greg Westbrook.

HE'D TAKEN a long shower, hoping to clear his head and calm his body. It hadn't worked. Greg could still feel the effects of touching Marissa. Kissing Marissa. He considered taking a run to blow off some sexual steam, but a thirty-mile sprint probably wouldn't help. He needed to take a step back before he did something irrational—like take Marissa's key, which he still had in his possession, let himself in like a thief and climb into her bed.

Instead, as he always did around this time of night, he automatically traveled to the opposite side of the house to tell his daughter good-night, before he remembered she wasn't there. He walked into Jen's room and immersed himself in all the reminders—her volleyball trophies lined up like gold soldiers on her shelves, weathered corsages from past proms anchored by pushpins on a corkboard. He turned his attention to the dresser that housed several photographs. Her first day of kindergarten, which he'd missed because he'd been a first-year medical student and working thirty-six-hour shifts. Her softball championship when she was twelve, an event he hadn't been able to attend due to his responsibility as chief resident.

But he'd been there for her sixteenth birthday, her first date and he'd taught her how to drive. He'd missed a good deal of her formative years, but he couldn't turn back time or regain what he'd lost, no matter how hard he tried. If he could do it all over again, he would do things differently. Yet that wasn't going to happen, so he would settle for being the best dad he could be now.

The high-school diploma proudly displayed on the wall reminded him that his daughter would soon be out of the house permanently, and that thought only increased his strong sense of loneliness. But Jen had to move forward with her life, without him, even if at times Greg felt as if he were at a standstill in his own life. That same sad state of limbo he'd resided in since the divorce. Maybe even before the divorce.

Not only had he failed his daughter, he'd also failed her mother in many ways. For that reason, he'd resisted becoming too involved with any woman. He wasn't sure if he'd ever be any good at any permanent relationship, but at times he wanted to try again. Ironically, that's where Marissa came into the picture. Granted, he wanted her in every way possible. Still, chemistry didn't necessarily make for a solid commitment when two people were at odds with their goals—even if he recognized that it went far beyond simple lust when it came to his feelings for his neighbor. But he'd held Beverly back from realizing her dreams for the sake of his own; he refused to make that same mistake with Marissa. Asking her to stay would be selfish on his part, and he'd become acquainted with selfishness on a very personal level.

Weighted by the familiar guilt, Greg walked onto the veranda outside of Jennifer's room, the place that served as his daughter's favorite refuge to talk on the phone with various friends—including more than a few boys. He dropped down onto the glider that faced Marissa's house, dangling the beer he'd brought with him between his parted knees. The curtains covering the wall of windows were open wide, allowing him a prime view into her empty bedroom—one room in her house that he'd never seen, though he'd been tempted to investigate while caring for the obnoxious bird. Respect for her privacy had kept him from doing that to this point. Since she was obviously still up and about somewhere else in the house, he decided to take a visual tour without her knowledge.

A floor lamp illuminated the double bed covered in some crazy leopard-skin print. Typical Marissa. She was definitely a contradiction—the independent woman who at times seemed vulnerable. He'd witnessed that vulnerability tonight. He'd witnessed a lot more than that, including a response to his kiss that he'd welcomed, even if he had taken off in a rush. But as he'd told her, if he hadn't made a quick getaway, he might be in her bedroom rolled up in that animal-skin throw, wrapped in Marissa's arms, jumping the gun before either of them was ready. After all, tonight was the first time their relationship had tilted toward anything beyond friendship. They needed time to get used to the change—unless she decided to move, and he ran out of time.

Releasing a rough sigh, Greg leaned back in the swing and set the glider in motion with his heel, rocking it back and forth while he continued to stare at Marissa's bedroom like some lunatic voyeur.

When the bathroom door opened and Marissa walked out with her hair wrapped in one towel and her body wrapped in another, Greg stopped the glider's motion. He knew in that instant he should leave, but as she perched on the vanity stool in front of the dresser's mirror, innocently readying for bed, he felt as if his ass had been glued to the wooden seat.

Hell, he was a voyeur.

Leaning forward, he watched her towel-dry her brown hair and run a brush through it several times with long fluid strokes. He missed the ritual of witnessing a woman preparing for bed. The soft scents keeping him awake, the soft body curled into his own. He and Beverly hadn't shared that kind of familiarity in the last few years of their marriage. The intimacy had been replaced by closed bathroom doors and closed-off emotions, a wide berth that neither had been able to span.

Marissa rose from the vanity, propped one foot on the stool, then began rubbing her legs with lotion. Starting with her calves, she worked her way up to her knees, then her thighs, parting the towel to immediately below the point of decency, luckily keeping everything vital from his view.

Greg wished he was applying that lotion, only he wouldn't stop at her thighs. His body burned and ached like he'd run nonstop for hours. More like one part of his body that had little to do with running. He continued to watch her, sorely tempted to go to her house and beg her to end this torture. Still, he didn't leave or turn away. He was paralyzed by some masochistic need to wait.

She glanced at the windows and he suspected she was about to shut the curtains. Shut out his prying eyes, because he didn't have the will to leave. For a moment he wondered if she could see him gawking at her through the darkness surrounding him.

Instead of closing him out, she stretched, tugged the towel away and dropped it to the floor. Even in the limited light, he could make out Marissa's soft curves before she slipped a plain cotton gown over her head and shimmied it down her body. And though she was now completely covered, his body still paid the price. He should have left while he'd had the chance.

He remained frozen in place when she tossed back the covers and slipped onto the edge of the bed. His heart pumped at an accelerated pace, every ounce of his blood seeming to settle in his groin. He'd never been so hard in his life. And she still had no idea he was spying on her. Or did she?

The question shot through his mind as she stood again and, before turning off the light, stared at him straight on. He saw the flash of her smile before the room went dark.

Damn her, she did know. What kind of game was she playing? Maybe she was punishing him for his behavior. But this wasn't simple punishment. This was the worst kind of torment—and he probably deserved it.

He pushed out of the glider and downed the last of his beer in two gulps, but it did nothing to rid him of the agony of wanting and not having. When he returned inside to Jen's room, he checked the bedside clock, noting it was now past midnight, the arrival of a new day, reminding him that he needed to turn on the TV and get the latest reports. If nothing had changed with the weather, he'd go to bed wanting Marissa, needing her with such severity that it was all he could do to hold on to his control. He would go to bed and consider that she might soon be leaving him, too. Just like his ex-wife had five years ago, thanks to him.

THE SOUND OF THE BLARING DISTRESS signal sent Greg off the sofa and onto his feet. Not knowing how long he'd been asleep, he glanced at the clock, noting it was almost five in the morning, and centered his attention back on the warning flashing across the screen.

The hurricane was heading straight for them, projected landfall—Panama City. Not more than fifteen miles away.

Dammit! Just when they'd begun to recover from the last barrage that had assaulted the state, here it came again. And worse, the hurricane had picked up speed in the past few hours, which meant they had limited time to prepare. No substantial time, in fact, according to the commentator. Four hours, tops.

After shrugging on his T-shirt and working his feet into his cross-trainers, Greg fished through his pockets for his keys, specifically Marissa's house key. Rather than call her, he decided to deliver the sorry news personally. As soon as he made sure she was awake, he would escort her to the local shelter before returning to the house to ride it out.

Her safety was foremost on his mind, the reason he warred with keeping her at his side and sending her off to huddle with the masses. But the high school was farther inland, built to survive the worst of the worst, and that would probably be best, even if he'd gone to great expense using the latest technology to hurricane-proof his own place.

As he headed toward the door, two words stopped him dead in his tracks and made his gut clench. Two words that no Floridian ever wanted to hear again.

Category 4.

"MARISSA, WAKE UP. We've got to get rolling."

Clasping the sheet to her throat with one hand, Marissa bolted upright and pushed her hair out of face to find her dream had come to life. Greg stood by her bed wearing a black T-shirt, faded jeans and a grave expression, looking as if he had the entire weight of the world resting on his broad shoulders.

She had to ask, yet she was afraid to ask. Afraid she already knew the answer. "What are you doing here?"

He rubbed one hand over the back of his neck. "It's heading this way."

She didn't have to ask what "it" was. After coming to her knees, she stared at him in disbelief. "How bad is it going to get?"

"Pretty bad. When it hit the Gulf, it got stronger and faster and it changed course. They've clocked the winds as high as one-forty. The storm surge could reach fifteen feet." He released a rough sigh. "It's a Category 4."

Marissa tried to catalogue all the facts, but her mind rejected the details—except for one. Category 4. "What do we do now?" Aside from panic, or have an emotional breakdown, which she refused to do, however tempting that might be.

"As far as this house is concerned, there's not much we can do," he said. "Some of the plywood in the garage is splintered so there's not enough to cover all the windows. We'll hope for the best under the circumstances."

And expect the worst, Marissa decided. "I have to do something. I can't just ignore this house." That would be like discarding her father's memory without a second thought.

Greg paced a few steps before he faced her again. "I'll do what I can with the windows, use what wood's available and tape up the rest. I'll also move some of the furniture and make sure the gas is shut off. Right now you need to grab a few things and I'll drive you to the shelter. After that, I need to secure the clinic and grab some supplies."

"Do you intend to stay at the shelter?"

"No."

Exactly what she'd expected. "Then I'm not going."

His eyes reflected an anger she'd never seen before. "Dammit, Marissa, you can't stay in this house and ride it out. It's not safe."

"It's held up through several storms, with only minor damage."

"And every time, the damage has been worse because of its age."

Marissa realized the validity in that observation, even if she didn't like it. "What will I do with Baby? I can't take her into a crowded shelter. She'll drive everyone nuts. And I'm not even sure they'd allow her to be there."

He looked at her as if she'd gone nuts. "I'll keep her with me."

She lifted her chin in defiance. "I go where the bird goes, so if she's with you, then I'm going to stay with you."

"No way."

"Why not? Obviously you think your house is safe enough."

She saw indecision cross his face then finally, acceptance. "Okay, you can stay with me. I'll take the bird to my place now and as soon as I get back from the clinic, we'll get settled in the safe room."

A minor victory for Marissa, one she didn't care to celebrate at the moment. She had too many other things to deal with, namely the angry bite of fear threatening her composure.

Greg picked up the clothes she'd laid out on the bureau and tossed them onto the bed. "Get dressed, and be sure to fill up the tub for washing up later in case a water main breaks. Only bring what you can't live without. Understood?"

His harsh tone made her cringe, and bristle. "Yes, sir. Captain, sir." She topped off the comment with a salute.

He dropped onto the bed and took her hands into his. "This is serious business, Marissa. We have to move fast."

"Don't you think I know that?" She sent a sweeping gesture over the room. "Everything that means anything to me is in here, and I'm terrified I'm going to lose it all." And that included him, too.

He pulled her into his arms and gave her a brief hug. Only minimal contact, but Marissa appreciated it more than he knew. "We'll survive this. You can count on me to do everything I can to make sure that happens."

She *was* counting on him, and that was odd considering she'd only counted on herself for many, many years. This whole scenario was surreal, and incredibly scary. But at least with Greg nearby, she would feel somewhat safer, whatever the storm might bring.

CHAPTER THREE

MARISSA DIDN'T KNOW what to take, and what to leave.
She possessed myriad keepsakes, some she had bagged
in plastic the night before. She chose to take only a few
souvenirs, including the scrapbook she'd kept for years.
And of course, she couldn't leave her notebook computer. All her important business files and contacts were
stored there, but luckily Susan had backup, and she
lived in Arizona. No hurricanes in Arizona, and that
seemed like a nice place to be at the moment, Marissa
thought as she crammed a couple of T-shirts and shorts
and a pair of jeans, along with a few pair of panties and
bras into the nylon bag. A bag that was so full it
wouldn't even zip. But that was okay. She didn't have
time to reorganize, and that was all too apparent as she
looked out the crack in the wood covering her bedroom
window to see the trees in the backyard bending like
sipping straws in the thrashing wind. The clouds looked
ominous and the rain had already begun. The skies had
darkened and although it was nearing eight a.m., it
looked closer to dusk than to dawn.

When the phone rang, she snatched it off the charger
and, for a split second, she expected a call announcing
it had all been a mistake. The hurricane had done an
about-face and was headed back out to sea. "Hello?"

"I'm about to pull into the driveway," Greg said,

without delivering a formal greeting. "Get your stuff and meet me at the front door. And hurry."

"Okay," she muttered before hanging up. She could barely draw a breath and almost froze where she stood. But survival instinct kicked in and sent her rushing into the living room, bag hanging from one shoulder, computer briefcase from the other, and the motley stuffed dog named Egbert hugged tightly in her arms. She'd had him since she was five, and as silly as it seemed, she couldn't force herself to leave him behind.

Marissa stepped onto the porch and, as soon as Greg's Lincoln Navigator pulled into his driveway, she turned to secure the door. The force of the wind blew it back so hard she thought it might rip off at the hinges. No need to lock it, she decided. If some idiot wanted to take on a hurricane and break in, they could help themselves to the TV and DVD player. Most of what she owned would mean little to anyone else, anyway.

The pelting rain stung her bare legs as she walked the path, battling the wind and her hair, which kept whipping into her eyes. She could see Greg standing on his porch wearing a yellow slicker, and she hadn't even bothered with a jacket. Her clothes were already soaked to her skin but her main concern was getting to the house. Getting to Greg.

Then something slapped her hard in the face, some piece of debris that had shot out of nowhere. She dropped Egbert on the ground, and when she reached down to pick him up, both bags slid off her arms. Her clothes fell out of the duffel and scattered about the yard, her forehead throbbed like the devil, and she was tempted to sit down and cry uncle. Or maybe just cry.

Then Greg was there, his large hands gathering her things, helping her up and cradling her elbow to guide her to safety. He didn't scold her, didn't say a word, in fact, until they were in his foyer and out of the brutal elements.

After grabbing up a square black case, Greg said, "Come on." She followed behind him like a lost child, and probably looked like one with her favorite stuffed animal still in her grasp and her wet hair stringing down in her face.

Greg strode down the hall that Marissa had never really explored before. At the end of the corridor, he opened the door to a bedroom that contained simple, masculine furniture and a king-size bed covered in brown suede. Obviously his bedroom. She had little time to survey the area before Greg bypassed her, crossed the room and opened a door. A metal door with several locks and a heavy latch. "In here," he said as he moved aside to allow her entry.

When she stepped inside, Marissa felt as if she'd entered a bank vault about the size of a double walk-in closet. Other than a built-in, multidrawer cabinet housing a small sink and refrigerator, and a double mattress covered by plain white bedding, no other furnishings existed. A few boxes lined the walls, and the area was illuminated by two lights set inside portable fans resting on the counter, casting the platinum walls in an almost eerie glow. Fortunately, she wasn't prone to claustrophobia, otherwise she might have hyperventilated when Greg closed the door, the sounds of tripping locks echoing off the metal tomb.

Persistent squawking drew Marissa's attention to her left, where a glint of gold against silver indicated Baby's cage set on the floor. She had to admit it, having Baby there made the place feel a little more livable.

She knelt in front of the cage and stuck her finger

inside to stroke the bird's forehead. "Hey, Baby." The macaw chirped another sound of protest. "I know you don't like this, being down on the ground, but at least you'll still have your feathers intact when this is over."

When Marissa came to her feet again, Greg breezed past her, grabbed a towel from the counter and handed it to her. "All your things are wet, so you're going to have to wear something of mine." He crouched down, opened the bottom drawer, pulled out a T-shirt and a pair of shorts and offered them over one shoulder. "This will have to do right now."

Considering Greg was at least six-two, and she was barely five-four, that could be interesting. But making a fashion statement certainly wasn't utmost on Marissa's mind at the moment. Surviving was.

When Greg turned his back, she pulled her soggy blue T-shirt over her head and wriggled out of the clinging pair of white cotton shorts then laid them out on the floor. She dried off as best she could and, although her bra was damp and so were her panties, she decided she could live with that. The replacement clothing was definitely too big, particularly the black jersey shorts that she cinched as tight as the drawstring allowed. They still drooped low on her hips, which really didn't matter since the white T-shirt hit her mid-thigh.

Taking the towel in hand, she began to pat her hair while she peered over Greg's shoulder. "What do you have there?" she asked when he slid several vials into the refrigerator.

"Mostly insulin," he said, without turning around. "It can be hard to come by after a major storm. I picked these up from the clinic and I keep nonperishable supplies in here to carry with me when the need arises.

I'm running short on a few things. I should have taken inventory last night, but I was a little distracted."

She heard a smile in his voice, which made her smile too despite the increasing sounds of chaos surrounding them. "Did you enjoy the little show from Jen's porch?"

"You could say that."

"Pretty girl," Baby chimed in.

"I couldn't agree more," Greg said as he sent a quick glance over his shoulder. "And I suppose I should apologize for staring into your window. I didn't realize a person could see into your bedroom from Jen's room."

She had a hard time believing that, but she'd give him the benefit of the doubt. Besides, she'd engaged in her own covert surveillance through his fence yesterday, so who was she to criticize? Not to mention, she hadn't minded knowing he'd been watching her. In fact, she'd been totally turned-on by that knowledge, and that had kept her awake much of the night—when she should have been worrying about the possible hurricane. "Actually, Jen and I have been known to hold conversations in the evening while she's on the porch. I talk to her through the open window. She likes to fill me in on the latest gossip in town. Riveting stuff—who got a new set of dentures, who's cheating during bridge games. That sort of thing."

"Oh, yeah?" He turned and leaned back against the counter. His smile suddenly withered into a scowl. "When did you get that cut on your forehead?"

Funny, she'd totally forgotten about that. "In the yard. Something hit me, although I don't know what it was. It doesn't hurt that much."

He pushed her hair away from her forehead to examine the wound. "Have you had a tetanus shot in the last ten years?"

"I'm not sure. It's been a while." A long while since a man had touched her the way Greg had, on so many levels.

"I can remedy that," he said, before turning to the counter and withdrawing a syringe from one of the drawers.

Darn, she should have lied. "How nice to be holed up with a needle-wielding doctor." When he turned and held up the hypodermic, Marissa cringed. "Where are you going to put that?"

He pushed up the T-shirt's sleeve. "Right here."

Marissa looked away while he gave her the injection, surprised that it was over before she'd registered the stick. She turned her face toward him when he stuck an adhesive bandage on the spot. "You're good, Dr. Westbrook. Just a minimal prick."

He looked up and grinned wide, showing his dimples to full advantage. "I've been called worse."

She rolled her eyes. "Very funny."

He discarded the needle in a nearby metal trash bin. "In case you haven't noticed, I can be fairly tough in certain situations." She had noticed, but the way he'd touched her face, with absolute gentleness, belied his assertion.

"I suppose that comes with the doctor territory," she said. "Saving lives is serious business."

"Yeah, it is." He turned around and rummaged in another drawer before facing her again with some sort of ointment. "This might sting."

It did, but Marissa was determined not to show it. He followed the ointment application with a bandage, then went back to unloading his supplies.

Marissa dropped down onto the makeshift bed and hugged the somewhat soggy Egbert to her. She could hear a slight groaning sound, as if the house protested the sudden invasion. She wondered how others were faring in the area, if they were safe or if the storm had already destroyed homes as well as lives. She didn't want to think about that. Didn't even want to consider what the winds might be doing to her aged house. If only she'd taken the time to do some updating, especially to the roof, aside from installing a few more braces and patching weathered wood. But that hadn't been a priority since the move, and she'd thought she would have more time. She'd been a fool.

Greg finally joined her on the mattress, keeping a moderate distance between them, and patted Egbert on his shaggy brown head. "What's the story behind this poor dog?"

"His name is Egbert." She held up the stuffed animal. "My dad won him for me at a local carnival when I was five or so. He's been with me ever since."

"You had a lot of good times with your dad."

Marissa glanced from Egbert to Greg, who looked surprisingly solemn. "Yes, and a lot of good memories. They tend to help with all the bad."

"Those associated with his death?"

She wasn't sure she wanted to talk about that, but Greg looked sincerely interested, and talking would at least serve to get her mind off their current predicament. "Lou Gehrig's isn't conducive to good memories."

"ALS is tough," he said. "Probably one of the worst diseases to deal with."

"Yes, it is."

"Was it familial or sporadic?"

Marissa tended to forget Greg was a doctor, and that he'd been sufficiently armed with extensive medical knowledge. Because of that, he could appreciate what she'd been through, probably more than anyone she'd encountered outside of her former support group. "Sporadic. After he was diagnosed, my dad did quite a bit of family research, I think mainly to put my mind at ease. He couldn't find anything to indicate anyone in our family ever had it. In fact, they all passed away from natural causes, most at a very old age."

"That's good. At least your odds of contracting it are remote."

The only good thing out of a horrible situation. "He put up a good fight for five years," she continued. "He went downhill on the sixth. I stayed with him as much as I could, but I did have to work though I'd already started the business from home by then. I bought Baby so she could keep him company when I couldn't. She talked to him when he wasn't able to talk himself. In a way, she's his voice."

He favored her with a reassuring smile. "Except for the 'Greg's a hunk' part."

"True."

She returned his smile, but Marissa got that same old substantial lump in her throat. Still felt that same old sorrow and sense of helplessness when the memories rushed in. The endless days and nights of caring for her dad. The continued life in his eyes even when he could no longer speak or move. "The worst part of it all—until the day that he died, he was still aware of what was happening to him. I've often wondered if he was afraid, but I'll never know because he wasn't able to tell me."

Greg rubbed his hand up and down her arm in a comforting gesture. "Sounds like you were a good daughter. And I'm sure he was okay since you were there with him through it all."

She willed the tears away with all the strength she could gather. "I tried to be there for him as much as I could be."

"What about your mother?"

"She died from an aneurysm while giving birth to me. My dad raised me all by himself. Walt Klein, esteemed history professor during the day, just Daddy at night."

"He never remarried?"

She crossed her legs and hugged Egbert tighter. "No. He always said that a love like his and my mom's only came along once. Not that he didn't keep company with a few women. He was quite the charmer. Kind of like you."

Greg looked somewhat self-conscious, and Marissa found that endearing. "I've never seen myself as being particularly charming."

If he could see himself through her eyes, then he might change his mind. "That's your appeal. Quiet charm, not overt."

"I'm surprised you'd say that after last night."

She could say a lot about last night, how she'd stayed awake just thinking about his kiss, about him watching her, all the while wondering what it would be like to go beyond the limit. Go all the way.

Marissa raised her hand and began fanning her flushed face. "It's warm in here. Are you sure we're going to have enough air to breathe?"

He pointed toward several vents. "We have passive air flow. It doesn't rely on any kind of power source so it doesn't matter if the electricity goes out."

"What about your generator?"

"I have a small one that powers the refrigerator in

here, and separate system for the house. I'll turn that on after the storm's over."

And she prayed it would be over soon, without incident. "Then it's going to get really hot in here before it's over?"

His eyes seemed to darken instantaneously. "That's entirely possible."

A few moments of silence passed, the tension as substantial as the rain outside while he continued to study her. She struggled for some cute comeback in response to his suggestive tone. *Promise?* was the first thing that came to mind, but she worried she might be misreading him.

Before she could respond, a loud bang followed by a mournful howl caused Marissa to physically jump while Baby released a screech. "What's that?"

Greg took her hand in his and rubbed his thumb along her wrist. "That's Hurricane Eden letting us know she's definitely arrived."

Marissa could use a diversion, and that prompted an idea. She pointed at the row of boxes. "What do you have in there?" she asked.

"Mostly Jen's things and some pictures."

"I'll show you my stuff if you'll show me yours."

He grinned again. "Now that sounds like a plan, checking out each other's stuff."

She sent him a quelling look though she reacted to his intimation with a pleasant little shiver. "The stuff in the boxes and my bag."

He looked sorely disappointed. "If that's the way you want to pass the time, guess I'm game."

FOR ALMOST TWO HOURS, they sat across from each other, telling childhood stories and revisiting memories as the radio commentator on Greg's battery-operated radio traced the hurricane's path and confirmed what they already knew. Eden was mauling the Florida Panhandle with a vengeance.

While the storm roared like a feral cat around them, Greg relayed the history behind the keepsakes in the boxes and Marissa did the same with the souvenirs she'd brought with her—while Baby serenaded them.

"Ninety-nine bottles of beer on the wall..."

Greg shot a fierce look over his shoulder at the bird. "Doesn't she know another song?"

"No, and she can't count past ninety-nine." Marissa came to her feet, grabbed a towel and draped it over the cage. "Go to sleep, Baby." Not likely that would happen with all the cacophony going on outside. But maybe the macaw would eventually tire out and give up in an hour or two.

After returning to the bed, Marissa rifled through her bag for the last of her mementos. She withdrew the weathered black scrapbook and opened it up on her lap, revealing her parents' wedding photo—her mother dressed in simple white lace and her father wearing a plain black suit and a total look of love.

She turned it around and showed it to Greg. "This is my mom and dad."

He studied it a moment before he said, "Nice-looking couple. Now I know where you come by your looks."

"I'm sure you say that to all the girls you entertain in your safe room."

He lifted his gaze from the photo and landed it on her. "I've never brought anyone in here other than my daughter, and that was during the last storm."

Very welcome news. Marissa certainly didn't like to think that he'd brought Sophie around for a quick roll on the mattress where she now sat. Returning to the photos, she pulled out another of her favorites and offered it to Greg. "That was me when I was twelve, right after I got my braces. As you can see, my father and I both loved animals."

"Two cats and a dog. That's a houseful."

She pointed at the obese gray tabby sitting in her dad's lap. "That's Lord Farley, named after one of my father's colleagues. The Siamese is Railroad, which is where we found him, and the mutt is Toe Jam."

Greg laughed. "You named a dog Toe Jam? And I thought Egbert was bad."

Marissa couldn't help but laugh, too. "I know. It's strange, but my father encouraged me to be creative in all endeavors. We just thought it fit him." As the melancholy settled over her, she sighed. "Sadly, they're all gone now." Everyone but her.

"That's the way life goes," Greg said. "Unfortunately, loss is a part of it."

How well she knew that sense of loss, but she refused to engage in self-pity. Right now she felt very lucky to be alive. Lucky to be in Greg's company. "The rest of this stuff would probably bore you."

"No, it wouldn't. I want to know all about you."

His genuineness touched Marissa and she regretted they'd waited so long to get to know each other better. Better late than never, she supposed, even if she might be leaving soon.

Greg moved to her side while she navigated the album, pointing out various stages of her life depicted in an assortment of souvenirs—from dance recital programs to report cards. When she reached one particular picture, she bypassed it without hesitation.

Greg flipped the page back over before she could move on. "Who's this?"

"That's Brian, an old boyfriend." She sounded as if she'd just downed a whole bottle of pickle brine.

"Someone special?" Greg asked.

She kept her attention on the snapshot of her and Brian during a ski trip, wondering what she had seen in him, and wishing she'd removed the photo a long time ago. "At one time I thought he was special. I was young and very stupid."

"You sound pretty bitter."

"I think we're done with my life story now." She closed the book before he started asking questions she wasn't sure she wanted to answer. Questions that would only serve to revive more resentment.

A whoosh followed by the clang of what sounded like metal against metal reminded Marissa once again why they were there in the safe room.

"Damn it to hell," Greg muttered, heightening Marissa's concern.

"What's wrong?"

He pinched the bridge of his nose between his thumb and forefinger and closed his eyes. "Nothing."

She tugged his arm to get his attention. "Don't tell me *nothing* because I know better."

He finally looked at her. "Either the winds are tearing up my shutters or some kind of debris hit the air-conditioning unit on the outside wall. Not much I can do about it now."

If the hurricane was destroying Greg's window armor, she didn't even want to consider what it might be doing to her barely protected glass.

When Greg stretched out on his back, hands laced

behind his head, Marissa could only stare before she asked, "How can you look so calm?"

"Because I've been through it before. We just have to wait it out."

She hugged the scrapbook to her chest as if it could provide a shield. "Well, I've never been through it before. It's scary as hell."

He patted the space beside him. "Come here and try to relax."

Relax? How could she relax when the world could be shredding at the seams outside? Still, being next to Greg would provide some much needed comfort, even if she couldn't divorce herself from the concern.

On that thought, she laid the book in the bag and stretched out on her back beside him. "Is it possible that the roof might cave in on top of us?"

"It's reinforced masonry, and this room was built to withstand hurricane-force winds. When I planned this house, I made sure it was as stormproof as possible."

Marissa sighed. "I wish I'd done more with mine."

"You can do it after this is over."

"If the house is still standing, and that's a big *if*."

He reached over and ran his knuckles along her jaw. "Hey, I had an older house that survived a pretty bad storm when we lived in Miami."

God love him for giving her hope. "You did?"

"Yeah, I did."

She rolled over to face him. "Why did you leave Miami to settle in Ocean Vista?"

He turned his attention from her back to the ceiling. "As a last-ditch effort to save my marriage."

Marissa had always been curious about the circumstances behind his divorce. Now she would finally get the chance to know a few more details. "Obviously the move didn't help."

This time, he sighed. A rough one. "Nope. Too little, too late. My job was a big part of the problem, so I decided that leaving the trauma scene behind might help." He hesitated a moment. "There was something else we needed to leave behind before we could begin to make it work. Actually, *someone* else."

Maybe she didn't want to know the details after all. Maybe it would be best if she could go on thinking that Greg was an honorable man who would never do anything to ruin his marriage.

But the maybes didn't really matter. She wanted to know. *Had* to know. Drawing in a deep breath, Marissa prepared to ask the question and confront the answer, whatever it might be.

"Did you cheat on your wife?"

CHAPTER FOUR

HE'D BE DAMNED if he'd walked right into that one. Greg hated to even think about it, much less talk about it, and he wasn't too sure he wanted Marissa to know the truth. But male pride had compromised his relationships before, and since this relationship with Marissa had a lot of potential—provided she decided not to move—the truth was important.

"Beverly cheated on me." When he heard the slight catch of her breath, he added, "And I can't say that I blame her."

Marissa rolled onto her back and remained silent for a few moments. "I think you just shocked me more than the surprise arrival of this hurricane."

That was definitely saying a lot, and he needed to say more. "Bev and I married too young. During midterms and after a few beers—we were barely of legal age to drink—she got pregnant. We'd only been dating a couple of months, but I decided to do the right thing. As it turned out, it wasn't right at all."

She rolled to her side, her elbow bent and her palm supporting her jaw. "Did you love her?"

A tough question, one he'd asked himself a lot over the years. "Yeah, but it wasn't always enough. I pursued my career, medical school and residencies, while she quit school and stayed home to raise Jen. We had some good times, but I was obsessed, and she paid the price."

"She never went back to school?"

"She planned to do that when Jen was older. By that time, I'd decided to take on another residency and went from emergency medicine to trauma surgery." At his marriage's peril.

"I had no idea you'd been a surgeon," she said. "I guess I just thought you were always a family doctor."

"Not until we moved here." To start over, only to say goodbye.

"Don't you miss operating?"

The understanding in her voice both surprised and pleased him. Beverly had hated his work long before she'd begun to hate him. "Yeah, at times I do. But at least I got to know my daughter better over the past few years. That made the switch worthwhile."

Marissa touched his arm. "I'm sorry your marriage didn't work out, Greg. But unfortunately, it happens all the time. Just look at the divorce rate."

He turned over on his side to face her so he could fully gauge her reaction to the next question he planned to pose. "Is that why you've never married?"

She lowered her eyes before again focusing on him. "I was actually engaged once, several years ago."

Another revelation Greg hadn't expected. "To the guy in the picture?"

"Yes. It's a long story."

"I want to hear it." And he did. He wanted to know everything, even though thinking about her with another man made his gut churn.

After a slight hesitation, she continued. "I was working at an advertising agency in Boston, and that's where I met him. We were both on the rise with our careers, young and successful. Seemed like a perfect fit. But when my dad was diagnosed, and I decided to move back to New Hampshire to be near him, Brian wasn't willing to do that. I had a choice to make then, stay with him and abandon my father, or call off the engagement. I called things off." She released a slow breath. "Amazing what you discover about people during a crisis."

Very prophetic, because Greg was learning more about Marissa with every moment that passed, and he liked what he'd learned. To this point, they'd kept everything on the surface, not once broaching anything too personal. The relationship was definitely changing, for the better, in his opinion.

He reached over and ran a palm up and down her arm. "I hate that he hurt you. You didn't deserve that, and he sure as hell didn't deserve you."

"I knew that it wasn't meant to be when it didn't take me that long to get over him."

Although she said it with conviction, Greg could still see a twinge of pain in her eyes. He wanted to take away that pain, at least for a while, so he did what he'd wanted to do since that morning. He looped his hand around her neck and reeled her in for a kiss. He kept it light, kept it easy, but he wasn't sure how long he'd be able to do that. Jen had claimed that he'd been engaging Marissa in an ongoing flirtation since the day eight months ago when she'd come over to introduce herself. He'd denied it then, but he couldn't now. He was tired of denying any of it. Tired of pushing aside all these feelings for her, the want and the need.

"Give it to me, Baby."

Marissa pulled away and sat up, thanks to the damn bird. "So much for Baby going to sleep."

Greg fell back onto the pillow and rested a forearm over his eyes. "Yeah. She has great timing."

"Maybe if we turn the lights off, she'll stay quiet."

That sounded like a plan to Greg. A good one. "We can try it."

"Fine, I'll do it."

When Marissa climbed over him, it was all he could do not to pull her against him without formality. Instead, he kept his hands to himself and his eyes covered until he felt the mattress bend, signaling her return.

"It's really dark in here," she said. "I can't see a thing."

But the sounds of the raging storm continued, including a loud series of firecracker pops that made Marissa gasp. "What was that?"

"Probably transformers," he said. "They can explode in severe weather."

"Oh, great."

Greg reached over and found her hand fisted at her side. "Come here."

He slid his arm beneath her shoulders and pulled her to him. She rested her head on his chest and, although he couldn't see her, he could smell the soft scent of her hair and feel her warm breath against his neck. He couldn't count the times he'd imagined this, having her so close, but not under these conditions. He'd wanted to arrive at this place because she'd wanted it, too, not because a disaster dictated the circumstances.

When another crack echoed through the room, her frame went rigid in his arms. "It's okay," he told her as he stroked her hair. "We're safe."

He felt her relax, at least for the time being. Now seemed like a good opportunity to tell her the truth, if only to momentarily divert her from the danger.

"I broke up with Sophie because of you."

"Because of me?"

Greg wasn't surprised by the shock in her tone. He *was* surprised that he'd said it without hesitation. "Every time I was with her, I thought about you. It got a little crowded in the bedroom."

"I didn't mean to—"

"It's not your fault. It just happened."

He gave her a few minutes to let that soak in before he continued. "Do you remember the day we played water volleyball before you left on your trip?"

"Yes. You and me and Jen and Sophie."

"Didn't you ever wonder why you were on my team instead of Sophie?"

"I just assumed that had to do with the height factor. You and Jen are tall, Sophie and I aren't. That made things more even, or so you'd said."

"Yeah, but it would have made more sense for Sophie to be paired up with me."

Marissa remained silent for a few moments before saying, "Come to think of it, yes, that would have made more sense."

"Truth was, I wanted you close to me, not separated by a net."

"Oh. I didn't know that."

She was about to gain a lot of knowledge. "Do you remember you and me fighting over the ball?" he asked. "We just stared at each other a few minutes before I finally let go."

"I remember. Then you suddenly got out of the pool and said you'd had enough for the day."

"I wanted to kiss you so damn bad I had to get away before I did."

"I had no idea you felt that way."

Maybe she just hadn't wanted to see it, but then neither had he. "Sophie noticed all of it. She confronted me later that evening. I denied everything, but then Jen started in on me, too. She told me she'd seen the way I looked at you. I didn't realize I was being so obvious."

"Was Jen angry?"

"Just the opposite. She told me I should dump Sophie and ask you out. She said we've been dancing around our attraction to each other for months, and I'd be crazy not to do something about it. I told her I wasn't sure you felt the same, and she claimed you did, even though you'd never admit it as long as Sophie was in the picture."

Again Marissa fell silent and Greg worried he'd gone too far. "I swear I'm not trying to put you on the spot. I just thought it was past time for me to let you know how I feel. I've had some pretty serious fantasies about you for a while now."

"I have to admit…"

When her words trailed off, he shook her slightly. "Admit what?"

"I've had a few fantasies about you on occasion."

"Just on occasion?"

She sighed. "Okay, on several occasions. I remember one particular day when…" She laughed. "God, I can't believe I'm about to tell you this. Maybe we should just drop it."

Greg began a slow burn below his fly and he figured it was about to get a lot worse. But he wasn't going to let her off the hook. "Tell me."

"Okay. One day you were sitting on the end of the diving board. Jen went in the house to take a phone call and I was lounging in a deck chair. Sophie wasn't around. Anyway, I had this image of you and me, on the diving board."

Damn. "What were we doing?"

She slapped his arm. "You know what we were doing."

He released a low chuckle in spite of his increasing discomfort. "Just one question. Who was on top?"

"I was."

That nearly sent him over the edge—the vision of Marissa taking him on a wild ride atop a diving board. "Might be interesting with the springboard motion."

"So now you know," she said. "I've had my fair share of questionable thoughts about you, too."

"I'm glad to know I'm not alone." Glad to know he hadn't imagined the constant state of awareness, the chemistry between them. "And it would be damned ironic if after all these months, we never had the opportunity to make the fantasies a reality." If she moved away, leaving him behind. Leaving him to always wonder what might have been.

The winds outside roared and the walls groaned, but the noise wasn't loud enough to drown out Marissa when she said, "Maybe we should take the opportunity now."

MARISSA WASN'T SURE what was making more noise— her pounding heart or the hurricane wreaking havoc on the house. For once she'd made a decision without hours of internal debate, and it felt great. Still, she had no idea how Greg would react to her proposition. No clue what he would say or do.

He didn't say a thing. He just took her mouth in a very deep, very persuasive kiss. He breezed his palms over her hips and nudged her closer, divided her legs with his leg and pushed against her. No doubt about it, he wanted her. And she definitely wanted him. Needed him. She needed to forget what might be awaiting her outside this steel harbor. She needed to feel alive, feel as if she could let go, if only for a while. Some might call her crazy, but even if this proved to be the first and last time they made love, she didn't care. Finally having all of Greg, exactly what she'd wanted for months now, was worth a bout of insanity.

He broke the kiss and whispered, "Are you sure?"

"Very." And she was.

"Then I want you out of these clothes," he murmured, as he tugged the T-shirt up and over her head. "If I can't see you, I want to feel you. All of you, without anything standing in my way."

Who was she to argue the point? Or argue anything when he reached behind her back and discarded her still-damp bra with ease. The too-big shorts followed, along with the last barrier—her panties. Now she was totally naked and defenseless, covered only by darkness. And definitely ready for what came next.

After plying her lips with another deep kiss, Greg moved away and although Marissa couldn't see him, she could hear the rustle of fabric and the rasp of a zipper. They were down to the wire, almost past the proverbial point of no return. That didn't deter her in the least. For eight long years she'd been alone, celibate, even though other opportunities had arisen from time to time. But not with a man like Greg. No other man had affected her so deeply or moved her so completely. She worried no other man ever would.

When the mattress dipped beside her, Marissa braced for the impact of having Greg so very close with nothing but bare flesh between them. Yet she could never adequately prepare for the unyielding plane of his chest pressed against her breasts when he took her back into his arms, the way his body fitted against hers and his undeniable state of arousal. They remained that way for a while, limbs intertwined, bodies meshed, hands roving over each other. No candlelight lit the room. No wine at hand. No romantic ballads playing in the background, just the low hum of the weather reports and a riotous storm providing a strange symphony, a reminder that they could still be in dire straits.

Marissa blocked the menace by concentrating solely on Greg. So much time had passed since she'd experienced this kind of intimacy, she wanted to savor every sensation, from solid muscle to hair-roughened thighs, a broad back and straight spine, all of which she explored with insatiable hands. And his mouth moving against hers, the soft, sleek glide of his tongue, well, that added more fuel to the already blazing fire. Yet she wanted to know more. Feel more.

Marissa opened her palm against his chest and slid it down the slight dusting of hair, down his ridged abdomen before curling her fingertips around his erection. As far as she was concerned, first-time lovemaking involved a little experimentation as well as some detective work. She touched him with hesitancy at first before growing bolder, exploring the territory while listening carefully for his reaction. The slight shudder coursing through his body told her she was pleasing him, and that pleased her. But she hadn't quite satisfied her curiosity before Greg caught her wrist, pulled her hand away and rested it against his chest.

"You've got me where you want me," he whispered. "Now it's my turn."

When he lowered his lips to her breast and drew a

nipple into the warmth of his mouth, Marissa released
a ragged rush of air. When his hand breezed down her
belly and curled between her thighs, she held her breath.
With the room completely dark, her senses were heightened, or perhaps it was just his skill that made it appear
that way. He made her feel weak and so…*hot*. Maybe
this was all he planned—mutual foreplay—since they
hadn't discussed birth control, a nonexistent priority in
her life. Maybe she should…

Stop thinking, and that's exactly what Marissa did
when Greg quickened his caress, slid a finger inside her,
and said, "Now I have you almost where I want you."

And he did, right on the brink of a climax. She held
on to him tightly while losing her grip on reality. Almost
too much, she thought. Maybe even more than she could
endure. But she had no will to stop him, no thought but
to give in to the orgasm's sudden surge that forced a low
moan out of her mouth as spasm after spasm hit her with
such force she trembled all over. As the wave began to
subside, she gripped Greg's solid arms as if he were a
lifeline, and in many ways, he was. He'd brought an el-
emental part of her back to life. In fact, she'd never felt
so alive, yet she still wanted more. She wanted it all.

"Greg, I need…"

"I know what you need. So do I." He feathered
another kiss across her lips before he left her again.

Feeling strangely bereft, she almost issued a protest
until she heard the sound of jingling keys followed by
tearing paper, and then she knew. Greg had a condom
in his pocket, indicating he was always prepared. Of
course he was. The man was equipped to handle every
situation. Definitely well equipped, she thought as he
moved atop her and eased partially inside her, meeting
a slight resistance.

"Relax, babe," he told her.

"It's been a while," she said.

"I know, and I don't want to hurt you."

"You won't unless you stop. Then I'll have to hurt *you*."

He released a low chuckle. "Believe me, I have no intention of stopping."

After a harder thrust, Marissa's body accommodated Greg. Accepted him. Welcomed him. With him seated deep inside her, she expected a mad rush. What she got was an easy rhythm and Greg's rough sigh.

"I wish I could see you," he whispered, while lining her jaw with kisses. "I'd turn on the light but I don't want to wake up the bird."

Baby's rendition of the beer song was a surefire way to ruin the mood. "Let's not do that."

"Then tell me what you're feeling."

How could she possibly put that into words? "I feel like I've been asleep for a long time, and now I'm awake. I can't remember feeling this good in years."

"Neither can I."

All talk gave way to another kiss and a faster pace, an almost desperate tempo. She tuned out the sounds of the crashing wind, the occasional crack, the hurricane itself. The twist of fate that had brought them to this point could only be appreciated now, despite the possibility of destruction. Life affirmation at its finest.

She soon learned two things about Greg—he had a lot of stamina, and he was determined. Determined to draw another climax out of her, which he did, using his hands and his body and some moves she had never before experienced.

"Man, I felt that," he said.

So had Marissa. Every pulse. If only she could see

him as he lifted her legs around his waist and thrust again and again, driving even harder. But she could imagine how he would look—imposing, powerful, gorgeous. She imagined his jaw tightening, his muscles straining, his dark eyes flashing. After a few more thrusts, his body tensed in her arms and he muttered a low groan before he buckled against her, the sound of his harsh breathing at her ear.

Marissa hated that it was over, hated that it might only be this once, but she didn't hate the way he felt against her, or his weight or his gifted hands continuously skimming over her body. She'd never been so content, so satisfied or so ready to do it again.

They continued to hold each other, their slick bodies still joined as the storm raged on. She drifted off to sleep with Greg inside her, and came awake when he rolled away.

"Did you have to leave so soon?" she asked.

"I'm not exactly a lightweight. It's also getting pretty warm. I didn't want you to be uncomfortable."

Marissa could get used to that kind of discomfort on a regular basis, even though her hair now clung to her damp forehead and it felt as if no air was stirring at all. A few moments ago, she hadn't minded the heat. The heat that Greg had generated. But without him in her arms, the room was stifling. "You're right. It's a sauna in here," she said, though she had no cause to complain. Not after what she'd experienced with him. "Maybe I'll lose that stubborn ten pounds I've been carrying around for a couple of years."

She hadn't realized Greg had moved until she heard the sound of running water in the sink. At least they still had water, a positive in a situation filled with negatives. A booming *thwack* coming from above them prompted

Marissa to close her eyes and served to reaffirm what they were still facing.

"Probably just debris hitting the roof," Greg said. "We'll have a lot more of that in the next few hours."

"Thanks for warning me." But all the warnings in the world couldn't dispel Marissa's fears. She imagined trees falling, strangers' cars whirling down the street, her cottage in ruins. She refused to think about that now, would prefer not to think about anything aside from their lovemaking, although that seemed highly illogical in light of the situation.

A gust of air and sudden beam of light caused her eyes to snap open. Greg had brought the fan/light combination to the side of the bed and set it on the floor, directing it at her. Now her bare body was center stage and spotlighted for his perusal.

"You don't need to lose any weight," he said as he sat on the edge of the mattress, his gaze raking down her then back up again. "You're perfect just the way you are." He said it with such certainty, looked at her with such marked appreciation, she actually believed him.

Assaulted by a bout of shyness, Marissa tugged the pillow from beneath her head and placed it over her eyes. "Is that light necessary?" she asked.

"I just want to see what I'm doing."

When she felt something damp grazing her neck, she lifted the pillow to find Greg with washcloth in hand, obviously intent on giving her an impromptu bath. "How does that feel?" he asked as he lifted her arm and ran the cloth down it.

She tossed the feather pillow behind her. "It feels great. It's definitely cooling me off." Sort of.

"Good. We might have to do this for several days."

He grinned. "You bathe me, I bathe you. Kind of makes the loss of utilities worth it."

Boy, did it. "That's mighty neighborly of you, Dr. Westbrook."

He bathed her other arm before moving to her chest, gently sweeping the cloth over her breasts before continuing on to her belly. "At your service, Ms. Klein. I aim to please."

She was definitely pleased, even though she felt incredibly selfish. While others most certainly struggled to survive the storm, she was being tended by a man determined to see to her comfort. She didn't have the will to protest as he washed her leg, concentrating first on her knee before sliding the cloth up her thigh. Although his ministrations to that point were innocent enough, Marissa reacted with a shiver that contrasted with a heady rush of warmth.

"Is the water too cold?" Greg asked, indicating he'd noticed her slight tremor.

"No."

He lifted her other leg and bent it at the knee, leaving her totally exposed. Vulnerable. Excited. "Are you sure? You're shaking."

"I promise it's not the water."

He skimmed the cloth up the inside of her thigh and along her pelvis. "You're still hot?" His tone was low, oh so sexy and very suggestive.

"You could say that my temperature is definitely rising."

And she grew hotter still when he focused his sponge bath between her legs. "Are you hot here?"

She shook again, only a slight tremor, but an obvious one. "Yes, and you're not helping the situation."

After tossing the cloth aside, he lowered his head and

placed a kiss below her navel, his dark eyes pinning her in place. "I've always believed that a little after play can do a woman a world of good."

After play? She was still reeling from both the *fore* and *during* play. She couldn't imagine she had anything left, but then his magical mouth swooped down on her. Marissa fisted the sheets and tipped her head back, her lips closed tightly against the threat of a loud moan. Maybe even a scream, something she'd never, ever done before during lovemaking. She couldn't quite fathom how she could still be so sexually keyed up, or why she was responding as if she hadn't had an orgasm in years, not minutes. But she *was* responding—to every pull of his lips and soft stroke of his tongue. In a matter of minutes, she was totally at his command, her hips lifting and shifting and her body racked with shock wave after shock wave, compliments of another powerful climax. The third one. How could that be possible?

Easy. This was Greg. He had completely ruined her for anyone else. He'd introduced her to his skill, meted out his mastery and turned her into a voracious female. Worse, he was quickly transforming her into a woman inadvisably falling in love.

"You don't play fair," she told him as he kissed his way back up her torso and stretched out on his side, looking very pleased.

He rimmed her breasts with a fingertip, causing her nipples to pucker. "You are one responsive lady."

"Only with you," she admitted. "I've never been... well..."

"That turned-on?"

She rolled over to face him and draped a hand over his bare hip. "Multiorgasmic. I've never had three before in such a short span of time."

"You've never been with the right man."

Very true. A little cocky, but right on target. Nothing wrong with a healthy dose of confidence. "I suppose you could say that." She sat up and nudged him onto his back. "Now it's my turn to bathe you."

"You won't get any argument from me."

After finding the discarded cloth, Marissa stood and walked to the sink to draw more water, not daring to look back even though she could sense his gaze boring into her. When she returned to the bed, she discovered he looked quite willing and submissive with his arms folded behind his neck. And incredibly sexy with his mussed golden hair and gorgeous body laid out before her like a manly buffet.

Kneeling on the floor beside him, she took in all the details as she bathed his body the way he had hers. She began with his arms, noting the fine-tuned definition, the supreme strength. She moved on to his chest, outlining his collarbone in small circles before paying special attention to each of his nipples as he had hers. She swiped the cloth down his belly slowly and kept right on going to her intended target. But before she could go any farther, he clasped her wrist.

"Whoa there."

She sent him a severe frown. "Hey, you didn't stop, so I shouldn't have to, either."

"I'm getting hard again just thinking about you touching me, and I don't have another condom."

"Are you absolutely sure?" Marissa couldn't believe she'd actually asked that, and with such all-consuming enthusiasm.

Greg responded with a laugh. "Unfortunately, no. I only keep one with me for emergencies. Unless you want me to take a chance and go into the bathroom to get some more."

"Of course not. That would be dangerous."

He took the cloth from her grip, tossed it aside and pulled her flush against him. "You're dangerous." He slid his tongue slowly over her bottom lip. "You make me want to forget my responsibilities and stay with you in here for days."

"That sounds like a wonderful idea, but you have to play doctor and I…" *Have to decide if I'm moving.* Now that decision had been further complicated by their love-making, and her recognition that she was falling for him. "I have to see if my house is still standing," she added, bounding back into reality and away from the bliss.

But the bliss returned when he tugged her to his mouth for another kiss. She could feel the temperature rising again, and that wasn't all. Breaking the kiss, she pulled back and looked at him. "Are you sure you don't have a condom in one of those drawers over there?"

"Yeah, I'm sure. And I'm tempted to make a run for the bathroom, to hell with the weather."

"I have a better idea."

He worked his hands into her hair as she lowered her mouth to his torso. "I might not survive your idea," he said.

She lifted her head and smiled. "You can handle it, Westbrook."

But just as Marissa set her lips in motion down his body, a sharp crackle filled the room, followed by the sound of a male voice saying, "Come in, Dr. Westbrook."

Greg raised his head and muttered, "Dammit."

"What is it now?"

"My job." After nudging her aside, he bolted out of the bed and retrieved a handheld, two-way emergency radio from the counter. "This is Westbrook."

"Hey, Doc, this is Charlie Godwin. I'm over at the high school. We've got a lady in labor here and the EMTs could use your help."

"What stage is she?"

"The paramedics tell me she's moving fast toward delivery and they need your help. The storm eye's passing over us now and should last another thirty minutes or so. That should give you enough of a break to get here."

"Okay. I'll be there as soon as I can get out. In the meantime, tell the EMTs to keep her on her side."

After Greg signed off, Marissa pulled the sheet up from the end of the bed and tugged it to her chin, fighting a piercing sense of panic. "You're going to have to leave?"

"Yeah. At least the high school's not that far." He pushed away from the counter and began to dress while Marissa watched, her mind a jumble of concerns. If he left, she would be alone in this metal bastion. That definitely wouldn't work.

She gathered her own clothes that she'd laid out to dry and began to put them on. "I'm going with you."

Greg paused with his hand on his fly. "No, you're not. The drive alone is dangerous. You'll be safer here."

"But you won't be here, and I don't want to be by myself." Maybe that sounded a bit like a petulant child, but she meant every word.

He nodded toward the cage. "You'll have the bird to keep you company."

She moved directly in front of him, hands braced on

her hips. "I'm going, even if I have to ride on your hood."

"No, you're not."

Time to bring out all the reasons she should. "I can help you."

He slipped his shirt over his head and leveled his gaze on her. "You have no idea what we might encounter in these conditions. If people can't make it to the hospital, some will come to the shelter. They may have broken bones and severe cuts. Some might even be dying."

Marissa swallowed hard. "I can handle it. When I took care of my father, I learned to treat bed sores and how to change out an IV. But even if I can't provide medical attention, I can give comfort, especially to the elderly." She sent him a pleading look. "Let me do this, Greg. I need to do something besides wait around until this hurricane goes away. Please."

He scrubbed a hand over his jaw and studied the ceiling for a good while. "Okay. But if I think it's not safe when we start out, then I'm bringing you back and going it alone."

She slid her arms around his waist and rested her cheek against his chest. "We'll be okay."

He circled his arms around her and held her tightly. "We have to be okay. You mean too much to me for me to let anything happen to you."

Marissa wanted to shout out her joy, but a sudden, imposing fear wouldn't let her. She was about to go outside to confront the storm's first round of destruction—and she prayed she would find her cherished cottage still in one piece. If not, her heart would surely shatter.

CHAPTER FIVE

THE EYE HAD PUNCHED a hole in the massive accumulation of dark clouds, allowing the sun to filter through in an almost surreal glow. A good thing, Greg decided as he backed the SUV out of the garage, which was fortunately still intact. So far the only damage to his house involved a few of the shutters. Not so with Marissa's cottage.

But she didn't even bother to look as they drove past her lot. She just sat in the seat, clutching a plastic bag containing towels, a few bottles of water, some snacks and the ragged dog, her eyes tightly closed against the scene.

"Is it still there?" she finally asked as he continued up the debris-covered street.

"Yeah, it's still there." But barely. A tree had crashed through the carport, landing on Marissa's sedan and crushing it. As best he could tell, the cottage's roof was half-gone, thanks to the winds and more trees that had fallen like matchsticks onto the structure. And that was just the front of the house. There was no way of knowing how much damage had been done to the back, or if it was still intact.

They would deal with it later, and he'd be there for her every step of the way. Right now he had to deliver a baby despite the deadly storm.

When he turned on to the main road, Greg encountered a patrol car and a sheriff's deputy directing cars containing a few citizens making a last-minute exile to the shelter. He pulled up alongside the deputy, powered down the window and flipped open his credentials. "I've got to get to the high school ASAP. There's a woman in labor."

The man braced both hands on the SUV's door and glanced up the road. "You're going to have a tough time getting through, Doc."

Exactly what he'd surmised. "I don't have a choice."

"I can give you an escort."

"I'd appreciate that. Any reports on serious injuries yet?"

"Just some scrapes and one broken leg. The paramedics took them to the school. A few minutes ago, rescue workers recovered five occupants in a house near the beach."

"What's their status?" Greg asked, although he already knew the answer by the sorrowful look in the man's eyes.

"All fatalities. And it's only the beginning. When the eye moves out and the northeast feeder bands move in, it's going to get a whole lot worse."

Greg noticed Marissa still had her eyes shut. He hated to see her suffer, but he'd witnessed her distress earlier when she'd said goodbye to the bird, as if it might actually be the last time she saw Baby.

He turned his attention back to the deputy. "I need to go now."

The officer pushed off the door. "Be careful. Lots of debris on the road. Just follow me."

Nothing Greg hadn't witnessed before. "I'm right behind you."

As he drove behind the deputy past the stream of traffic, Greg flipped the radio on to listen to the current updates, none of which were good. Before the storm was over, more lives would be lost, more property destroyed, more heartache for the Panhandle inhabitants.

Marissa remained silent even though she'd finally opened her eyes. He wished she'd kept them closed, especially when they passed a group of houses—or what used to be houses—that now looked as if they'd fallen victim to a car bomb.

"Oh, my God."

He saw abject fear in her expression, her hand pressed against her mouth. "It's bad," he said. "But that's not entirely unexpected."

"I know my house will be leveled, if we even survive to see it."

Greg reached over the console and took her hand. "We're going to be okay. Right now we have to get to the shelter." He said it with as much assurance as he could muster, even knowing that anything could happen. The high school could suffer damage, maybe even a collapsed roof. He didn't need to tell her that, because she probably already knew. He prayed that he could keep her safe. That they would all be safe.

As he drove on, he encountered several downed power lines snaking along the side of the road. A child's bicycle blocked the lane, causing both Greg and the patrol car to move over to the side and off the pavement. Fortunately, neither got stuck in the soaked soil. He momentarily wondered how the clinic was holding up. Probably sufficiently flooded, he decided, because of its proximity to the beach along tourist row. If it wasn't completely destroyed. He could rebuild if need be, just as everyone else would. Right now, safety was his main concern.

When they finally reached the high school, he found the parking lot full and several people sprinting into the building. The wind was starting to pick up again, signaling the return of the hurricane. Now if Eden would only show them a little mercy so Greg could do his job, be there for those who needed him. And that included Marissa. Especially Marissa.

MARISSA FOLLOWED Greg into the high school, not knowing at all what to expect. The last time she'd been in this particular gymnasium, she'd watched Jennifer Westbrook playing basketball, vying for the district championship. Today, no scoreboard lit the room; in fact, it was almost completely dark except for a few flashlights, indicating the power was out. No rowdy sounds of fans echoed off the walls, only muffled voices. The cavernous area was incredibly warm and filled with people. The small hamlet of Ocean Vista catered to the tourist trade, with less than a thousand permanent residents. She could almost swear all those residents were crammed into the gym. At least she hoped so. But she knew that wasn't true. After all, the deputy had said five had already perished. How many more would join them?

A man wearing a blue EMT uniform and wielding a large emergency light approached them. Marissa decided he wasn't much older than twenty, perhaps even a student in this very high school a couple of years ago. He looked incredibly young, and somewhat fearful although he tried to hide it with a solemn face.

He offered his hand to Greg and smiled. "I'm sure glad to see you, Dr. Westbrook."

Greg gave the young man's hand a fast, hard shake. "Good to see you, too, Adam. What's going on with the woman in labor?"

"She's having a tough time, sir. I think she's getting real close." He scrubbed a palm over his forehead. "To be honest with you, I've never delivered a baby before. Not too many opportunities in Ocean Vista since most of the folks here are way past childbearing years."

"Who's with her now?" Greg asked.

"My partner, Raleigh, sir. The rest of the crew left to transport some serious cases to the hospital in Destin while they could. Raleigh's never delivered a baby, either."

He patted Adam's shoulder. "That's okay. I've done my share. Does she have a husband?"

"Yeah, but he's active duty. Navy, I think. He's training on the West Coast. She says he wanted to catch a plane but he can't get close since all the area airports are closed."

Marissa's heart ached for the woman she had yet to meet. She couldn't imagine having a baby all alone, although that could be the only way she would ever have a child. Alone.

Adam hooked a thumb over his shoulder. "She's in a classroom right outside the gym."

"Let's go," Greg said.

Marissa wasn't sure what to do, stay or follow. "Greg, should I…"

"Come with me," he told her. "She could probably use your company."

And Marissa could use some strength. She'd never seen a baby being born, had never really had a close pregnant friend. But she could do this. She would stay with the woman and provide comfort even if she could do nothing more. The rest was up to Greg, and she had no doubt he would handle it well. Very fortunate for the mother-to-be that he was available.

As they carefully worked their way through the sea of humanity, shining their flashlights on the ground to avoid stepping on anyone, Adam filled Greg in on the pregnant woman's condition. Her name was Amanda Stapleton, she was all of twenty-two, and this was her first baby—a baby that wasn't due for another three weeks. Not surprising, according to Greg, who claimed stress could bring on labor, and so did barometric-pressure drops.

Marissa followed behind the men, sending brief greetings to several familiar faces—Nancy from the flower shop, Sam from the grocery store and Isabella from the boutique. She saw families huddled together on sleeping bags set out on the floor, the majority retired couples who had opted to spend their golden years in Ocean Vista, in homes that they'd worked all their lives to buy. Homes that could be destroyed at the speed of a gale-force wind.

After they left through the double doors and stepped into a pitch-black hallway, Adam led them across the corridor and into a small room lit by several battery-powered lanterns. Marissa could make out a form on a blanket on the blue-carpeted floor, but not much more. Moving closer, she finally saw the young woman lying on her side, facing the door, her cheeks damp with tears, her blond curls clinging to her face, her eyes firmly closed. A dark-haired young man was kneeling behind her, his gloved hand resting on her shoulder. He looked up and relief washed over his expression. Obviously, this was Raleigh, and no doubt about it, he was definitely thrilled to see Greg, too.

The men exchanged brief greetings while Marissa stood back, awaiting instructions.

"I'm Dr. Westbrook, Amanda," Greg said as he crouched down by her feet and opened the black case he'd brought with him. "If you'll turn onto your back, we'll see what's happening."

Amanda opened her eyes and lifted her head. "You're a real doctor?"

Greg gave her a reassuring smile. "Yeah. Board certified and everything." He pointed at the bag Marissa clutched in her arms. "I need the towels now," he told her as he worked a pair of latex gloves on his hands.

"Sure." Marissa fumbled through the sack's contents and, when Greg took the towels from her, he followed with a brief touch on her wrist, letting her know her presence was appreciated.

"Amanda, this is Marissa Klein," he said, with a nod in her direction as he unfolded one towel. "She'll be with you if you need anything."

Taking her cue, Marissa set the bag aside in the corner, moved to the pallet and sat next to the woman, legs crossed before her. "Hi, Amanda," she said softly. "I'm right here, so just let me know if I can do anything for you."

The young woman stared at Marissa with tired brown eyes. "A baby would be nice…" She grabbed her belly and groaned. "I need to push. Now!"

"Don't push," Greg said as he lifted the sheet covering her legs and bent her knees. "Just breathe through the contraction and then I'll check you."

Amanda rolled her head from side to side. "I don't think I can stop it!"

"You have to try," Greg said. "For the baby's sake."

Marissa wasn't sure what to do now, but when Greg

said, "Help her, Marissa," she recognized she had to do
something, so she took Amanda's hand in hers. "Hang
on to me, sweetie, and look at me. Just breathe."

Amanda locked onto Marissa's gaze and blew out
several breaths in rapid-fire pants. "That's good,"
Marissa said, even though she wasn't sure if Amanda
was doing it right. That didn't really matter, as long as
it worked.

Finally Amanda's expression relaxed, and so did
her grip on Marissa's hand. "It's over now," she said,
followed by a long, slow breath.

"Move that light a little closer," Greg said, and after
Adam complied, he told Amanda, "I'm going to see
what's happening now."

The young woman closed her eyes again and tightened her grasp on Marissa's hand while Greg performed
the examination. "She's fully dilated," he finally said,
then looked up at Amanda. "On the next contraction,
you can push."

Amanda lifted her head again. "I can?"

Greg grinned. "Yeah. And hopefully you'll have a
baby in a while."

But a while turned into several minutes, and several
minutes turned into an hour as the storm charged back
in, bringing with it more discordant sounds, some loud,
some eerie, while Marissa provided as much comfort as
she could to this poor woman giving birth without her
husband, in the midst of a hurricane. No nifty epidural,
no hospital bed, no significant light. What a nightmare.

At least Amanda had Greg in attendance. And
Marissa had something else to concentrate on aside
from the storm's pounding, namely the young woman
who was growing more tired with every unsuccessful
push. When she proclaimed she'd changed her mind

about having a baby, Greg announced, "You're almost there."

"You can do it," Marissa told her. "It's going to be over soon."

A rap sounded at the classroom door followed by a masculine voice saying, "Dr. Westbrook, we need you out here. We've got a man having chest pains."

"Dammit," Greg muttered. "I can't leave now. The head's crowning. You two go check it out."

Adam came to his feet and Raleigh followed. "We'll handle it," Adam said, sounding almost relieved. "We'll let you know if we need you."

Greg glanced up long enough to send the EMT a look of gratitude. "Thanks. Hopefully I'll be finished here soon."

After the men left, Greg turned his attention to Marissa. "Looks like it's just you and me and the mom-to-be. So let's get this baby born."

With renewed strength, Amanda bore down while Marissa cajoled her and congratulated her when the baby's head, covered in downy dark hair, finally emerged. Yet when Greg told Amanda to push once more, then suddenly demanded she stop, Marissa knew something was terribly wrong.

"What is it?" she asked.

"Shoulder dystocia," Greg said. "The baby's shoulder is caught beneath your pelvic bone, Amanda," he explained. "I need to dislodge it. I also need you to move behind her, Marissa, and pull her legs up as close to her ears as you can to open her pelvis."

"Okay." Marissa couldn't panic now, not in light of the current complication. She had to stay strong, stay focused. She worked her way behind Amanda and followed Greg's instructions, knowing it couldn't be comfortable for the woman. But labor wasn't about comfort, that much she realized.

Greg laid one palm below Amanda's distended abdomen and applied pressure, causing Amanda to wince. "This is going to be tough, but it's the only way."

Amanda simply nodded, a steady stream of tears flowing down her face. Marissa spoke soft words of support as Greg worked to deliver the baby for what seemed to be endless moments. She couldn't exactly see what he was doing, but she could see his brows drawn down in concentration, his grim expression. She could also see what it was doing to the young mother, could hear it when Amanda let go a long, keening cry.

"Hang on, Amanda," Greg said. "I've got to be careful so I don't injure the baby's shoulder."

Marissa had never felt so helpless in her life. She briefly thought of her own mother then, how she had died giving birth to her only daughter. And she wondered what would happen if this didn't work. Would the baby die? Would Amanda? She quickly pushed those thoughts away. Greg wouldn't let that happen. She had to believe that.

"One more push, Amanda," Greg commanded.

Marissa wasn't sure Amanda had anything left to give, yet she tucked her chin to her chest and bore down, the strain on her face reflecting her efforts.

"It's a boy," Greg said, bringing Marissa's attention back to him. She relaxed her grip on Amanda's legs when she saw the baby safely cradled in the doctor's arms. A beautiful baby boy, wet, motionless. Silent.

"Is he okay?" Marissa asked. She prayed he was.

Without responding, Greg dried the infant vigorously with a towel while he suctioned his mouth and nose.

Marissa noted the distress in Amanda's eyes, heard it in her voice when she asked, "Why isn't he crying?"

At that moment, the little boy answered his mother with a very loud, and very welcome, wail.

They all laughed then, even Amanda who had basically been through hell to see her child born. After cutting the cord, Greg laid the baby on the new mother's belly and smiled. "He's well over eight pounds. No telling how big he would have been if he'd waited until his due date."

"His father's a big guy, too," Amanda said as she laid a hand on the baby's head. "He's going to be so proud of you, little boy."

Marissa watched with wonder as the bond between mother and child forged right before her eyes. She couldn't count how many times she'd imagined this happening to her. How many times she'd dreamed that one day she would have a baby. But in the past few years she'd intentionally tossed aside that dream, believing it was too late for her. Too late to find the right man, although she realized how much she wanted that man to be Greg. But even if that was a possibility, he already had a child and he probably wouldn't want another. She wasn't even sure if he really wanted her, at least in the way that she wanted him. Yet when he glanced up at her and she saw gratitude and pride in his eyes, and maybe even more, a little glimmer of hope came calling.

"Thank you both so much, Dr. Westbrook," Amanda said. "You and your wife make a great team."

Greg pulled his attention away from Marissa and gave it back to the young mother. "We're not married. We're just neighbors."

Just neighbors. Nothing more. And in that moment, Marissa's hope faded away like early-morning fog.

Feeling the need to flee, at least for a while, she came to her feet. "I'm going to be outside if you need me."

That was all she could manage before the emotions went into a full-fledged assault. Luckily she had the strength to stop the breakdown until she arrived in the hall. Once there, she strode down the corridor, into the darkness. Away from possible discovery. She collapsed onto the floor on her knees and, with the winds whining around her, she cried for what she'd never had and what might never be.

AFTER VERIFYING the man with chest pains was suffering from a bout of angina, and Adam had returned to watch over the mother and baby, Greg went to search for Marissa with flashlight in hand. He finally found her sitting on the floor several yards down the hallway, her back against a row of gunmetal-gray lockers, hugging her knees to her chest, her head lowered. When she hadn't immediately returned, he'd begun to worry. He was still worried.

After taking the spot beside her, he set the light on the ground and draped his arm around her shoulder. "Are you okay?"

She turned her face into his chest and that's when he realized she was crying. He stroked her hair and held her as she quietly sobbed, all that he knew to do. He'd been wrong to ask her to help, something he should have recognized from the beginning. The birth process wasn't always pleasant, and this particular delivery had been tougher than most. But because Marissa was strong, he'd assumed she could handle the situation. He'd grown so accustomed to the procedure he'd totally disregarded her feelings. Still, she'd been a rock the whole time, more help than she realized, and that's where he needed to begin.

"You did a great job in there," he said. "Amanda told me to thank you."

She turned her face toward him and swiped a hand over her eyes. "Amanda did all the work. I didn't really do anything much. Just a little hand-holding."

"Don't sell yourself short, Marissa. It wasn't a good situation. A lesser person might have buckled under the pressure, but not you."

"It wasn't that bad at all. In fact, it was miraculous. I'm glad I was there to see it."

"Then why are you so upset?"

She lifted a shoulder in a shrug. "It doesn't have anything to do with the delivery itself. It just reminded me of a few things."

"What things?"

A few moments passed before she said, "My mother, for one. And what I've missed out on in my life. I'll never know what it's like to see my own baby come into the world."

He gave her a gentle squeeze. "You're talking like it's too late for you. A lot of women are having families later in life. There's no reason you can't do the same."

"I suppose I could visit a sperm bank once I get to Chicago," she said. "Or maybe find a willing man to get me pregnant."

He didn't want to think about her living in Chicago. He definitely didn't want to consider her with another man. "Just don't do anything desperate until you've had time to think about it."

She rested her cheek against his chest. "Right now I'm too tired to think about anything at all. I just wish this hurricane would go away."

"We still have a few more hours to go before this is over."

A few hours before they returned to the neighborhood and assessed the damage. Before she had to witness her house in total ruins, as he knew it would be. According to the latest weather reports, delivered by Adam, the winds had been clocked at one-hundred-thirty miles per hour, with some gusts at one-forty. Now was not the time to reveal the sorry state of storm affairs to Marissa. She needed a few moments of peace, and she probably needed some sleep.

On that thought, he straightened his legs and patted his thighs. "Lie down and take a nap."

"What about Amanda and the baby?"

"You mean little Gregory? He's fast asleep in his mother's arms. They're both asleep."

She laughed. "She named him after you?"

"Yeah, she did. I'm not sure how her husband's going to feel about that since he was counting on a junior."

"I'm sure he won't care once he learns what you did for them both." She shifted onto her back and laid her head on his thighs. "You were so wonderful. I can't imagine what would have happened if you hadn't been there."

Greg didn't want to imagine it. A wrong move could have resulted in a baby with a brachial plexus injury, even possible paralysis. Inability to dislodge the shoulder could have resulted in an emergency C-section, the worst possible scenario. "I've had some practice with tough situations, delivered quite a few babies in my time, including Jen."

Her eyes went wide. "You delivered your own daughter?"

"Yeah. I didn't exactly plan it. Bev couldn't wait

until we got to the hospital so I pulled into a convenience-store parking lot. I was a first-year medical student and damn scared. I didn't know what I was doing at all." He traveled back to those moments in his mind. Good moments. Great moments. "Jen was so little. I remember how small her hands were and that the first thing I noticed were her dimples. That was after I realized she was okay and I hadn't done any damage when I caught her."

"Wow." She took his hand in hers and flexed his fingers back and forth. "You didn't want any more children after that?"

"I wanted more. Bev didn't. She said she didn't want to raise another child alone." And he'd deserved her scorn, her punishment, at least to a point. He hadn't deserved her unwillingness to work it out after they'd moved to Ocean Vista.

"You can still have more," she said. "Men have the option of impregnating women well into their golden years."

Greg let go a cynical laugh. "I'm not too keen on being a father again at the age of sixty."

She covered a yawn with her palm. "I'm sure you could walk out into the gym and find several women willing to have your baby right now."

But he only wanted one woman—Marissa. And as screwy as it seemed, he'd have a baby with her. Several, if that's what she wanted.

"Get some sleep while you have the chance," he told her. He was unsettled by his increasing feelings for her and shocked that he would actually think about having a baby with her when he wasn't sure how she felt about him. He was getting way ahead of himself.

Greg snapped off the flashlight, leaned his head back

against the locker and closed his eyes, but all he saw was Marissa. All he could think about was making love to her again and again. Having her in his bed—a real bed—for as long as she wanted to be there.

He just wanted her in his life, period.

MARISSA WOKE with a cramp in her neck and a pain in her back from the unforgiving industrial-tiled floor. She no longer had a set of solid thighs supporting her head, just a rolled blanket beneath her neck. Alone, but no longer in darkness. Either the electricity had been restored, or a generator had kicked in. She was betting on the latter.

Rising on rigid legs, Marissa started down the hall in search of the bathroom. She found one nearby, took care of business, then decided to check on the mother and baby, and hopefully find Greg in the process. As she walked the corridor, she was struck by the silence. No crunching or grinding sounds. No whining winds. With any luck, the storm had finally ended.

Quietly she opened the door into the classroom to find Greg sitting in a chair positioned next to Raleigh and Adam and Amanda, who was propped up on several blankets, holding the baby close to her heart.

Marissa made her way to the pallet and smiled down on the new family. "Hi, there. You look a lot better."

Amanda smiled back. "I'm much better. A little tired, though."

"That's understandable." Marissa knelt beside her and took a long look at little Gregory. "He's absolutely beautiful."

"Do you want to hold him?" Amanda asked.

She glanced up to see Greg's gaze leveled on her. "Sure, I'd love to."

When Marissa held out her arms, Amanda slid the towel-covered little boy into the crook of her arm. "He's precious," she said, around a growing tightness in her throat. "Perfect." And he was, with a cap of black hair and chubby little cheeks. "Does he look like his dad?"

"Right down to the cowlick on his forehead. Allan's going to freak when he sees that. I just wish he would get home soon."

"I'm sure he'll be here as soon as he can get in." When the infant began to fuss, Marissa handed him back to Amanda. "Here's your mommy."

"I think he's hungry again," Amanda said as she began slipping the buttons on her shirt.

In order to give her some privacy, Marissa stood, grabbed the bag she'd left in the room before the delivery and headed toward the door. "I'll be there in a minute," Greg called after her.

Marissa waited in the hall until he joined her. He looked tired, she noticed immediately, his hair unruly and his eyes reddened from a lack of sleep. But none of that detracted from his handsome face. "I take it you didn't get much of a nap."

"Nope. Too much adrenaline."

She held up the bag. "Want some water or maybe some cheese crackers?"

"No thanks. I'm okay." He rubbed a hand over his nape. "The storm's heading out, but they'll be moving more of the injured in here. I'm probably going to be treating people all night until they give the all clear. I could take you home if it's safe."

If she had a home left, which she probably didn't. "I want to stay. I can help out. Be an extra set of hands." Like any good *neighbor*.

"I'd appreciate that." He sounded like he truly did.

"What now?" she asked.

They stood in silence for a few moments before he tugged her into his arms and kissed her. A lingering kiss that almost caused her to drop the bag and poor Egbert for the second time in less than a day.

After a time, Greg released her and stepped back. "Now that I have that out of the way, it's time to go to work."

"Where do we start?" And when would it end, this soul-deep longing for him? Probably long after she was out of his life, if ever.

Greg pointed toward the double doors. "We'll start in there."

FOR SEVERAL HOURS, Greg mended minor cuts and doled out pain relievers. Fortunately nothing major had come his way. Yet. All the while, Marissa stayed by his side, offering comfort and quips. She was definitely the best medicine around.

Bev would never have done the same for him, that much he knew. Not that she wasn't caring. She'd spent a lot of time volunteering for several causes during their fifteen-year marriage. But she'd considered medicine his mistress and hadn't wanted to be a part of it. She'd never visited him at the hospital, had rarely asked him about his day or his work. He'd tried to talk to her about his concerns, his fears, but she'd tuned him out. Eventually, he'd stopped trying.

Marissa was sincerely interested. She'd asked questions and listened carefully to his answers. Right then she was standing in the corner of the gym, talking to Alice Hawkins, the owner of the local dry cleaners. Alice's elderly mother, Vera Malone—one of his patients—was curled in the corner in a fetal position, her mournful cries rising above the hum of conversation. Alice had cared for her mother alone, rejecting any suggestions that she put her in a convalescent home. He could certainly understand why Marissa related to Alice's situation. She'd been through it herself.

When Marissa caught sight of Greg, she left Alice and strode toward him. "Can you do something for her?" she said with a nod toward Vera.

"She's end-stage Alzheimer's. Not much that can be done."

She hugged her arms tightly around her middle. "She's so upset. I feel so bad for her. And Alice. I know how tough it must be for her."

"Let me see what I can do."

Her smile brightened the entire, crowded room. "Thanks."

He placed his palm in the small of her back and guided her to the corner, where Alice rose and sent him a small smile. "Hello, Dr. Westbrook."

"Hey, Alice. I'll see if I can help." When he approached the elderly woman, she let go a bloodcurdling screech, causing Greg to back off.

Alice gave him a bewildered look. "She doesn't remember you."

"Either that, or she does. I'm probably not her favorite person at the moment."

"Nothing seems to help anymore," Alice said. "I'll just have to hope she goes to sleep soon."

"Buddy," Vera moaned. "My Buddy?"

"Is Buddy her husband?" Marissa asked.

Alice shook her head. "Buddy was her dog. A spoiled pug that she loved to extremes. He's been dead for ten years. Every now and then, she calls for him because she doesn't remember he's gone. But then, most of the time, she doesn't remember me."

"I have an idea." Marissa spun around, crossed the room, then came back with the bag. "Maybe this will help." She pulled out the scruffy stuffed Egbert, knelt by the elderly woman and laid the animal in her arms. "Here, Mrs. Malone. Here's your Buddy."

The woman stared at the dog, unresponsive, while Marissa stroked her hair and softly crooned words of comfort.

Greg still had things to do, people who needed his attention, yet he stayed to watch the scene playing out before him. Marissa's shirt was wrinkled, her hair a tangled mess. The bandage he'd applied to her forehead had dropped down below the cut. Her blue eyes looked fatigued even though she smiled. And he couldn't remember her ever looking so beautiful. But that was his heart talking as much as his head. Witnessing her compassion and caring moved him in ways he'd never been moved before.

"I can't believe how wonderful Marissa is with her," Alice said. "My mother has become so frightened of strangers, but right now she looks as if she's always known her."

As far as Greg was concerned, Marissa was just plain remarkable. "She has a way with people." She definitely had a way with him.

A few moments later, after Vera closed her eyes and grew quiet, Marissa joined them again. "That seems to have calmed her down a bit."

Alice drew her into a long hug. "That was so sweet, honey. I'll make sure you get your dog back as soon as I know she's asleep."

Marissa took a meaningful look at her longtime companion, Egbert. "You don't have to return him. She needs him more than I do."

Knowing what the stuffed animal meant to Marissa, knowing that it was directly tied to memories of her own father, Greg recognized the depth of her unselfishness. Recognized that she was a one-in-a-billion lady. And in that instant, he also realized that he was completely, without question, in love with her.

CHAPTER SIX

NEARLY TWENTY-FOUR HOURS after the beginning of the ordeal, they were told they could safely leave. The hurricane had moved north, dumping torrential rains on neighboring states and spawning tornadoes, according to the latest reports. They'd also heard that most of the beach houses in Ocean Vista were gone and that the center of town—the tourist hub—including Greg's clinic, had sustained major roof damage and severe flooding. Still, Greg had insisted they go home first—if they even had homes to go to—and Marissa dreaded that very thing.

The rain fell gently as they pulled out of the high-school parking lot, and the morning skies were as gray as Marissa's mood. Greg's SUV was fortunately still operable even though the back window had been blown out. A few of the smaller cars had literally been picked up and set down helter-skelter, some on top of other cars, stranding many of the shelter's inhabitants. Several sheriff's deputies, as well as volunteers, had offered to escort those without transportation to their homes. What was left of their homes.

While they drove on, they discovered the side of the road littered with more random items. Twisted metal and planks of wood that had yet to be cleared away turned the street into an obstacle course. As they drew closer to their own neighborhood, Marissa considered begging Greg to turn around or to keep driving. But that would only delay the inevitable. She needed to see what remained of the cottage, if anything could be saved.

When they turned onto their street, she was impaled by total shock. The street sign was gone and although only a few houses had been built on the rural road, most of them had suffered considerable damage. Roofs were gone, trees had been uprooted, furniture was strewn about the curbs as well as articles of clothing. Some telephone poles were leaning, others had toppled over like dominoes. Several neighbors stood on lawns that now looked like rolled-up carpet, staring at the carnage. Some picked their way through the ruins, most likely looking for anything they could salvage. Marissa wondered if she would soon be doing the same and realized, when they pulled up to the curb in front of the cottage—what used to be the cottage—she had nothing to save.

Her beautiful sanctuary, her refuge, was little more than a tangled mass of splintered timber and mounds of soaked insulation, a partial frame with little roof left covered in a sickly shade of green chlorophyll. Her car was beneath the old oak where the wooden swing her father had made for her once hung. The trees that remained upright had been stripped of leaves and sections of bark, nothing more than skeletal figures set against the hazy sky. Clothes, a bureau she didn't recognize and a patio table were only a few of the items strewn across the area.

She opened the car door that seemed as if it weighed two tons and stepped onto what was left of the lawn. Beyond that, she couldn't move, couldn't speak. She could only stare at the destruction, totally sapped of strength.

Marissa was mildly aware of the sound of an opening car door and footsteps behind her. Even Greg's arms coming around her from behind couldn't stop the chills, the rock of nausea in her belly.

"Do you want to see what we can find?" he asked.

She shook her head, and even that took great effort. "No. I can't handle that right now."

"Then let's go to my house."

His house. Marissa looked to her right to see that the Westbrook fortress was still standing. Yes, the yard was destroyed and littered with refuse. Yes, a few of the metal shutters were bent and twisted. But other than that, it looked little the worse for the wear. She wanted to resent him for his lack of loss, but she couldn't, considering that his house had kept her and Baby safe.

Baby.

She regarded him over her shoulder. "I need to see about the bird."

He lightly kissed her cheek. "I'm sure she's okay, but let's go check."

Marissa took one last look at the devastation. As she'd predicted, her decision had now been made for her.

She turned into Greg's arms and saw compassion in his beautiful brown eyes. "At least I have a place to go."

"You can stay with me as long as you'd like."

"Not your house. Chicago."

FOR THE PAST TWO DAYS, Greg had worked with the medical-emergency team to triage the injured. He'd slept in fits and starts, eaten on the run, returning home only for an hour or two between shifts. He'd tended wounds and assumed the role of counselor. He'd seen his fair share of tears—from men, women and children alike. He'd listened patiently to stories of survival, of shattered lives. He'd done his best to heal, but some things just couldn't be fixed. And that included Marissa's current state of despair.

She'd refused to sift through what remained of her house, or contact the insurance agency. He had tried to console her, yet she'd continued to shut him out. Depression wasn't uncommon at times like these, but he suspected it was more. Much more. He had no idea when she planned to leave for Chicago, but in many ways he felt as if she was already gone.

Now that the search-and-rescue operation was over and most of the injured treated, Greg was determined to make Marissa talk to him. If she was serious about moving, he wanted to hear her say it. What he would say after that was anyone's guess. He wanted to ask her to stay, but he had no right. He wanted to turn back the clock and regain the time that he'd wasted in pursuing a relationship with her, but that wasn't possible. He wanted to tell her he loved her.

He didn't intend to apply any undue pressure, but he sure as hell couldn't let her walk away without giving it his best shot.

After pulling into the driveway, Greg shut off the engine and sat for a few moments to gather his thoughts and his courage. He got out of the car, struck by the smell of food grilling in the neighborhood. The electricity had yet to be restored for those who still had a sufficient roof over their heads, and many were outside barbecuing what they'd recovered from their freezers, as if everything were back to normal. Far from it. Normalcy wouldn't return anytime soon, but Floridians were survivors, and eventually life would go on. So would his life, and possibly without Marissa.

He strode to the backyard and entered the gates to find several tree limbs and a lot of debris clouding the pool, something he needed to take care of eventually. But not before he took care of his houseguest.

When he entered the family room, Greg found Marissa in the same spot where he'd left her that morning—curled up at the end the sofa where she'd slept the past two nights. He crossed the room, tossed his keys on the end table and dropped down beside her.

"Did you watch TV today?" he asked her.

She shook her head. "The electricity's still out."

"The generator's working." Exactly what he'd told her yesterday, and the day before.

"Oh." She toyed with the corner of a throw pillow, failing to look at him. "It doesn't matter. I took several naps. I can't seem to catch up."

"I know what you mean."

"The water's back on," she said in a listless tone. "I don't think we're supposed to drink it yet."

"Probably not a good idea until they're sure it's safe. But that means we can take a shower instead of a sponge bath." That called up memories of their lovemaking three days before, although right now it seemed like thirty. She hadn't acted as if she'd wanted his attention. Hadn't even touched him.

Finally she raised her gaze to his. "You must be exhausted."

"I am." But not so tired that, if she made one move toward him, he wouldn't gladly carry her to his bed. "I should have a break until I can get the clinic up and running again."

"Then they've found everyone?"

"Yeah. Only nine fatalities, although we have a few people we transported with critical injuries. Relatively speaking, we're lucky. It could have been much worse."

"It's bad enough." She stretched her arms above her head then dropped them back onto her lap. "Guess I should go take care of Baby. She's all I have left."

She still had him, if she wanted him, and right now he wasn't sure she did. When she started to stand, he caught her hand and tugged her back down on the sofa. "We need to talk."

"About what?"

"About—" The shrill of the cell phone housed in his pocket prevented him from finishing his sentence. At least service had been restored, but that also meant he could be summoned to help out some more. He'd take this call, then he'd turn the damn thing off, at least until he said what he needed to say.

He flipped the phone open and muttered, "Dr. Westbrook."

"Oh, my God, you're okay!"

"Jen?" Exactly what the doctor needed, to hear his daughter's voice.

"I was so worried when I heard about the hurricane. Is the house still standing?"

"Yeah. Just minor damage. Where are you?"

"In Paris. Marissa's house, is it okay?"

"No."

"But she's—"

"Right here with me."

"I'm so relieved you're both all right. Let me talk to her, then she can put you back on."

He offered the phone to Marissa. "It's Jen. She wants to talk to you."

Greg leaned back against the cushions and waited

while Marissa spoke with his daughter in a low voice, even though he really wanted to pace.

"It's okay, Jen. Don't cry. Everything will be okay."

Marissa had faced the loss of her house and she was still consoling his daughter. Just another display of her compassion, and only one of the many reasons he loved her.

A moment of silence passed before she said, "Yes, probably. But I promise not to leave before you get back, as long as it's okay with your dad if I stay here. I doubt I can find a hotel room within a hundred-mile radius."

It was more than okay with Greg. At least it might buy him some more time. More time for what? To convince her to stay? Apparently she'd already made up her mind, and that shot a sick feeling straight into his gut.

After she said goodbye, Marissa handed him the phone then went back to fidgeting with the pillow.

"Are you enjoying yourself, kiddo?" he asked Jen, while keeping his gaze centered on Marissa.

"I was but now I'm worried about you two. I could come home early. Mom would understand."

Greg highly doubted that. "You need to stay. It's chaotic around here. By the time you get back, hopefully things will be back to almost normal."

"If you're sure."

"I'm sure."

"And Daddy, try to talk Marissa out of taking that job in Chicago. I don't think she really wants to go, and I know you don't want her to leave."

No, he didn't. Not in the least. "That's not up to me, Jen."

"It's up to you to finally tell her how you feel about her. She's in love with you, you know."

"No, I don't know that." But he could hope. He still had time for that.

"Well, she does love you, and I know you love her, so don't let her get away, okay?"

"I'll do what I can." And he would, come another hellacious hurricane or more high water.

"Good. I'll see you in a few days. And Daddy, I love you."

Those three words meant more to him that his daughter would ever know. Now if only he could hear the other woman, not quite out of his life, say it. "Love you, too. Be safe."

After he hung up, Greg set the phone aside on the end table and leaned forward, draping his forearms on his legs. "It was good to hear from her."

"Yes, it was," Marissa said. "And if you don't mind, I'd like to borrow your phone and call the Chicago office tomorrow to let them know I'll be taking the job. My phone's dead."

"Not a problem," Greg finally said. But it was a problem. A big one.

He checked his watch and decided to force her hand. Snatching the phone from the coffee table, he offered it to her again. "Call them now. No reason to put it off any longer."

She stared at the cell for a few moments, indecision warring in her expression. "I'll call them in the morning. Right now I want to take a shower."

"Suit yourself. But it sounds to me like you're not sure about taking that job."

She pushed off the couch, rounded the coffee table then faced him. "What options do I have, Greg?"

He came to his feet. "You could rebuild."

She shook her head. "It wouldn't be the same."

Time for the first request. "You could stay here, with me."

"I don't want to wear out my welcome." She pointed over her shoulder. "I'm going to shower now, if that's okay."

Dammit, he wasn't handling this well at all. "Be my guest."

When she spun around and headed away, Greg cursed his sudden spinelessness. Cursed his inability to lay it on the line. But it wasn't too late. Not yet. Not until she got on a plane bound for Illinois. He didn't plan to wait that long to spill his guts. In fact, he didn't plan to wait a minute longer.

On that thought, he strode down the hall and into his bedroom, pausing at the bathroom door to hear the sound of the shower. He kicked off his shoes, shrugged out of his lab coat, yanked off his shirt, pants and briefs, then walked into the room as if he'd been invited, which he hadn't.

When he opened the transparent shower doors and stepped inside, Marissa gasped and dropped the bar of soap. "What are you doing?"

He fought to keep his attention on her eyes, not on her body. "I need a shower, too."

"You couldn't wait until I was finished?"

"Nope. I have some things to say to you and I figured if I'm going to do some soul-baring, I might as well do it completely bare."

She folded her arms across her breasts, providing him with some minimal relief. "By all means, go ahead. Don't mind me. Just make sure I have some hot water left."

"It won't take that long." The spray was boring into his back so he pushed the nozzle toward the wall. He didn't need any more distractions. "First, a question. How do you feel about me?"

She grabbed a washcloth and ran it over her face. "What do you mean?"

"You know what I mean."

"I think you're a wonderful neighbor. A great doctor. The best father."

"How do you feel about me as a man?"

A small smile started to creep in. "You're a hunk. Is that what you wanted to hear?"

"No. I want to hear that what happened between us in the safe room the other day wasn't just a diversion."

Her smile faded altogether. "It wasn't a diversion. I wanted to be with you. I told you that."

"But you haven't let me touch you since we came back here. Hell, you wouldn't even consider sleeping in my bed."

"You were gone much of the time."

Here it came, his job running interference again. "I had to help out."

"And I totally understand that. People need you."

"I need you. I've needed you for months now, and especially the past two days. We need each other."

That caused her to look away. "If we let things progress between us, it would complicate everything. We'll just grow closer—"

"And you don't want that?"

"I want..."

He took a chance and moved toward her, stood right in front of her with only a small space separating them, at least physically. "What do you want, Marissa, because I sure as hell can't read your mind."

"To finish my shower. What do you want?"

"I want you to stay."

She fisted the rag in her hands. "Because you're afraid you won't find a suitable neighbor?"

"No." He sucked in a deep breath and prepared to drop his guard and lay his heart at her bare feet. "Because I love you."

BECAUSE I LOVE YOU...

The declaration nearly caused Marissa to wither onto the slick shower floor in a heap of suds and disbelief. Or maybe she hadn't heard correctly. Regardless, she wanted to hear it again. "What?"

"I love you."

How could that be? How could he be standing there, opening up to her so easily, when this had been the answer to her dreams? "That's what I thought you said. I'm just trying to wrap my mind around it and figure out why you're telling me this now."

"Because I was afraid you would leave before I had a chance to tell you. I don't want that, even if I don't have a right to ask you to stay."

No, he really didn't have that right. Not yet. "Why do you think you love me?"

"I don't think, I know." He forked a hand through his now-damp hair. "Since the day I met you, I looked forward to seeing you every time you walked into a room. I missed you when you weren't around. And I can't tell you how many times I wanted to follow you home when you left. It wasn't just about sex, either." He cracked a crooked smile. "Even though that was great."

How well she knew that. "Keep going."

"I love you because you understand me. Understand my work. You're the most compassionate woman I've ever met. Sometimes you frustrate me because you're too cautious, but I can overlook that, as long as you overlook my habit of rushing into things first and asking questions later."

And that concerned her the most. "Is that what you're doing now?"

"No. I've given my decision a lot of thought. In fact, this is all I've thought about for the past two days. You're all I've thought about and, I swear to God, if you walk out my door and never come back, I don't know what I'll do."

Walking away didn't seem at all appealing. In fact, it seemed like the worst thing she could do, leaving behind the possibility of having Greg in her life permanently. "If I do stay, what comes next?"

"We'll see how it works, although I already know it's going to be fine. It's going to be great."

"But no guarantees," she said. "There's always the chance that we might decide we don't work. We could even decide we don't like each other."

"That's not going to happen."

"How can you be so sure?"

"Because I wouldn't marry a woman I didn't like."

Marry? Okay, that did it. Any minute now, she was going to give herself that standard pinch to make certain she wasn't dreaming. "Are you serious?"

He pulled her into his arms. "Dead serious. We don't have to get married today or tomorrow or even in the next six months, just as long as we do it eventually."

Marissa let go a laugh even though she wanted to cry. Joyful, not sad, tears. "I never thought I'd receive a proposal in the shower. But then I never thought I'd make love in a safe room, either." And that's exactly what they had done—made honest-to-goodness love, although she hadn't realized it at the time.

He cupped her face in his palm. "I never thought I'd get married again, but that was before I met you. And you still haven't said how you feel about me."

Time for her to tell the absolute truth. Time to tell him what she'd wanted to tell him for days. "I do love you. I have for a while now."

He rubbed his hands down her spine then back up again. "Jen was right then. She told me you did."

"Smart girl."

"Then you'll marry me?"

Marissa wanted to scream *Yes!* but one thing was holding her back. She wouldn't be satisfied until she had her own answers. "I admit, I want it all. A good career. A home. Even a husband."

"I want you to have it all. I'd be willing to move to Chicago. I can work in the ER—"

She stopped his words with a kiss. Just a small one, for now. "It's a lot to consider."

"We can and will work around it, Marissa. As long as we're together."

She hesitated a moment, pretending to think. "You know, it is a good opportunity, thrusting myself into the world of lubricants."

"You really want to hawk lubricants?"

Her smile arrived full force. "No, not really."

He slid his hands down and kneaded her bottom. "Who needs lubricants, anyway?"

Certainly not Marissa, thanks to Greg, who had her body weeping for him in a matter of moments with a slow kiss and a thorough touch. They explored each other with the enthusiasm of two people who had never known such pleasure, until they were both winded and wanting more. But when Greg backed her against the wall, and slipped inside her, Marissa snapped into reality mode.

"The condom, Greg," she said, although speaking through her rapid breathing took great effort.

He tipped his head against her shoulder and stood stock-still. "I know. I'll go get one, if you think we really need it."

Need it? "I could get pregnant."

"I realize that, but I'm not worried about it."

She pulled his head up and forced him to look at her. "You're willing to take that risk?"

"First of all, I know you want a baby, and I sure don't want you to have one with anyone else but me. Secondly, like you've said before, I'm not too old to start another family. And lastly…" He kissed her softly yet soundly. "I don't consider it a risk. I consider it a blessing. All I have to do is look at Jen to know the truth in that."

All Marissa had to do was look at him, to see the sincerity in his eyes, hear it in his voice, to know he spoke the truth. "If I got pregnant right now, you'd be happy about it?"

He moved inside her without missing a beat. "Does this answer your question?"

Yes, it did, and Marissa couldn't think of a better answer, or a better way to show their love for each other. She tuned into his every move, the sound of his voice as he told her that he loved her again while he filled her completely, both body and soul. She'd never felt so liberated, so in love, and she briefly wondered how she had gone so long without these feelings, until she could no longer do anything but give everything over to her lover. The man she loved.

In the aftermath, they remained in each other's arms awhile until Greg pushed away and turned the faucet toward her. They bathed each other then, exchanged more kisses, and by the time they finally left the shower, the water had grown cold. They dressed in T-shirts and jeans with some difficulty since they couldn't seem to keep their hands off each other.

Once they were proper again and back in the family room, Marissa slid her arms around his waist. "I'll go see what I can find for dinner. You look like you could use something to eat."

"I could use your answer. Are you going to marry me, or do you need a year or two to decide?"

Before Marissa could give that answer, the doorbell rang, bringing about Greg's string of muttered oaths aimed at the intruder.

"This better be good," Greg said as he let her go. "Maybe it's the electric company delivering good news for a change."

"Would they really be here so soon?"

Before he disappeared into corridor leading to the front entry, he turned and said, "We can always hope," then left the room.

Marissa hoped for many things, that if she agreed to Greg's proposal, she wouldn't be making a massive mistake. They had just now acknowledged their feelings for each other, and taking that next step was a little intimidating. So was giving up the opportunity to work for a major company. Somehow, that didn't seem as important now, but being with Greg did. Loving Greg did. After all, he had said he'd be willing to move to Chicago. But could she ask him to leave Florida, farther away from his daughter and the town he had grown to

love? The town that loved him as well? The place she
loved as well.

The sound of voices drew her from her typical delib-
erations and into the hallway, where she saw Greg
standing at the open front door. He gestured toward her
and she strode the rest of the way to see Ruth Silver-
stein, a slip of a woman with neatly coifed white hair,
standing on the front porch, a foil-wrapped bowl
balanced in her hands. Her husband, Ira, an equally
small man with thinning silver hair and mischievous
dark eyes, stood immediately behind her. Marissa had
known Ruth and Ira for years through her father. Many
times she'd visited the library where Ruth volunteered
to discuss their favorite books. And she was both
relieved and thrilled to see the couple looking quite
well.

"Ruth, I'm so glad you're okay." She breezed past
Greg and gave Ruth a hug. "Did the retirement community suffer much damage?"

"It's still standing." Ruth waved a hand above her
head. "Such a mess, all the rubbish in the parking lot.
No electricity or water. But we are all safe." She offered
the bowl to Marissa. "I've made some of my special
soup for you. It will cure all that ails you."

"It's the brandy," Ira muttered. "Don't take too much
at a time."

Ruth sent him a quelling look. "Hush, old man. You
have lived this long because of my special recipes."

He laid a hand on his wife's shoulder. "And I will live
much longer, my dear, as long as my liver holds out."

"I'm sure the soup's wonderful," Marissa said, and
so was the obvious love the couple had for each other,
although she wasn't sure spiked soup would help clear

her head. She took the bowl and handed it off to Greg. "I can't tell you how much I appreciate this."

Ruth patted her cheek. "That is what community is all about. Caring for our own, as you will soon see. Now you must come with me."

When Ruth offered her hand, Marissa glanced around to find Greg had gone back in the house although the door was still open. Curious, she allowed Ruth to guide her into Greg's front yard and onto the littered path that had once led to her house. But before she took more than a few steps, she tugged Ruth to a halt.

She'd heard the hum of heavy equipment all day long, but she'd assumed it had been coming from somewhere down the road. Yet there it was, a bulldozer pushing fallen branches into a pile next to a mound of fractured aqua wood that used to hold the walls of her cottage together. Now the cottage was little more than a battered frame, a hollow shell with only a scrap of a roof.

Clusters of people milled around, picking through the remains and carrying personal items to place in another pile. She recognized several of the citizens—Grady from the local diner, Cindy Deason, Greg's nurse, and her husband, Bill, along with their teenaged son, Billy Jr., who'd delivered her newspaper every morning without fail. Even Sandy and Jim from up the street, practically newlyweds, had joined in the efforts, though their own house had suffered major damage as well.

Ruth slipped an arm around Marissa's waist and gave her a squeeze. "It's a terrible thing, losing your home. But at least you have your health. If your father were here, he would tell you to go on with your life. To live as if each day were your last."

Exactly what he would have said, Marissa thought.

But he wasn't here, and neither were all the little reminders of him.

"Your closet is still intact," Ruth said, pointing a bony finger toward the back of the frame. "I told everyone to leave it be. A woman's closet is her business."

Marissa gave Ruth a shaky smile. "Then you arranged for all of this?"

"Oh, no, dearest. Not me. Dr. Westbrook did. He treated several of these people here over the past few days, refusing any kind of pay. When they asked what they could do, he told them that you needed help. And they have all answered the call."

"Yes, they have, and it means more than they know."

Ruth dropped her arm and patted Marissa's back. "You must come see what you can find before they cart it all away tomorrow."

For the first time, Marissa felt she had the strength to do that. After all, the community had come to her aid, and she couldn't hang back and let them do the job alone. But before she moved forward, a young man dressed in navy khakis approached her, hat in hand. He was tall with a large frame, his brown hair close cropped in military fashion. He stuck out his hand and smiled. "Ms. Klein, I'm Chief Petty Officer Allan Stapleton, Amanda's husband."

She shook his hand enthusiastically and almost hugged him. "I'm so glad you made it back. When did you get in?"

"Last night. I just wanted to stop by and let you know I'm grateful for everything you and the doc did for my wife and baby. She says she couldn't have done it without the two of you."

"How are they doing?"

"They're doing great. I brought them home from the hospital a few hours ago." His expression and tone reflected his pride.

"And you should be with them," Marissa said.

"I'm heading back now, although I can lend a hand in a day or two. I just wanted to come by and thank you. Amanda says she'd like you to stop by when you get a chance. Our duplex is over on Cook, not far from the school."

"Then your place is okay?"

"We've got some damage to one side, but it's livable."

That relieved Marissa, and it also made her realize that Amanda and the baby needed a roof over their heads much more than she did. "I'm glad. Give Amanda my best, and now you get home to your family."

"I will." He shook her hand again. "Take care, and I'm real sorry about your house. I hope you get it rebuilt soon."

As he walked away, Marissa took another long look at what remained. She could rebuild, but as she'd told Greg, it simply wouldn't be the same. At least she had her pictures, even if she didn't have most of her things. But she had Greg, and that mattered most. Still, she needed to see what else she could find. See if any more of her keepsakes had survived.

Just then, she felt two arms come around her from behind and a warm kiss on her cheek. "They've made a lot of progress."

She looked back at Greg and smiled. "And I can't believe they're practically ignoring their own places to take care of mine."

"Yours was the worst around here, Marissa. At least, of all the houses away from the beach. They want to help. They always do, every time we have a storm. That's just the way it is here."

And Marissa wouldn't have it any other way. She pulled Greg's arms tighter around her and took a few more moments to watch the neighbors banded together to clean up the mess. Watched as they joked with each other as they worked, exchanging good-natured barbs and affectionate insults. Watched a community of survivors come together in the aid of one.

The shrill of a loud whistle caught her attention, followed by Adam, the youthful EMT, calling, "Hey, Doc, what do you want me to do with this?"

Marissa's hand fluttered to her mouth and her eyes clouded with tears. Yet she could still see it—the black rocker, even more cracked and peeling, but still in one piece. "That's my father's favorite chair," she said, through an onslaught of emotions.

"Carry it over to my house," Greg called back to Adam. "Guess that's a sign to let you know he's still with you."

Marissa loved Greg for that, loved that he understood what that aged piece of furniture meant to her. And she realized how much he meant to her as well.

How could she leave any of this behind? How could she ask him to leave? She couldn't. One decision that was all too clear.

"Yes," she said without hesitating.

"Yes, what?"

"Yes, I'll stay. Right here in Ocean Vista, with you, in your house. And I'll marry you, too, since we need to set a good example for your daughter."

Clasping her shoulders, he turned her around. "Are you sure?"

Exactly what he'd asked her before they'd made love

the first time, and her answer was the same. "Very sure. My father grew up here. He loved Florida and he taught me to love it, too. I do, almost as much as I love you. I want our children to grow up here."

"Then we'll stay."

As they walked hand in hand to join the crew, Marissa's heart didn't seem quite as heavy as before. Yes, her lovely cottage was gone, and so were most of her things. But things could be replaced; love couldn't. Yes, the storm had taken many reminders, but it could never take the memories. She had them stored in a safe haven in her heart—both the old memories as well as the new. A place to shelter all those yet to come.

With Greg at her side—the doctor next door, her friend, her lover and soon-to-be life partner—she would make many, many more sweet memories. They might face storms in the future, but they would face them together. And, God willing, they would have a new family, a new beginning. New hope.

EPILOGUE

THREE WEEKS AGO, she came into the world appropriately during an April shower, a tiny, red-faced protesting tempest, delivered by her father, who'd insisted she arrive safely into his hands, that his touch was the first she would know. She was blessed with golden hair, bright blue eyes, a matched set of deep dimples and a fierce determination. She was also blessed with two parents who loved each other well, and told each other often, who'd exchanged vows with each other, including one to keep her safe and secure, no matter what it took.

Her day began and ended in the room next to her big sister's, her crib positioned near the window that overlooked where her grandfather's house had stood before the storm, now recently replaced by a delightful playground with a wooden swing set and fire-red slide—built lovingly by the same neighbors who had assisted in clearing away the debris, but never the memories. One lone oak tree remained, a monument to the strength of community and stalwart survivors. The park awaited the day when she would be old enough to venture outside to explore, to know how it felt to walk on bare feet in the grass, immersed in the scents of the sea, the sun warm on her face.

In the corner of the room sat a chair once cracked and

peeling, now covered in buttercup fabric, the place where her mother fed her and her father rocked her to sleep. On that chair rested Egbert, returned several months ago by a grateful daughter claiming the rag-tag puppy had been a guardian angel for its interim owner, who had peacefully passed away with "her Buddy" cradled in her arms. Downstairs, a musical macaw periodically sang a lullaby, remarkably in tune. A sun-catcher hung in the nearby window, splashing a primary-color prism on the walls, providing the infant with her own personal rainbow—the symbol of hope—and that was her name.

Hope Klein-Westbrook represented the good that had emerged from the devastation. She was her big sister's joy, her daddy's next best girl, and her mother's miracle. She was also Greg and Marissa's testament to love's ability to overcome adversity. The precious child was their future, conceived in love, born into love, a Floridian through and through.

Their everlasting Hope.

WILDFIRE
Laura Wright

* * *

Absence diminishes small loves and
increases great ones, as the wind blows out
the candle and fans the bonfire.
—François de la Rochefoucauld

This story is dedicated to all the smoke jumpers in the US. You are amazing people, who risk your life every day, and even though you all seem to dislike the word – you're heroes and heroines in my book (literally).

Acknowledgements

To my friends and fellow authors Kristi Gold and Kathie DeNosky. Ladies, you're talented, wonderful and kick-ass women!
Thank you for thinking of me!

To Tina Colombo, thank you for your hard work and patience.

To Julie Ganis, thanks for your help and support. You are truly the greatest of friends.

And to smoke jumpers Robert Bente and Wayne Williams. Thank you for taking the time to help me. I admire you both so much, and hope we can meet some day.

PROLOGUE

JUMPING STRAIGHT into the smoky fingers of a four-acre blaze might seem like a suicide mission to some, but to Gabriel London it was just another Tuesday.

That being said, there was one thing that never got easy. This moment—the one when he sat at the Cessna's door, legs hanging out into the slipstream, engines screaming in his ears like ravenous lions.

Gabe stared down at the charred landscape of the Shasta Trinity National forest, his brain running a million miles an hour. Acres upon acres of California pine were up in flames and spitting smoke. Somewhere inside, two Forest Service workers were trapped.

His guts rolled over, tossing around the quick breakfast he'd scarfed down an hour ago. But he hardly had time to think on it. He felt the slap on his back and instinct took him. Like a bullet in a chamber, he shot forward and out of the plane into the hot summer air. In an instant the world went quiet and silently spun around him. The wind pitched his limbs from side to side, and he felt more vulnerable than a lame bunny as he plummeted down at ninety miles an hour. He didn't count, had never taken to that bit of rookie training. He knew when to grab the green rip cord, knew by instinct when his chute needed to be open. After ten years, he'd damn well better know.

Gabe said a prayer as he covered the last two hundred feet.

Don't let the wind change.

Actually more of a demand than a request, but he wasn't any good at asking. His heart seized and he grabbed for his steering toggles, moving himself into the upslope of breeze. For just a moment, he forgot all irritating tugs of fear and enjoyed the moment of pure flight. Then, he was back to work. He spotted Ty Matheson zeroing in on the jump spot and yelled a good-natured, "You're coming in too fast, bro."

"I bet I'll be getting there before you," Ty shouted back.

Just seconds after Ty, Gabe slammed to the ground, abrupt and shocking to the system. Pain seared into his bad knee, but he ignored it.

They had work to do.

Ty signaled the plane to drop gear and after they rescued the packs from the trees, they slung their bags over their shoulders and started up the hill.

Though the fire was a half mile off, the heat was almost unbearable at times. The stench of smoke hung in the air and visibility was poor, but Gabe was used to the conditions. So was Ty. They'd jumped side by side for ten years, been in the same rookie training at the Redding Base and worked well together. They hardly needed to speak anymore, their actions and reactions were so similarly understood.

The sky burned pink as they hiked through the thick brush. They'd flown over the ranger station a thousand times, seen it live and in person more times than they could count as rookies and as jumpers. They didn't need a map to get there.

"Wind's shifting," Ty said, his voice calm as they set out.

Gabe swung his bag to the other shoulder. "Sooner we get to them and get out the better."

Twenty minutes later, and a good quarter mile from the station, they found the forest workers. The two men were lying by a stream. In a state of panic and exhaustion, they told Ty and Gabe the station had been overcome by fire and they'd hightailed it out of there.

Ty took on the younger man, whose ankle had been busted by a fallen tree. He gave him some water as he set the bone. Realizing that Ty's pace would be slow carrying the man, Gabe urged Ty to start down the hill and he'd catch up, then turned his attention to the older man, Mel.

Mel was pretty out of it, and couldn't stop throwing up. Gabe knew they'd better get moving, but he couldn't push the guy. He offered Mel a few minutes to get a hold of himself before urging him onward.

It wasn't long before Gabe realized this was not the best decision he'd ever made. A dry wind had moved into the area quick as hell, and Gabe knew that the fire would move with it, onto steep slopes and into the dense, highly flammable pines surrounding them. His blood pumping fast, Gabe gripped the man close and retraced his steps, pretty sure he could get them back to safety without having to open his pack.

But within seconds, another blast of wind kicked up and a wall of flame raced down the hill toward them. The fire was narrow but pretty long, and it was burning up fir trees and dry grass, hungrily eyeing more rich clumps of trees ahead.

Gabe stopped in his tracks. He didn't have time to

remove lower limbs from the trees, and there was no good black area for an escape route.

With deft fingers, he quickly opened his pack and took out his fire shelter. He grabbed Mel and hauled him underneath the tiny aluminum tent. Every muscle in his body felt pinched. He could hear the fire blistering, snapping, then screaming over and around him. The sound became deafening, and beside him, Mel moaned and prayed, begging God to deliver them both from this true-to-life hell....

"THAT'S INCREDIBLE! So how did you two get out of there?"

Knocked back into the present, Gabe looked up from his untouched burger and into the deeply interested, pale blue eyes of Nora Wallace. The journalist for the extreme-travel magazine *EDGE* was one of the most ir-ritatingly persistent people Gabe had ever met. For the past three months, she'd badgered, cajoled, pleaded and finally convinced him to do an interview for her magazine. Nothing personal, she'd promised, just a regular day-in-the-life kind of thing.

"You were under the tent," she prompted eagerly, clearly riveted to his story. "Mel was praying for your lives, and..."

Gabe knew it was sexist as hell, but before he and Nora had met he'd thought: journalist, men's magazine, extreme travel—the woman was going to look like Paul Bunyan's sister, right?

Wrong.

His gaze on hers, he continued, "The fire passed over us and I got Mel back down the hill. He kept saying his prayers had been answered. Maybe so. I don't know about that, but we were alive." Gabe took a swallow of beer. "It was close to sundown when the helicopter arrived. Winds had shifted again and new crews were being flown in to battle the fire. I have to say that I had an urge to stay with them, but I had a job to finish, so I helped Mel onto the chopper and took off back home, back to the base. And that's it."

"Wow. What a story." She was writing demon-fast on her yellow legal pad, her long auburn hair falling forward in ginger waves.

When she looked up she'd catch him staring, Gabe thought without much care. Odds were pretty good she was used to men staring at her. All that hair and soft skin combined with those mile-long legs and an epic chest.

He took another pull on his beer. The real kicker was the lady had a brain, too. Gabe hated going into any situation blind, so he'd done a little homework on her. Magna cum laude from Stanford.

Bummer.

He might've asked her out. But he preferred his dates to have more bed smarts than book smarts.

"So, Mr. London," she began again in the husky tone that went straight to his zipper. "You had a pretty cushy life in Hollywood before this, didn't you?"

"Before this, I went to college, then worked a Hotshot crew."

"Hotshot?"

"A firefighter who works the ground during a wildfire."

"I see." She returned to her legal pad. "And before college?"

"Grade school, high school."

"Your father was a major player in Hollywood, wasn't he?"

"He produced some high-quality films, yeah. *Evil Cows From Jersey* was one of my particular favorites."

She dropped her all-business facade for a minute and laughed. Damn smile lit up the room, and those full pale pink lips…was it too much to hope she'd gotten a C or worse in her advanced Physics class in high school?

"I'll have to rent that." She popped a French fry into her mouth. "Sounds like a classic."

"For some. Truth is, my father hated the kind of films he produced, but they brought in ungodly amounts of cash—and that he could be proud of."

"And was he proud of you, too?"

The question hit him between the eyes. He'd thought about his father many times since his death, joked about him, the six women he'd married after Gabe's mother had walked out on them, and the kind of bourgeois life they'd led—but he'd never gone *there*. Sentiment was for fools and saps. He never looked at his past with any amount of seriousness. Over the din of the crowded diner, he told Nora Wallace, "My father died when I was nineteen, so he basically saw me at my teenage worst. He didn't know what I wanted from life or what my plans were."

She didn't write that down. "What do you think he would've thought of you now? Would he have acknowledged your 'hero' status?"

"I'm no hero, Miss Wallace."

"Many would beg to differ."

He shrugged. "Just doing a job. No jumper worth his rocks would consider himself, or herself, a hero."

"Which ironically makes you even more of one."

He stared at her, this formidable woman with the brain of a Nobel laureate and the body of a vamp, and tried not to sweat. He nodded at her relatively untouched plate. "You going to eat that?"

She smiled and eased her plate toward him.

"How old are you?" he asked, as if it mattered.

"Why? Because I'm acting like a smitten teenager?"

"You're smitten?"

She inhaled deeply, thoughtfully. "I think so."

Well, what do you know? The electric charge he got just looking at her went both ways. He slid a French fry into his mouth.

"Tell me about the rest of your family," she said. "How do they feel about what you do?"

He stared intently at her. "You said we weren't going to get personal here, and that seems to be the road we keep traveling down."

She lowered her pencil. "You can always tell me to go to hell, Mr. London."

"Well, that wouldn't be very neighborly of me, now would it?"

She smiled.

He sighed, sipped his beer. "I have no family. My mother left when I was five and I barely remember her. She's not a part of my life."

"No sisters or brothers?"

"Just the ones that work the fire line."

She nodded her understanding, picked up her pencil again. "I like that. Can I use it?"

"Knock yourself out."

He watched her write, watched her hand grip the pencil with a sort of teasing pressure. It was erotic as hell, and he eyed the glass of ice water at the next table. "Not going to say you're sorry that I'm an orphan or offer me a sympathetic word?"

Her brows drew together. "Are you a man who needs sympathy?"

"No."

"I didn't think so."

He chuckled. "And something tells me that you're not the kind of lady to offer any, are you?"

Her eyes sparkled with humor and she slowly shook her head. "We do have similar pasts, you know? I'm an only child, too. My parents have been gone for five years now. And you know what?"

"What?"

She gave him a soft smile. "I pretend it doesn't bother me, either."

He leaned toward her. "You're a real piece of work."

Their waiter suddenly appeared beside the table. "Dessert?"

Gabe shot her a wide grin. "Dessert, Nora?"

Given her bold, straightforward manner, Gabe was only mildly surprised that right there, in front of God, the pimply faced waiter and a crying baby in the next booth, Nora Wallace gathered up her paper, pencil and purse and said plainly, "Do you want to come home with me?"

CHAPTER ONE

Four months later...

HE WAS NO ROOKIE, but the rush he got from hardcore PT was a beautiful thing.

Even if that physical training came calling at four in the morning.

The girth of the walnut tree's trunk was nothing to its height, and Gabe felt like he'd dropped into a vat of sweat at midpoint. Suited up, with a full pack strapped to his back, wind tilting him sideways, he dug his spurs into the bark of the tree and fought his way up. The climb took about twenty minutes, but it felt like hours.

It was 0500 and already working its way to another hot summer day when he rappelled down. First thing he saw were a couple of new rooks heading over to the obstacle course. He grinned as the two former marines taped up their hands and looked bleakly at the O-Course, especially The Mutilator and monkey bars.

War of attrition, fellas. Better get used to it or you'll wash out in a hurry.

"Hey there." Ty Matheson was jogging toward him, heading for the parking lot.

Gabe called out, "Where you off to? You're usually nose-deep in a plate of eggs at this time of day."

"Heading over to the Trinity Mountain Resort area.

Fire up there. Nothing major yet, but firefighters are evacuating the locals and I got a sister living up there."

Gabe's insides fisted with tension. He had no sister, but he sure as hell knew someone who lived around there, who had a cabin about two miles from the Trinity Resort.

Four months dropped away like they'd never existed to begin with, and all he saw was her face, her pale blue eyes jumping with hunger as he pushed deep into her body.

Gabe dragged a hand through his sweaty hair. The need for her hadn't vanished after that first night they'd shared—a new thing for him. He usually got bored. But with her, it hadn't been just about the way her body moved in perfect rhythm with his or the way she took control—or gave it up—at the most perfect times. It was how she'd managed to stroke each scar on his body until he told her how they'd come about, how she watched him as he came inside her—no timidity, only need and passion. The woman could've swum inside his very soul and he would've offered no protest.

But she'd burned him.

"See you later, bro," Ty called to him as he headed for his car.

His muscles tight, Gabe sprinted after him. "I'm going with you."

"Why?"

"I got something I need to check out."

Ty grinned as he tossed his pack into the back of his car. "Something or someone?"

"Shut up."

Ty chuckled. "We might have to talk our way past the line."

Gabe threw back the door to his truck. "Wouldn't be the first time. Let's go."

Once upon a time, Nora Wallace had offered his mind and heart a place to open up, to rest, for just a minute. He'd fought against it with everything that was in him, but in the end he'd allowed himself to trust her.

"Fool," he uttered darkly as he turned the key and shoved the gearshift into reverse. She was practiced, and she'd gotten exactly what she'd wanted—the story that she'd been after—Millionaire Playboy Smoke Jumper caught with his pants down and his guts hanging out.

Sure, she'd tried to explain, but by then he was deaf.

As far as she was concerned, anyway.

Gabe gunned the engine and flew out of the parking lot. He didn't want to think about her ever again, and yet right now that seemed like an impossibility. The cabin they'd shared for two nights might be in the path of the fire, hell, might already have been eaten up by the blaze.

He slammed his palm on the steering wheel. If he had any brains left, he'd leave the evacuation to the fire-fighters. But he was an idiot, and he wouldn't allow her death to be on his conscience. Odds were she was back in L.A., but he had to be sure.

THE STENCH OF SMOKE was unmistakable.

Feet thrust awkwardly into sneakers, Nora ran for the front door. Her heart thudded painfully in her chest and her legs felt heavy and gangly as she grabbed the doorknob, turned and yanked it back. A bluish light of predawn mingled with the cautious invasion of smoke rising from the valley below. In what seemed like slow motion, she rotated around, nearly tripping on the rug as she headed for the bathroom. She grabbed a wet washcloth from the rim of the sink and slapped the white cotton against her mouth as she rushed out the front door.

The phone lines were down.

She had to get to her car.

If she could just get to her car, she could outrun what was on its way.

Ash pelted her as she jogged down the stone walkway. Heat assaulted her skin and smoke made her eyes burn. But she kept going. There was no driveway, just a spot of grass down the hill where she parked her car. Her pajamas felt confining, and she had an odd desire to strip bare.

Coughing, she tripped coming down the hill. When she got to her feet, she froze.

Fire.

Orange devillike flames were eating up the brush between her and her car.

She turned back, thinking fast, weighing her choices.

If she retreated to the house, she was going to die. Her only chance was to hike up into the hills.

GABE PLOWED HIS TRUCK through the brush, his headlights cutting the thin veil of smoke. He'd left Ty two miles back, on the trail headed for his sister. All he wanted to do now was get to Nora's cabin, find it empty and head back to the line to offer some help to the firefighters and hotshots.

But as he came over the rise, he found two things he didn't expect. A ridge fire, and Nora Wallace in her pajamas. A strange roll of emotion flooded him, among them relief and annoyance. He didn't want to deal with her, their history or getting her out, but he shoved back his weak thoughts and pushed himself into action mode.

He came up alongside her, breaks squealing to a stop, and thrust open the passenger door. "Get in."

She stuck her head in the car, squinted at him. "Gabe?"

"Uh-huh."

She just stared at him, like he was a figment of her imagination or something.

He sighed. "Do you want to get out of here or not?"

"What are you—"

"Get in the truck," he interrupted angrily. "We don't have time for this."

Her lips pulled tight against her teeth, but she did as he said. Once she was beside him, Gabe slammed the pedal to the metal and they whizzed back around and headed away from the fire. But the wind changed again, and they'd barely gone a quarter mile when flames shot up in front of them, blocking their way.

Ashes from the main fire were spitting out spot fires around them. Gabe went on automatic pilot; his brain serving up every plausible scenario. The road was blocked off by fire. Wild sage grew in abundance here. Fire would eat that up in a hurry. It was late summer— bone-dry tinder everywhere. If they retreated, all they'd find were more flames, more smoke. Dammit. He could do nothing, not alone and not with Nora in tow. They needed to ditch the truck and go on foot—higher up into the mountains until the fire burned out.

"C'mon." Gabe hauled Nora against him and out the driver's-side door. She was quiet and responsive, even stayed close to his side as he snatched his spare pack from the bed of his truck.

He could smell the sickly sweet stench of burning sage and pulled on Nora's hand to hurry her forward, through thick brush and over rocks and hills. He felt useless as hell, running from a fire. As the smoke eased, he had the urge to drop Nora's hand and run back to it. But he pushed onward.

After about twenty minutes and only a quarter of a mile up or so, Nora's breathing began to sound labored. Gabe slowed and let her rest. After all, the air was becoming thinner, and clearly she wasn't used to the exercise. He watched her sit down on a bed of dried pine needles, coughing a few times.

Like a wary animal, he paced, jumped up on rocks and sniffed the air. They didn't have much time to sit here. When he turned around to face her again, she was watching him with those pale blue eyes. Even in her baggy nightwear, she looked tempting. Her auburn hair was down and bed-worn, her beautiful face was stained with ash, but she still looked good.

"Nice jammies," he muttered drily.

She didn't say thank-you. Instead, she shook her head. "What are you doing here?"

Trust Nora Wallace to get to the point. He shrugged casually, though his body was tight and ready to move on, get to higher ground. "I've been asking myself that same question."

"Did you come for me? Did you come to rescue me?"

She made such a thought sound totally implausible. Sure he thought she was a shallow, unethical, do-anything-to-get-to-the-top kind of woman, but that didn't mean she wasn't worthy of a rescue. "I heard about the fire and didn't want your death on my con-science, that's all."

She stared at him, then a brush of humor touched her mouth. "That's very sweet, London."

"I thought so."

"So, what was your plan? To drive in, pick me up and drop me off in town?"

"I didn't even think you'd be around to rescue. And you're welcome by the way."

She sighed then, came to her feet. Around them the sun was rising high and pink, while the air remained thick and heavy. She walked right up to him, her gaze direct. "I'm sorry I'm being a little brusque here. I'm just confused and freaked-out." A breeze kicked up and she hugged her arms, looking serious and sincere. "Thank you for helping me. I really appreciate it."

"Don't mention it," he uttered, fully ready to get back on the trail. "But do me a favor and try to keep up. We can rest when we put another mile between us and the fire."

"I'll do my best," she said with a twinge of pride to her tone.

"That's all I ask." He was about to turn toward the trail, when something caught his eye. It was Nora. His gaze roamed over her, then narrowed. He cocked his head to the side. "Something's different about you."

"I would say so. I'm wearing wrecked sneakers, sushi pajamas and I've tossed out my blush for this lovely inky ash color."

He shook his head. "No, it's something else. Have you gained a little weight?"

"What?" she gasped.

He shrugged, his eyes dropping to her breasts. "Something's different."

Nora bristled. "Your charm's really wilted in the last few months."

"Didn't know I had any to begin with," Gabe shot back. "Wasn't one of the attributes you mentioned in your article. There was my money, my job and my affinity for life under the sheets, but no charm mentioned."

Bars seemed to slam shut all around her, and she tilted her chin up. "I think we should find a way back to the road, don't you?"

"Nothing would please me more, but there's no way to do that right now." He grabbed his pack and swung it over his shoulder. "That spot fire is going to pass over and through us if we don't keep climbing."

CHAPTER TWO

AFTER THREE HOURS of hiking under the hot summer sun Nora's legs burned, but she wasn't about to complain. She'd had about all she could handle with this fire—life and death, the possible destruction of her family's cabin and the forced proximity to a man who thought she was pretty much the scum of the earth.

She ventured a glance in his direction. Tall and broad like the trees that surrounded him. Dark hair, cut short and spiky against his tanned neck. Black eyes that watched every movement, every flicker of wind, every possible danger or way out. She had the urge to curl into him, feel his warmth, capture the resolute strength he always seemed to possess. She knew he had curbed his pace for her. She knew that, without her, he could have been more than a mile farther than where they were, and again she wondered why he'd left his world and stepped back into hers when he'd sworn he'd never darken her door.

Was it possible he knew her little secret?

She shivered, goose bumps playing over her skin. Yes, she *had* gained a few pounds. And she could recall with absolute clarity how that circumstance had come about. Two nights of the most amazing sex of her life— two nights that had spun her around, knocked her out and changed her forever.

Her mind spit out the decadent images she'd tried like hell to forget over the past four months. The two of them in bed, nude and shaking with the force of their climaxes. Gabe on top, Gabe on the bottom, Gabe behind her, Gabe holding her to him as they let their bodies cool, only to heat up again.

"Maybe you should tell me your name now."

They'd met just hours ago and now here they were in bed. A grin on her face, Nora buried her head in Gabe's chest, her skin still prickling from the rush of heat and electricity. "Don't even joke about something like that."

"Why not?"

"Makes me sound easy."

He chuckled. "C'mon, Nora. We're grown-ups. We don't need a long courtship if we don't want one."

"My mother lived her life that way. Pure pleasure. Fast and amazing. And it brought her plenty of trouble—until she met my Dad, at any rate."

"This is different."

"Is it?" She wasn't at all sure.

Gabe turned, slipped her beneath him and held her with his gaze. "I think so."

The weight of him felt divine, so comforting yet erotic as hell. "Like maybe I've met the right guy, too?"

He grinned. "Could be." He brushed her hair back from her face in the gentlest way. "Like I told you, I had a father who played fast, too. I know what you're feeling. But you can't give everything a definition."

"So you're saying we should just enjoy this?"

"Think you can do that, Wallace?" he said, his head dipping to her breast.

"I'll...wow, I'll do my best," she murmured as he circled her nipple with his tongue.

"Watch out!"

Nora slammed back to the present just as she was about to collide with the trunk of a ponderosa pine.

"No daydreaming," Gabe admonished, taking her arm and guiding her back onto the rustic trail, the landscape completely devoid of cabins, only wildlife and forest. "Gets you hurt."

"Right." After four months of daydreaming, she should know better.

"And I don't want you hurt. We'll move even slower if I have to carry you."

"I got it, London," she said testily, feeling very tired all of a sudden.

"This trail leads to the summit, and we need to cross that ridge…" Gabe stopped talking, looked at her and studied her again. "You look pale, Nora. Maybe your blood sugar's low." He glanced at his watch. "Close to noon."

"Too bad there's no Denny's around here, huh?"

"Here." He opened his pack, grabbed a baggy, then handed her a piece of jerky. "Make it last."

"Thanks."

The meat tasted slightly off, but she didn't care. She was hungry and light-headed and she had to put something in her stomach. She chewed the dried meat and continued to hike, and after a while she felt that new and oh, so comforting, so wonderful tapping against the rise of her abdomen.

She ventured a glance at Gabe and idiotically wondered if he could feel it, too. She rolled her eyes. All the guy felt was contempt for her.

What the hell was she going to do? Tell him the truth? She had inadvertently deceived him once before with that damn article. Was she going to do it again? With him right here, beside her?

Her heart flipped over as she walked, the sun waging war on her exposed skin. Should she try again to tell him the truth? Right now?

She shook her head. The last time she'd tried to tell him the truth had been a disaster. She remembered that day like it was an hour ago. She'd gone to the Redding Base, ready to face him, and had only managed to find him in the arms of another woman; a tall blonde with an enormous rack and what had seemed like six exploring hands. But the octopus lady shouldn't have mattered, right? Nora should have walked right up to the pair, pulled them apart and told Gabe the truth.

But she wasn't that brave, it seemed.

Just then, Nora gasped and stopped dead in her tracks. That lovely kick she'd experienced a moment ago had morphed into a full-fledged pain inside her. She gripped her belly.

"What are you waiting for?" Gabe turned around and stared at her, brows lifted. "I don't have any red wine to go with that dried-up piece of steak."

For just a second, Nora debated whether or not to tell him that she wouldn't be drinking wine for at least another five months. But the impatient, untrusting expression on his face had her pressing her lips together.

"Let's go, London," she said as the pain subsided, then vanished. "For today, I follow where you lead."

He sniffed. "For today?"

She nodded and pushed onward. "That's all I can spare."

BY FOUR-THIRTY that afternoon, the wind had shifted again, even picked up speed, and Gabe was on his guard for more spot fires. Hot embers from the ash of the existing fire could travel a good distance on the breeze, and if it hit a patch of receptive fuel, he would have a big problem on his hands.

Another big problem.

He heard the weary footfall of the woman behind him. He knew she was ready to drop. With just a cut of jerky and some water in her stomach, mixed with the fear of the fire and anxiety over the fate of her home, he felt sympathetic. But his sympathy wouldn't allow him to put them both in danger by making camp on unsafe, unstable ground. No. He'd taken them up the mountain another mile to the rock caves. It was a pretty isolated spot, no cabins, no nothing, but the fire was far enough away to not pose an imminent threat. They could get to the ridge and down the other side in another day or so if they picked up their pace a little.

Gabe dropped his spare pack next to the lip of a cave. He wished he'd tossed a radio, cell phone and some food into that pack before he'd left base, but he hadn't made the time—hadn't thought she'd be in the cabin—hell, he hadn't thought, period. They'd just have to make do with the flashlight, blanket, mini first-aid kit, cooking pot, boy's ax, rope and water purifier.

"We're going to make camp here," he announced, gesturing to the cave.

Nora stared at the opening to the rock. "I don't think so."

"What do you mean, you don't think so?"

"It's not right."

"Why the hell not? Worried you'll wreck your manicure on those scratchy rock walls?"

"Oh please. I don't care about things like that."

"Then I don't see a problem." He didn't have time for strange feminine ideas or phobias, whatever was making her uneasy. There was work to do before it got dark. "Why don't you clean up the cave a bit, lay out this blanket, while I see about some food. Wild potatoes grow around here." When he looked back at her she hadn't budged.

She sighed, looked heavenward. "All right. The thing is, I can't go in there because if the fire found its way up here, passed over us, the smoke could do some damage not only to us but—"

"The amount of smoke that's going to follow us will be minimal. Just the same as when we were walking."

"Yes, but we were outside, in the fresh air. In a cave, it collects and—"

"And what?" Gabe was on the verge of really losing his temper now. "What are you talking about?"

Moments passed, wind blew leaves and ash around them. Then finally, Nora sank to the ground and found his gaze. "You were right. I have gained weight."

He cursed. "Oh, Nora, for God's sake—"

"About five pounds actually." She tossed him a grim smile. "I'm worried about inhaling too much smoke because I'm pregnant, Gabe."

CHAPTER THREE

IN THE PAST YEAR, Gabe London had faced a thousand-acre brush fire, the retrieval of a man's lost limbs after a helicopter accident, and the near death of a fellow smoke jumper. He should've been able to hear this news with little more than a blip on the old heart monitor.

But he actually felt light-headed, and a strange pain was shooting up his arm—not the heart attack side, thankfully, but it freaked him out all the same. "How pregnant?"

She picked up a pinecone and fiddled with it. "Is that your gentlemanly way of asking if the baby's yours, London?"

He crouched next to her on her ground, in no mood for word games. "How far along are you?"

"Nearly four months."

"Damn, Nora!" He stood up again, paced like an angry wolf. Warring emotions raged inside of him; thrill and punching anger. He felt sick to his stomach, actually scared for the first time in a long time. He practically choked on the words that tumbled from his mouth. "And what? You weren't even going to tell me?"

"You didn't want to see me again."

"You, not a baby!"

She looked as though he'd struck her. Pale with only a hint of that kick-ass, war-of-the-words journalist he'd been so messed up on four months back, the woman he'd actually thought was *the* woman—the one he could be with for more than a minute.

He turned away, forgot about the fire down below, the smoke, the caves that sat before them. He wanted to slam his fist into something, break a bone, feel the pain surge through his blood. She'd been carrying his child around in her belly for four months and he'd been completely oblivious. He shook his head, bone tired all of a sudden.

"Gabe," she began quietly. "There was no baby to see. Not yet."

"So you would've called me when you went into labor?"

"I don't know."

His jaw dropped, and so did his heart—right into his gut, which was churning sickly. "You don't know?"

She sat forward. "What would you have thought if I'd have called you? Seriously?"

His jaw worked. He couldn't believe this was happening. He'd always been so careful, just not with her. He should've said no to that interview, no to the night at her cabin—no to all the hours they'd shared afterward. And no to himself when they'd run out of condoms.

"I'll tell you what you'd think," she said tightly, two pink spots now coloring her once-pale cheeks. "You'd think that I got pregnant to gain access to the Gabe London Vault." She studied him, then nodded. "You're thinking it now, aren't you?"

Six stepmothers in fourteen years. Six women who lived for three things—Harry Winston jewelry, Spago restaurant and plastic surgery. His father had funded it all, then passed his fortune on to Gabe when he'd died.

Gabe had experienced only one moment in his life when he'd forgotten to add that ingredient into the mix of his date and that moment had been in Nora Wallace's bed, hours before he'd found her article and realized she was just like the rest of them.

Gabe grabbed his pack and dug around for a length of twine, then took a stick from the ground. "I've had enough of this conversation. There's no more jerky, and I need to find us some food before it gets dark."

NORA FELT like a cat curled up with the sweetest bit of nip she'd ever come across. She was in bed, totally satiated and it was close to dawn on the third day she'd held Gabe London captive at her family's cabin in the woods. She smiled into her pillow. Well, she hadn't locked him away exactly, but she'd done her very best to keep him from leaving. Not only was he amazing in bed, but he made her laugh, made her feel feminine, made her feel alive instead of the emptiness she'd been enduring since her parents' deaths.

When she returned to L.A., she was going to kiss her boss for suggesting this assignment.

"Nora?"

Gabe's surly tone had her turning toward him. Not fifteen minutes ago, he'd gone to the kitchen for a drink. Daydreaming, she hadn't realized he'd been gone so long.

In the gray light of the coming day, he appeared pale. His eyes were frighteningly black, furious, and his mouth, once wet from her kisses, was now dry and thin.

He held up a sheet of white paper. "What the hell is this?"

She eyed the paper and shook her head. "I have no idea."

"That's a pretty unoriginal line for a writer, don't you think?" He thrust the paper at her.

A sinking feeling moved through Nora as she took the paper from him. Totally blank, except for the headline her editor had written a week ago screaming up at her. She closed her eyes and exhaled.

"Millionaire Playboy Smoke Jumper."

Gabe chuckled sardonically. "So this is the serious, honest interview you're going to do?"

She found his gaze and gave him an emphatic no.

"Dammit, Nora! This is a fluff piece. A total upthrust middle finger to every jumper I know. I told you I would never go for something like this, and you told me this was absolutely not what you were after."

She wasn't. "It's just a title. It was my editor's suggestion."

"I don't give a damn."

"She wants to sell magazines and she thinks this is the only way to do it," Nora explained, suddenly feeling very naked beneath her gray comforter. "I'm hoping I can talk her into a different type of story."

"And if you can't?"

She didn't know. And her hesitation said so.

Pure disgust etched his features. "I've been with my share of women, Nora, but I don't play them, and I sure as hell don't deceive them. Clearly, you don't subscribe to that belief system."

THE SUN HAD SET half an hour ago, but in the distance the orange glow of a still-raging fire had Nora's stomach in knots. She had little hope for her family's cabin, but her main concern was her baby. No matter how disconnected she felt to its father, she would do everything Gabe asked. He was the professional here, and knew his way around this forest just as she knew her way around the Los Angeles library.

Gabe had returned to camp with a huge bunch of wild potatoes and was now cooking them over a small fire in a very small pot he'd had in his pack. As Nora sat across from him, under a smoky yet starry sky, she felt determined to make some attempt at peace, even if it was just an apology. But he'd barely looked her way since his return from the woods, wouldn't even allow her to help him clean and cook the potatoes.

Clearly he hated her guts. Firstly, because she'd tossed out all her moral fiber and submitted that article, and, secondly, because she'd kept her pregnancy from him. He had a right to his anger over both, but she had the duty to explain her reasons behind her choices, even if he pretended not to listen.

Nora watched him stir the potatoes as she ran through several openers to the discussion in her mind. When they all sounded forced or just plain stupid, she sighed heavily and confessed, "Listen, Gabe, I hadn't planned on submitting that story."

"What story?" he said, as though he had absolutely no interest in the conversation.

She frowned but continued. "In fact, I held on to it for about two weeks before I decided to stuff the entire thing right into the shredder."

"Well, thank God, it was saved before its untimely death. What would *EDGE* magazine have put in its place? Real Live Saints Swim the Nile?"

"My boss called and demanded I submit it, Gabe."

"Of course she did," he said with deep sarcasm. "And you just couldn't say no."

She shook her head. "No. I couldn't." She'd wanted to. So badly it ate right through her soul. But by then she'd known that she needed the medical benefits, and there was no way she was walking away from that. "My boss wanted tabloid, not truth. What I originally wrote made her laugh. She threatened my job."

"There are other jobs—"

"No," she assured him passionately. "Not with hours and flexibility and income and insurance like this one. I'd just found out I was having a baby."

He stopped with the potatoes and looked up at her. The anger in his tone faded a touch. "You could've called me."

"I know." She scrubbed a hand over her face and gave him a regretful smile. "Or I could've come to see you."

Gabe looked abruptly cautious. "What?"

"At the base. I could've come to see you, talked to you, tell you that I was pregnant with your child."

"Yeah," he said earnestly. "You could've."

"But if I'd done that, I might've found you in the arms of another woman."

His lips thinned. "I don't get this."

"I might've found you kissing a very hot little blonde against the door of your truck."

Gabe blinked, then sighed and swore.

Nora sat up tall, her tone as even as she could make it with a heart that was pounding furiously inside her chest. "So, maybe it was a good thing that I didn't come there. Maybe it wouldn't have been the right time to tell you."

"Nora…"

She shook her head.

But he continued. "That was…nothing…"

"Not my business," she assured him as every ounce of the pain she'd felt that day, watching him, came back to her tenfold. "I just wanted you to understand where I was coming from on this, London."

He looked unconvinced, shook his head. "Well, what do we do now?"

There was a fire inching its way toward them, a baby growing inside its mother's belly and two people who were determined to misunderstand each other so neither one of them got hurt again.

A pang of desire moved through Nora. Not sexual exactly, but fierce nonetheless. She wanted Gabe to hold her, just for a minute so she could stop shaking inside. She wanted him to give her some indication that he had anything other than disdain for her. She wanted his forgiveness, and a hope that her baby would know his father's love.

But she didn't go there. Instead, she helped him take the potatoes off the fire as she said, "For now, let's just get out of this mess alive."

Gabe took a deep breath and stared down the mountainside. "That's the easy part."

CHAPTER FOUR

GABE COULDN'T SLEEP.

He was too keyed up. Several times throughout the night, he'd left the cave and clambered up a boulder pile to watch the blaze, watch as patches of the smoky orange blanket dropped back and died, watched as timber flew and ashes sailed on the wind, docking on beds of what was, no doubt, dry timber. He felt useless, and wondered if his bros had been called out.

He'd see the plane, surely.

Or hear it if the smoke got too thick.

He pushed off the thick rock and landed with a thud on the ground below. His knee buckled and he swore at the pain. His first thought was that he'd wake up Nora. Boy, he'd really left his balls back at the base, hadn't he?

After returning to the cave, he switched on his flashlight and aimed the light on the rocky wall above where she slept. Eyes closed and breathing easily. All he needed to know, yet he kept the light where it was. She looked really young and vulnerable, like one of those pretty female mountain lions who lured you in with their innocent veneer, then had your hand for breakfast.

His gaze dropped to her belly. Her pajama top was riding high and he could just make out the gentle hill of his child. A vise gripped his heart. He had a kid coming into the world and he didn't know a damn thing about being a father. Sure, he was dependable, proud, could get things done, but what did he know about love?

Not a damn thing.

The unconditional kind, at any rate.

A scratching outside the rock walls had Gabe instantly on alert. Silently, he reached into his pack for his ax, then trained the flashlight on the mouth of the cave. He saw nothing, yet still heard the animal. Scratching, walking over pine needles. Sounded like something bigger than a rabbit, maybe a deer or mountain lion. Of course, in the dark, it was really hard to gauge the size of something. A raccoon could sound like a bear, and a bear could sound like nothing more than a person out for a stroll.

The loud crack of a stick breaking had Nora sitting up, bleary-eyed. "What was that?"

"Quiet," Gabe uttered sharply.

Nora didn't say anything, but her breathing was heavy and anxious as she sat beside him. Gabe had heard the same sound on the survivors of that helicopter crash earlier this year. Fear—plain and simple. And he didn't blame her for feeling that way. Whatever was out there sounded pretty damn big.

"You know," Nora whispered, "it could be a person. Someone else might be lost out here, too."

Gabe glanced over his shoulder and whispered back, "We're not lost, Nora."

"You know what I mean."

"I'm going to check it out."

She grabbed his arm as he made to leave. "Why?"

"It's better to know what we're dealing with."

On a sigh, she released him. "Machismo is just oozing from you right now, London."

"Would you rather the thing find its way in here?"

"No, I think I'd rather it just went away without knowing we exist."

Gabe snapped off his flashlight, eating the regret that knocked at his gut for having turned on the light in the first place. His night vision was pretty wrecked now and it was going to take at least forty-five minutes to get his full vision back. He breathed deeply, trying to get his eyes to adjust to blackness.

"Whatever's out there probably smelled the potatoes," Gabe whispered as he headed for the mouth of the cave. "Just have to scare it off."

"While you're out there wrestling with a bear," Nora whispered after him, "should I stay here and whimper with fright as I clutch my belly?"

"Nope. Too loud," he uttered before disappearing altogether.

Alone in the pitch-black cave, Nora felt as though she were still dreaming, that those cracking sounds were happening outside her bedroom window at the cabin, not outside a remote cave high up in the mountains.

She sat there waiting and listening, deciding to give Gabe five minutes to return, and if he didn't she was going after him. But lucky for her, he did come back and just under the wire, flashlight under his chin like a creature in a horror flick, his expression thoroughly annoyed.

"No bear," he muttered. "No mountain lion—not even a rabbit."

She didn't get it. She shook her head. "Was there anything—"

She stopped short. Ambling into the cave on tiny white legs was the little something that had been making that big racket.

A dog.

A very ugly dog. It was black and white and seemed to be a combination of about fifty breeds. But with those enormous brown eyes, the little dog had an immediate friend in Nora. And he knew it.

With a few clicks of the tongue, Nora opened her arms for the dog. It scampered over to her and lapped at her face.

"Don't encourage him," Gabe grumbled, still hanging out by the entrance to the cave.

"Why not?"

"He could be rabid."

"Get serious," she said on a laugh, giving the dog a scratch behind the ears.

"I'm serious."

She glanced up at Gabe and smiled. "The big, strong, smoke jumper isn't afraid of a little bitty dog, is he?"

"He may be little, but he's got sharp teeth. I had a dog bite me when I was a kid."

Her gaze swept over him. "Where?"

"I'm done swapping scars with you, Nora," he said moodily.

She shrugged. "Well, then don't expect any sympathy from me or appeasement from Ashes, here."

"You can't name him." Gabe pushed away from the doorway and sat down across from her, his back to the wall. "Clearly, he belongs to someone," he added, pointing out the collar, sans tags.

"Maybe he does, but he should have a name, at least until we can get him home." She drew her brows together. "How do you know it's a he?"

Gabe rolled his eyes. "There are just some things you can't hide."

"Come here, Ashes," Nora cooed, inviting the dog to curl up next to her.

The little mutt was sweet and warm, and Nora put her arm around him and closed her eyes, looking content for the first time since they'd escaped the fire.

Gabe felt a stab of jealousy looking at the pair, then brushed it off.

Jealous of a dog.

Damn. Jealous period. What was wrong with him? He needed to get them all off this mountain and back to civilization. He just needed those flames to cross the ridge, then they could backtrack over the safe zone and head down the mountain to the road.

He stared at Nora and the pooch, eyes closed, bodies relaxed. Unlike the two of them, he wasn't going to sleep tonight. He pushed to his feet and stalked out of the cave. The air was gray and heavy, and as he climbed up the cave wall and sat, perched on top of the rock, he saw what he expected to see—the fires still burning down below.

The sight was priceless.

Nora remained where she was, lying on the blanket. She didn't want Gabe to know she was awake, or wake him up for that matter. He looked insanely handsome in the pale smoky light of dawn—just how she remembered him on those mornings when they'd greeted the day with a round of slow lovemaking. He looked sort of disheveled, his chin dusted with stubble. He also looked approachable, his eyes closed, locking away that imperious, hard stare that made her belly flip with both desire and unease. But the picture that really had her staring transfixed was a little black-and-white dog, its petite yet sadly dirty mug draped over Gabe's thigh.

She muffled a laugh.

As if he'd heard the slam of a tree coming down instead of a hushed chuckle, Gabe's eyes shot open. "What was that?" His dark eyes narrowed. "What are you staring at?"

"I really wish I could sell tickets," she said with a wide grin. "How many of your smoke jumping bros would pay to see this, do you think?"

Gabe's brow furrowed, then he glanced down. "Oh, you've got to be kidding."

"You make a lovely couple."

"He's a good-for-nothing oaf," Gabe grumbled, yet he didn't make a move to shove the still-sleeping dog off his lap. Instead, he settled back against the wall, his gaze serious, all-business. "I've devised a new plan for today."

"You were up pretty late."

"Just shut my eyes an hour ago. I wanted to watch the movement of the fire."

"And?" Nora sat up and hugged her legs.

"Well, it looks like it's fairly contained, but the wind keeps shifting, so there could be hot spots." Seemingly unaware, Gabe stroked the top of the dog's head. "I've figured out a different route back to the main road. But it'll be a lot of hiking. Think you're up for it?"

"Not much choice, is there?"

"We could stay here. Wait it out. Hope it doesn't hit us."

"We?" she repeated, her heart pinging with emotion.

He shrugged. "Or I could hike down, get some help, maybe a chopper—"

"But?"

"But I don't want to risk that."

There was no hint of warmth in his eyes, but his words were enough for her. "It's no problem," she assured him. "I can make it."

"You'll let me know when you need to stop and take a breather."

"I will."

He seemed satisfied with this, and gestured to the covered pot in the center of the dead fire. "Have that last potato. I'll catch something for lunch on the trail."

Her stomach rolled over. "Catch something?"

He laughed. "Game can be pretty tasty when you're starving."

She nodded, her lips pressed tightly together. "I'm sure."

"Unless you wanna give ol' Ashes here a try?" Gabe said, patting the dog's shaggy head. "He's small, but there might be some good meat on him."

She gasped. "You wouldn't dare."

Humor danced in his eyes.

She laughed, forgetting about the fire, her family's cabin, everything terrible for a moment. "All talk and no action, London."

A chuckle escaped his throat. "Get serious." His gaze slid to her belly. "Because we both know that's not true."

The playful moment continued and Nora swiftly moved with it, hoping it wouldn't shatter, like a child trying to catch a bubble. "Hey, the action started right here. It was me who came on to you first."

He eased the dog off his lap and started filling his pack. "Sure you did, but we're talking about follow-through—that's where all the action happens—not in the initiation."

Nora grabbed the blanket and rolled it up. "Oh, so now I didn't follow through? I never heard you complaining."

He glanced up, his gaze heavy-lidded and sexy. "That's because I'm *no* talk, *all* action."

She shook her head, rolled her eyes.

He laughed. "I'm going out to watch the fire. You eat that potato and get yourself together." He held up a hand. "Five minutes of girl time, then we're out of here."

Nora watched him walk out the cave door, Ashes at his heels.

ABOUT THREE HOURS into their hike and five seconds before Nora was about to ask for a respite, Gabe spotted a large rock and pointed to it. They sat down side by side, Ashes at their feet, and Gabe offered Nora and the mutt some water. They both drank richly, and when Nora was done she thanked him, then let her head fall back against the smooth boulder.

"You okay?" he asked.

"Sure. Just a little achy and sore, that's all."

"What hurts the most?"

She sighed. "My feet. I swear to God, it's like walking around on bricks sometimes."

Without a word, he scooped up her sneaker-clad feet and placed them in his lap. With deft fingers, he removed her shoes and gently began to rub the pads of her feet with his thumbs.

Heaven.

"You've got great hands, London," she said earnestly. "But that's old news." He glanced up, staring at her. She shrugged. "I'm not going to blush or get coy. The truth never embarrasses me."

He shook his head, chuckling. "So, have you thought about a name?"

Deeply tucked into the haze of pleasure he was giving her with his large, strong hands, Nora could only murmur, "What?"

"For the kid. Have you thought of a name?"

A name.

Wow, that brought her screaming back to reality. "Oh. No. Not really."

"Elizabeth is nice," he said with an offhanded shrug.

"Sure."

"It's my grandma's name, that's all."

Her heart pulled and she gazed up at him with a flood of tenderness. "It's beautiful."

"Course, it might be a boy."

"There's that fifty-fifty chance."

"My grandpa's name was Percy, and I'm just not going to do that to a kid."

She smiled. "My grandfather's name was William."

"Will…or Billy. That's good." He stopped with her feet, placed them on the ground beside her shoes. On a heavy sigh, he said, "You knew I wanted a kid, Nora. Hell, you pulled that fact out of me in your interview. How could you not tell me?"

"When I saw you with that woman—"

"That was just a one night…" He shook his head. "No. You had plenty of other opportunities after that day. Did you just take the coward's route or what?"

Sure, she was never embarrassed by the truth, but she'd run from it many times. "I was afraid."

"Of what?"

"How you'd react."

"Nora—"

"The thing is," she said quickly. "I could handle being rejected by you."

He looked away.

"But I couldn't stand the thought of you rejecting our child."

He looked outraged, stunned even. "That could never happen."

"How would I know that?"

Lines of anger bracketed his mouth and he spoke in low, uneasy tones. "You would've known if you'd have found out about me—not the Playboy Smoke Jumper—but me. Dug a little deeper. I'm a good man, honest and real. I'm the guy who never looks for a family, but in his gut wants one real bad."

Tears pricked her eyes, and she felt deeply and profoundly ashamed. She'd pulled a few stories out of him during that interview, a few juicy tidbits about his past. She'd found out that he wasn't looking for anything serious yet wasn't closed to the idea of a child. She'd found out his favorite music, favorite food and what he did when he couldn't sleep, but she'd never probed his heart.

And yet, she'd solely blamed her boss for that article.

Words and academia and tests and work had all come too easy to her. She'd gotten lazy. And it had cost her this man. Why hadn't she seen that before? Why hadn't she made the relationship with her baby's father a priority? Why hadn't she understood that really loving her child meant giving that child a father?

She swallowed the heaviness in her throat. She should've fought for the article she'd originally written, and she should've delved deeper into Gabe London.

Her gaze found his and she reached for his hand. "I'm sorry."

"I want this child, Nora." With their intertwined hands, he touched her belly.

The gesture nearly killed Nora, and she forgot about his anger, her stupidity and the future. She cupped his face, drew him to her and kissed him. At first, Gabe stilled, then with a throaty moan, he gave in. In seconds, he seemed to devour her, angling his mouth, swiping the inside of her cheek with his tongue, nipping at her lips until Nora thought her body had turned liquid.

Then an image of his angry eyes flashed against her lids and she eased away from him.

"Hey," Gabe murmured huskily, still half-lidded and sexy as sin.

Nora exhaled. "This is probably not the best idea."

"Huh?" He came awake slowly, his expression moving from confused to edgy and irritated. He disentangled himself from her touch, shook his head. "Dammit, Nora. Why are you the one backing off? I'm the one who should push you away—I'm the one who has the right to be pissed off."

"I know," she said. "That's why I did it. I could feel your anger through that kiss."

He took a moment, then nodded. "I want you, Nora. My teeth ache I want you so bad. But I haven't forgiven you."

Her heart dropped into her shoes, but she managed a solid "I know."

Gabe looked pained, confused even, then something startled him and he lifted his chin, shot to his feet. "Damn."

"What?"

He helped her up, pointed over the ridge. "There's a fire close by." He grabbed his pack and slung it over his shoulder. "Damn wind. Why does it feel like we're being trailed by this blaze?"

On a sigh, Nora followed him. "You know what Francis Bacon said, 'Things alter for the worse spontaneously, if they be not altered for the better designedly.'"

He glanced over his shoulder. "What the hell does that mean?"

"I don't know. That perhaps the movement of this fire is calculated. Forcing us to run, forcing us to work together, forcing us to deal with the reality we've created."

"And you know what Bob Dylan said?" Gabe asked, turning back to the trail.

"I don't think I've ever understood what Bob Dylan's said."

"This one's not too hard. 'Blame it on a simple twist of fate.'"

CHAPTER FIVE

SWEAT COATED Nora's skin and clothes by the time they reached what Gabe called checkpoint three—a thin, shallow river bracketed by black cottonwood trees. On a steady diet of smoke, hard ground and endless hiking, this lush, eternally green site looked like a little piece of heaven. Nora's throat fairly ached for water, her sweaty, ashy skin, too. Over the four-hour hike, Gabe had made sure she'd stopped and rested, but her thighs and calves felt as though they'd been twisted and poked, and she was grateful to sit down on the soft grassy hem of the riverbed.

In contrast, Gabe looked as though he'd only taken a walk around the block and could go fifty more laps if he didn't have a tired, pregnant lady on his hands.

Nora watched him set down his pack then seize the blanket inside. He handed it to her. "Take a few minutes to clean up, bathe, whatever."

"Thanks." His tone was even, cool, and Nora wondered if he was still annoyed with her over the abrupt ending to their kiss.

"I'll be over here," he said, turning around and heading up the grassy bank, Ashes beside him.

"Over where?"

He stopped, pointed to the left, to an enormous cottonwood, its branches dipping delicately into the two-foot-deep river. "On the other side of that tree."

"Opting for a little privacy, huh?"

"Don't want to tempt you twice," he tossed over his shoulder.

"I think I can resist you," she called after him.

"You sure?"

"Yep."

"Well, just to be safe…"

Gabe grinned to himself as he hiked up the quick hill and past the cottonwood. That woman could make a man crazy if he let her. But she was right about one thing—he was having trouble resisting her. He wouldn't have believed it, after all he'd done to rid her from his thoughts and memory over the past four months, but she'd burrowed under his skin again.

And with only one kiss.

Her mouth was like candy, a sugar rush that had him staggeringly, damagingly high.

He paused at the cottonwood and leaned against the massive trunk. He wanted to turn around, and, if she was nude or close to it, he just wanted to watch.

The faint stench of smoke drifted past his nostrils, but for once he didn't jump to attention, didn't race off to find the highest point to view the fire. Instead, he turned around and peered through the tree's accommodating branches. Nora had removed her pajama top and was washing her arms, breasts and belly with small hands and delicate fingers—fingers that had once stroked him as carefully.

Gabe felt as though fire had consumed his body, taken over his mind as his eyes zeroed in on the woman who was carrying his child. She was the same, yet different. Her body had grown lush with pregnancy: extra curves, swollen breasts and a slightly rounded belly, and he adored the enhancement.

A mad grip of possession moved through him as he watched her wash—along with a Stone Age desire to haul her against him, show the trees, water, air and fire just who she belonged to.

Then sense wormed its way into his muddled brain and he relented. His job was to get Nora back to the road, back to safety and back to reality. A quick rinse in the river for both of them and they could be on their way.

He was about to turn to leave when Ashes, who had run back down to the riverbed with Nora, came bounding toward him, yapping his fool head off, ready to play hide-and-seek or some other idiotic diversion.

"Quiet, you mongrel," Gabe uttered fiercely.

Clearly liking this game, Ashes kept on barking and jumping, until Nora looked up from what she was doing. For one moment, their eyes caught and held. She didn't rush to cover herself, only gave him a soft smile.

"Now, who can't resist who?" she called.

"Dammit." Gabe turned around and headed for his side of the riverbed and the cool water that he so clearly needed.

It was close to four o'clock and the sun was threatening to sink farther behind the mountains when they finally stopped for the night. Ashes took off into a clump of trees to relieve himself and Nora and Gabe hunkered down in the middle of a clearing.

They were deep on the other side of the mountain now and the stench of smoke was practically nonexistent. Nora put a hand to her belly and sighed. By this time tomorrow, if she was lucky, she'd be soaking in a hot bath. Though exhausted, she felt lighter, easier about the remainder of their journey, because no matter what lay ahead for her and her home and Gabe and the child, at the very least they had outrun the fire.

The only danger that remained seemed to be the sparks that flickered between her and the man before her.

"We should be on the road home tomorrow," Gabe told her, setting his pack down on a patch of cleared earth.

"I hope so," Nora remarked, gathering up all the dry sticks around her for the fire she knew Gabe would be building later. "I have to find out what happened to my cabin." She glanced up at him. "Do you think it's possible that it's okay?"

She didn't miss the quick drop of his eyes, the pull of his jaw. "Don't know."

But he did, she thought. Even she had surmised by now that the odds were slim to none that her family's place was still standing. Gabe was just being a nice guy.

"We'll have to wait and see," he concluded, digging in his pack for supplies.

"Oh, look at that." Nora smiled. A few feet away, two little gray creatures were sniffing around, completely oblivious to the human intruders.

"What?" Gabe asked, not sounding all that interested.

"Those two rabbits playing in the brush."

At that, Gabe's head shot up, though his voice dropped to a whisper. "Don't move."

"Why not?" she whispered back. "What are you thinking?" Her stomach began to turn then twist as her mind tossed out one very nauseating, though no doubt practical theory. "Oh, Gabe. No. You're not going to…"

Crouched beside her, he lifted one dark eyebrow. "You're hungry, aren't you?"

"I don't know anymore."

"You've got a baby growing inside you, Nora," he reminded her. "Don't get squeamish."

"Pregnancy gives me the right to be squeamish."

"Not out here. It's survival, plain and simple."

The rabbits' cute little cotton tails shifted as they hopped from plant to plant. Survival, huh? She leaned toward Gabe and whispered, "Well, is there a plan here or do you just run at them and fling your body over them?"

THIRTY MINUTES LATER, Gabe had successfully trapped, caught, skinned and cooked the two rabbits.

All while Nora wrestled with her conscience.

But as the delectable scent of cooking meat met her nostrils, she surrendered. It wasn't the first time. Five years ago, she'd tried to become a vegetarian with absolutely no luck. After three weeks of lentils, rice and pasta, she'd flung herself on the first burger that happened her way. She was a carnivore through and through, even more so since she'd become pregnant.

Gabe slid the meat off the roasting stick onto a large maple leaf and proceeded to cut it into chunks with his hunting knife. He handed her the largest portion and kept about a quarter for himself.

"Pretty good, isn't it?" Gabe said, handing her the filtered water bottle from his pack.

"I'm sorry to say that it's delicious," said Nora, after swallowing a very juicy bite before grabbing the water.

Out of the corner of her eye, Nora saw Gabe slip Ashes a few pieces of his meat. When she lowered the water bottle again, Gabe was ignoring the dog. Nora grinned in spite of herself, and when Ashes trotted over to her she made sure that Gabe saw her give the dog a few extras tidbits.

"The dog could lose a pound or two, but you can't," he said gruffly.

"It's just a couple of bites."

"The mongrel will be back in front of his feed dish tomorrow. He can survive."

"Do you think so?"

"Sure, it's just a few days and I'm giving him water."

"No," she said softly, feeling melancholy all of a sudden. "I mean about him being back in front of his dish. Do you think someone will claim him?"

Gabe gave the dog a pat. "Don't know why they'd want to, but probably."

Ashes' low growl interrupted their dinner conversation. Gabe stood up, looked around, then said quietly, "Don't move, Nora."

"Not more rabbits," Nora said glumly, as Ashes started barking yet oddly backing up.

"No." Gabe's voice was grave. "Coyotes."

CHAPTER SIX

NORA'S HEART LEAPED into her throat. Just ten feet away was a coyote. He was tan and skinny and not all that scary looking, but her hands starting shaking anyway. "They won't hurt us," she whispered. "I live in L.A. and they only mess with cats and small animals."

Slowly Gabe reached for his knife. "Nora, we've got a small animal."

Nora glanced at Ashes, who was doing an odd dance of cowering back, then jumping forward on his tiny white legs.

"And after being fed in the park by idiot tourists," Gabe said softly, "they've got no fear of humans anymore."

"But we're bigger than they are," uttered Nora nervously.

"They smell the rabbit and see the little dog. No doubt they're hungry, and they're obviously willing to risk it."

The coyote snarled and inched closer, his eyes fixed on Ashes. Nora stared, fear gripping her. Then, out of nowhere, a second coyote appeared from behind the first, catching Gabe off guard.

In some strange protective show, Ashes ran forward, barking furiously. Then realizing he was in big trouble, he froze where he stood, right in between the coyotes and Gabe. Sensing a meal in sight, the coyotes snarled at Ashes, then rushed him. Knife in hand, Gabe charged at the animals, trying to scare them off. One coyote dropped back, but the second, running on instinct and need, took a swipe at Gabe and caught him on the hand.

Gabe cursed darkly, gripped his hand.

Instinct overtook Nora. She remembered something from an article she'd written on animal behavior and she stood up. She walked toward the coyotes and a noise so loud and frightening erupted from her throat that she actually scared herself.

Gabe shouted after her, tried to grab her arm. "Stop, Nora!"

But Nora barely heard him. She lifted her arms above her head to make herself look larger and she rushed the coyotes.

They froze in place, stared at her, then took off, into the woods and out of sight.

Her heart in her throat, Nora turned to Gabe. She swallowed several times, feeling nauseous and exhausted with anxiety, her bravado now extinct.

"Come here." Gabe opened his arms to her and she lowered her head and walked straight for him, gripping him around the waist, clinging to him as Ashes circled them.

He felt whole and real, and Nora wanted to sink into him as her heart thudded in her ears. She didn't say anything, didn't move for the next ten minutes. Finally, she exhaled and dropped her head back to look at him. "Well, that was the best and most blatant example of karma I've ever seen."

Gabe stared at her mouth. "What are you talking about?"

"This afternoon. Your hunt. Our dinner."

"The connection escapes me."

She sighed. "The hunters become the hunted? Think about it, London."

He cursed. "Coyotes don't hunt humans. They were starving, and that one only nicked me because I got in front of him and this dog."

"Ashes tried to protect us."

"What?" he said incredulously. "He couldn't protect a flea."

"He did his best."

"He's a good-for-nothing dog."

Nora blinked. She knew better. "Why'd you step in front of him and that coyote then?"

Gabe shrugged. "Maybe because you like him. I don't know." He gripped her tighter, moved his hand up her back and then scowled with pain. Stepping back, he cupped his hand. "Don't look like much of a hero now, do I?"

Nora leaned forward to inspect the wound. "You look like a man who's bleeding."

"It's nothing."

"Let me see it."

Gently she took his hand and held it in hers. Thankfully, the scratch wasn't deep, but there was blood. She bent down, rummaged through his pack and came out with a first-aid kit. She did her best cleaning the wound and patching it up, and when she was done she did the oddest thing—she kissed the bandage.

Gabe cleared his throat, then uttered hoarsely, "Uh, Nora?"

"Yes."

"You need to stop touching me right now."

She looked up at him. His eyes were the color of coal, fire-bitten coal, as he gazed down at her. Desire ripped through her, and she saw the same need reflected in his expression.

She asked him, "Why did you come after me yesterday?"

"It's what I do."

"No, it's not."

"Well, it's part of what I do."

She couldn't stop herself. "Do you still have feelings for me, Gabe?"

Gabe stood motionless, his features tight. "How do I get you to stop talking?" His gaze flickered behind her. "Oh, yeah. Now I remember."

As he guided Nora back against a tree, a shot of panic whipped around in her chest. She wanted him to touch her, wanted him to make her feel, wanted him to let her give him pleasure, but she was afraid to feel close to him again.

His jaw flushed, rigid with tension, he slowly lowered his head. Nora didn't move. She held her breath, her body shaking, her legs watery. She waited for him to kiss her, but he didn't. Instead, he dropped to his knees and eased her pajama bottoms down around her ankles.

Panic jumped into her blood again. "What are you doing?"

"You know exactly what I'm doing," Gabe said, his mouth on her belly, his hands on her thighs, pushing her legs apart.

"Here?" she said, feeling his warm breath slide over her skin. "I don't think this is the place."

He nibbled at her hip bones. "I think this is the perfect place."

Gasping, Nora plunged her fingers into his hair for balance.

"Easy now," he whispered.

Nora couldn't think or follow directions. He had splayed her wide as he dipped his head. She moaned, sucked air through her teeth as his tongue drew a path up her sex, then burrowed inside to find the hidden cleft beneath.

An ache of all-consuming pleasure wove like a snake through her body. After they'd parted ways, she'd thought she was doomed to a life of celibacy. She'd felt that if she couldn't have the man she wanted, she wanted no man at all. But here she was, and here was the right man, the man she had fallen for four months ago, the man who had rescued her—the father of her child.

Gabe's mouth worked her with gentle flicks of his tongue. Her back against the rough surface of the tree, Nora moved with him, thrusting herself forward, angling upward to feel the hot, electric charges that came right before she did. Then she'd eased her hips back to prolong the sweet torture.

But when he grasped her hips, his fingers digging into her flesh as he nuzzled her deeply, she couldn't pull away. She could only thrust and thrust as he circled her cleft, licked her with his tongue, bit her with his teeth.

Until she throbbed too desperately to do anything but cry out, bucking as heat enveloped her.

CHAPTER SEVEN

HE WAS WEAK.

He was hard as hell, too.

But even so, he gently pulled up Nora's pajama bottoms, stood and took a step back.

He didn't want to look in her eyes, but the pull was too strong, as was his masculine pride. He wanted to see if she'd enjoyed herself.

When his gaze found her, he saw that she had stars and moons and the damn sun shining in her eyes. Smiling, she said huskily, "I want you to make love to me."

The shudder of her climax, the taste of her on his tongue was still with him, had his body and mind reeling with desire. He wanted her, against the tree, her legs around his waist, riding him. But they were in a totally different place than they had been four months ago. He wanted her, but he didn't trust her. That had never been a problem for him in the past, but with her everything was different.

He shook his head, feeling like a grade-A jerk. "No."

Her brows knit together. "Why not?"

He shrugged. "Timing's off."

Her gaze dropped to his fly. "That's not what it looks like to me."

Why was she so fearless? And why couldn't he put

all the b.s. from the past aside for about thirty minutes? He was about to explode, and she wanted him inside her.

"What's going on, London?" she asked when he didn't say anything. "What's this all about?"

He didn't think, just said the stupidest thing possible. "A thank-you."

Her eyes widened, her lips parted and she stared at him, through him actually. "A thank-you?" she repeated in a dangerously low voice. "For what exactly?"

He had unwisely dug himself a hole, he thought, so maybe he should just jump in and break a leg while he was at it. "Scaring off those coyotes and patching me up."

He'd never seen a woman look at him with such disgust, such revulsion. He didn't want that look coming from her of all people, and he despised himself more than she did at that moment. But even so, he wouldn't take it back. To do so, would mean he was letting her believe there might still be something between them.

And there could never be.

"Well, you're welcome," she said tightly, palms in the air. "But it was nothing, really. Nothing."

"Nora, look—"

"At least I got the answer to my question."

As she walked over to where his pack sat open and took the blanket out, he asked, "What question is that?"

Then she paused, eyed him critically. "If you still had feelings for me."

Slightly stunned, Gabe said nothing, just watched her spread out the blanket beside the fire. Her back to him, she lay down and presumably went to sleep while the sun set around them.

ASHES KNEW something was up.

Nora felt the dog close to her leg as she hiked down

the mountain the following day. No longer did Gabe push the mutt away, insult him or anything of the kind. He actually seemed to want Ashes near him, but ever since last night, since Gabe and Nora had argued, Ashes had been glued to Nora's side.

And she couldn't help but feel comforted by his attention.

As she walked, Gabe in front of her as usual, she no longer smelled smoke, but the fear in her heart was stronger than ever. They were very close to the road, and soon she would know the fate of her cabin. Soon she would walk away from Gabe with a proposal to stay in touch.

And nothing more.

In the wee hours of dawn, she'd come to the realization that her child needed a father and that she would work to make it easy for them to have a relationship. But that was it. She wanted nothing to do with him personally. She'd apologized, tried to make amends in as many ways as she could, but Gabe didn't want to forgive her. He had made his feelings about her plain as day—he'd had his revenge, made her feel like scum, and now it was time to face reality and move on.

"Only about an hour, I'd say," he called back to her.

"Good to know," she said softly.

He glanced back over his shoulder. "You okay? Need to rest or anything?"

"I'm fine."

I'm fine had been her clipped and curt sentence of choice since this morning, since Gabe had eyed her warily, remorse etching lines on his handsome face. Perhaps it was childish to throw around *I'm fines,* but what was the alternative? Really? Give him the honest lowdown on her feelings? He didn't want her feelings. He didn't want her.

An hour and a half later, they stepped onto pavement. It was a beautiful feeling. Nora sat down on the side of the road with Ashes, drank some water and heaved a sigh of relief as Gabe attempted to flag down a car.

The first truck that passed them flew right on by, but the second stopped and gave them a ride to the country store at the highway junction where the firemen were camped out.

When they were dropped off, Gabe immediately made a phone call as Nora got some water for Ashes. When Gabe returned, he forced Nora to sit back down and have some food and some water herself. But food was the last thing Nora wanted. She was desperate to ask the firemen about her cabin, but they were deep in conversation and she didn't want to interrupt them.

In less than ten minutes, two trucks pulled up and two young men got out. They were tall, thickly built and had ash and muck coating their skin and clothing. They walked over to Gabe and gave him a sly grin. The blond guy with a lazy smile spoke first, "Found her, huh?"

Gabe shot him a glare. "You're such a wiseass, Matheson."

The man with pitch-black hair and eyes the color of sage slapped Gabe on the back. "Couple more days and we would've come looking for you."

"How nice," Gabe said sarcastically, then turned to Nora. "These are a few of my buddies. Ty Matheson and Will Hutchins."

Nora gave the handsome men a weak smile. "Nice to meet you both." She tried to force some small talk from her throat, but nothing would emerge. She was on edge. She needed to make a plan to get a ride, or call a friend in L.A., or something—maybe find out where the other evacuated people had been shuttled off to. But most of all, she wanted away from Gabe. She stood up and nodded at the men. "Excuse me."

When Nora walked away, Gabe stared after her. She was on a mission, he knew. And the first firefighter in her path, a tall good-looking guy, got the series of questions she'd been holding on to since they'd driven away from her cabin.

A wave of jealously threatened to choke him as he watched her chatting up the firefighter. He didn't like the feeling, but he hated watching her with another man even more.

"Fire's romantic in the abstract," Ty needled him. "But set it loose and you got a real problem."

"Big problems," echoed Will.

"Shut up." He raised a brow at Ty. "Did you bring the keys, or what?"

Ty snorted, tossed the set into Gabe's hand. "Don't scratch her."

Gabe cursed, then left Ty and Will and followed Nora, who had just turned away from the fireman. "What are you doing?"

She was looking past him, not at him. "I'm trying to see if my cabin's still standing."

"They won't know for a while yet," Gabe informed her.

"I know." She shrugged. "So, I'll have to find out for myself."

"They won't let you past the line. And even if they did, I wouldn't let you pass."

"You wouldn't *let* me," she repeated coolly.

"That's right. Fire's out, but the ground's still hot."

She seemed to think about this, her jaw tight. Then

she lifted her chin. "I don't feel like staying at the high-school gym like everyone else, so I'll get a hotel room and wait until things cool off."

Gabe felt a rise of panic in his gut. He'd rescued her from the fire and now she didn't need him anymore. She was totally self-sufficient. If he didn't act, then she was really going to walk away and take care of herself. He shook his head. "No. No hotel. You're coming home with me."

"Not a chance," she said icily.

"I'm going to take care of you whether you like it or not."

"Gabe, I appreciate what you did. The rescue, the hike. Hell, even the little *thank-you* against the tree, but we're done here."

He moved dangerously close to her, put his hand on her belly. "You know as well as I do that we'll never be done."

"Only when it comes to my child."

"Our child," he corrected, his tone impatient.

They stared at each other, the heat of anger, desire and fear pulsating between them.

Gabe sighed. "Look, you want the mutt with you, don't you? And the truth is you can't bring him to any hotel around here. They have rules about fleas in their beds."

The anger in her muscles relaxed just slightly. "He doesn't have fleas."

Gabe shrugged. "He could sleep out on the hotel balcony, I suppose. Cold doesn't seem to bother him much."

"It's eighty degrees out."

He pulled out his buddy's cell phone. "I could try and find his owner."

"No!" The word was spoken so loudly several of the firefighters actually turned around and stared at them.

"Not ready for reality yet?" Gabe asked.

Her lips thinned and she held up a finger. "One night."

He covered her hand with his and tugged. "Let's go. I've got an extra room for you and an old pillow for the mutt to sleep on."

"He'll sleep with me."

"For protection?"

She shook her head. "No. Clearly, I'm in no danger where you're concerned."

CHAPTER EIGHT

GABE WAS a wealthy man, but his house was all about natural beauty and comfort.

Nora found herself sighing as she walked around his home. The two-story ranch-style house sat serenely on four wooded acres. It was painted red and had a beautiful wraparound porch that brought summer lemonade and backyard barbecues to mind. Inside, there were comfortable furnishings, lots of brown leather, hardwood floors and a brick fireplace that just ached to host a Christmas tree beside it.

If Nora hadn't turned her heart off to Gabe last night on the mountain, she'd probably be thinking, rather foolishly of course, that she belonged here, in a house like this one, with the mutt and the man.

But this was for one night only.

Until she found out what had happened to her cabin and all the memories that had been collected and saved there.

"Chinese food?"

Nora turned away from the open French doors leading out to the backyard and found Gabe standing against the kitchen counter, all hard angles and tempting expression. The man hadn't showered in days, had three five-o'clock shadows to shave off, and yet he was unbelievably sexy. She almost warned herself to have more careful thoughts, then quickly remembered that Gabe London didn't want her.

She gave him a nod. "Chinese would be great."

He snatched up the phone. "Spicy chicken and string beans and vegetable fried rice, right?"

"Right," she said tightly. They'd had Chinese on the second night he'd stayed at her cabin way back when. They'd eaten it in bed. Devoured spicy chicken before devouring each other.

Did he remember the night as well as the food? she wondered, only half listening as he placed the order. And if he did, what message was his suggestion of having it again sending? She shook her head and turned back to the deck. Ashes followed her, weaving in and out of her legs. She and Gabe were going to know each other for a long time. They were sharing a child. But that's where the line had to be drawn, for them both.

She heard him come up beside her. "I'm going to run next door and get some dog food for Ashes. They have a crazy old sheepdog next door who, I swear, eats a bag a day. I'm thinking they can spare a small bowl."

Plastering her best roommate face on, Nora turned to face him. "Can I set the table before I get cleaned up? Or do you need to eat something quick and get back to work?"

"I'm not going anywhere tonight," he said softly, his eyes steady.

Desire flooded Nora's entire body and she wanted to kick herself. She blamed these rampant twinges on hormones.

Had to.

A strange expression crossed Gabe's face, frustration mixed with need, but he turned away and gestured to the staircase. "Up the stairs, down at the end of the hall.

There are clean towels in the bathroom if you want to take a shower."

"Thanks."

"There's a clean robe behind the door, too."

She nodded. "Thank you."

When he was gone, Nora left the deck and went upstairs. She was on her way down the hall when Ashes whizzed past her and took a sharp left into a room. Calling after him, she followed him and found herself in what she immediately surmised was Gabe's bedroom.

Tan and white and comfortable. Totally Gabe. Big windows, open to the woodland beyond. And a big bed with a little dog stretched out on its tan comforter.

"Off, little man," she said, patting Ashes' backside until he acquiesced.

She was about to head out the door and to the bathroom when something stopped her.

Gabe's dresser.

It was an old-fashioned piece that was weathered but stained a nice walnut color. It held a scattering of frames, and she couldn't help herself from examining them. Dad and son at the Santa Monica Pier, the cheerful Ferris wheel in the background. Gabe looked about five or six and was barely smiling, and, though his father wore a wide grin he wasn't touching his son.

Nora wondered if this picture had been taken around the time his mother had walked out. She put down the frame and picked up another. His smoke jumper bros. Arms tossed casually over shoulders, beers in hand. Gabe looked happy, content, and a surge of guilt over the article she'd forced herself to write settled painfully over her heart.

She placed the photograph back where she'd found it. But she didn't leave.

She should have, but she didn't.

Instead, she slid her hand along the top drawer of his dresser, then grasped both wide black knobs and slid it open. She had no idea what she was looking for or what she expected to see, but she had this strange ache of longing that seemed to control her movement. With deft fingers, she took out a white cotton T-shirt and, without thinking, pulled off her dirty pajama top and slipped the shirt over her head.

Her heart slammed against her ribs, and she closed her eyes. Soft clean cotton, his soft cotton, against the sensitive tips of her breasts. That ache shifted to her heart. Feeling like an obsessive lunatic, she took off the shirt, folded it, put it back in the drawer and headed for the bathroom.

GABE FOUND a sleeping dog on his bed and didn't chuck him off.

In fact, if there was an elephant, two porcupines and three chest-beating gorillas hanging out on his bed, he'd probably walk right past them.

That's how distracted he was.

Mere feet away, the shower was running, and he knew who was in there—nude, wet and sliding his Irish Spring soap between her thighs and up between her breasts.

He surmised that going back downstairs and waiting for the grub would be the best course of action. After all, Nora was mad at him, confused by his desire-laced anger. Hell, he was confused by it, too. But what he knew for sure was that he wanted to see her, her body, her belly, her face more than he wanted his next breath of air. And nothing, not even her ire and his attempts to remain impassive, were going to stop him.

The bathroom door was ajar a half foot, no doubt from a retreating Ashes, and Gabe pulled it wide. Her silhouette through the shower curtain had his mouth scraping the floor.

"Need anything?" he asked from the doorway.

She gasped, gripped the shower curtain, then swore at him.

He chuckled. "Sorry. Didn't mean to scare you. Just thought you might need some more soap or a hand."

The last part hovered in the steamy air around them, but Nora wasn't giving in to his worn charm. She said rather tightly, "Nope. All set, thanks."

"Water hot enough?" he asked.

"Blistering. Just the way I like it."

"Well, let me know when you're done." His tail shoved between his legs, he turned to go. "I'm next."

"I won't be long, and I promise to alert the entire household to the completion of my shower."

A wicked grin split Gabe's features. Shaking his head, he turned back, headed straight for the shower and whipped back the curtain. "You're a real smart-ass, you know that?"

She was facing the shower spray, her sweet, round backside accosting—hell—tempting his vision. "And you're a little too interested in my bathing practices."

"Well, who could blame me?" he said huskily, ready to eat her up if she'd give him one sign she'd be willing. "Look at you."

She turned to face him. "Fat and sassy?"

His gaze moved over her at a leisurely pace. Pale skin, flushed cheeks, curved hips, slightly rounded belly, beautiful, heavy breasts and long, wet hair tickling her rosy nipples. The mad ache in his gut dropped, gave him a painful hard-on. He inhaled deeply through his nose. "I know you know how seductive you look, Nora. You've got enough confidence for two. And I'm pretty sure you get how on edge you make me."

Her expression changed from easy to hard in an instant and she swiped at a few water droplets slipping down her face. "Maybe. The problem is we never get you *over* the edge, London."

"You're right. I've been stalling."

"Why? Something tells me you never had to trust any of the women you've slept with."

"You're different, and you know it."

"Well, my confidence is waning."

"We don't want that." Gabe gripped the hem of his T-shirt and pulled it off.

Downstairs, the doorbell rang.

Nora's insides jumped at the sound. The shower and the heat had warped her perspective somewhat, made her feel lighter, ready to wrap her legs around Gabe London, the man she'd sworn off just an hour ago, if he'd stripped completely naked and joined her in the shower.

She raised a brow at him. "That would be my string beans and your kung pau."

Gabe didn't move. "Maybe not. Could just be my neighbor with more of those pig's ears he tried to force on me for the mutt."

Her hands seemed to move independently of her body, covering her breasts. "I'm pretty ravenous," she said, eyeing him speculatively. "And from the look of you, London, you need to tuck in before you drop."

He shook his head, a roguish grin on his lips. "I've got enough in me to hold you up against that wall for the next thirty minutes."

A helpless struggle rose up in Nora. She wanted to

hate him, wanted to break away from him and not have to deal with the fact that she was in love with him. But he kept coming back.

His gaze moved over her hungrily. She actually felt on the verge of climax she ached so badly. She longed for his touch, even arched her back at the thought, but her mind flashed images of that tree and the words that were spoken there. "That's got to be our dinner," she murmured. "But even if it isn't, do you really think we should risk it?"

Gabe's jaw tightened, then slowly he backed away from the shower. "You've got a way with words, Nora."

"So they say," she said miserably as she eased the curtain closed.

NORA HAD NEVER SEEN a man eat so much in her life.

"You were right to give me the shove off," Gabe said with a wide grin. "I didn't realize how hungry I was."

"Glad I could help," Nora said with dry humor.

They sat at the dining-room table, looking out at the wooded acreage of Gabe's property. The sun was setting spectacularly well out the floor-to-ceiling windows, but Nora felt only mildly relaxed even with the hot shower and food, which she was actually inhaling faster than Gabe. And faster than Ashes, who seemed to be having a feast of his own courtesy of their host.

The little black-and-white mutt had already polished off his bowl of kibble and was now sitting expectantly at Gabe's feet. Every once in a while Gabe dropped his hand to the dog's mouth and offered him a bite of egg roll.

Nora suppressed a smile. Gabe had a tough exterior, but he was soft on the inside. Why couldn't he give her a little of that soft side, a little forgiveness?

The query made her pause, chopsticks halfway to her mouth. Did she deserve forgiveness? If the tables were turned, would she have reacted the same way he had—or worse? Did it matter now? she thought wearily. She'd told him how sorry she was; she'd given him her body, offered him her heart. He'd toyed with both then tossed them back in her face.

Her stomach did a flip-flop and she pushed aside her string beans and reached for a fortune cookie. Ripping the plastic off, she cracked the cookie in half and popped one side into her mouth.

"You're not really going to do that, are you?" Gabe asked, when she unraveled the white strip of paper inside the cookie.

"Read my fortune?" She grinned. "You better believe it."

He snorted. "So what's the story? Money or fame?"

Her heart dipped. That was really the question, wasn't it? That's what Gabe thought Nora and every person with two X chromosomes wanted from life—or from him. He'd been schooled to believe that all women were after his fortune, all women wanted to use him for fame. His father had been a living, breathing example.

She searched for a clue on Gabe's rough exterior, a sign that he wasn't as jaded as he seemed. But she didn't find it on his skin or in his eyes. She found it under the table.

Ashes.

The little mutt was now lying in Gabe's lap, snoozing away.

Gabe London had one face he showed to the cruel world, and another when he thought no one was looking. She'd felt that side when he'd touched her, when he'd stared longingly at her belly in the shower, and she'd seen it in action when he'd driven through fire to rescue her.

An easy smile affixed to her lips, she inched the remaining fortune cookie toward Gabe's plate.

He chuckled and snatched up the cookie, then tossed it into the air and caught it. "You've got to be kidding?"

"I have the distinct feeling there's a fortune-cookie skeptic in my midst."

"That's not true. I have no doubts—" brow raised, he leaned forward "—that these things are complete crap."

"Oh, London," she said, shaking her head. "You're way too jaded, and you're missing out." She held her hand open. "Give it here."

He dropped the cookie into her palm. "Have at it."

Plastic off, cookie broken, Nora unraveled the fortune and read it. When she had, she laughed uproariously.

Gabe tried to focus on what was left of his kung pau, but after a minute or two he caved and dragged a hand through his damp hair. "All right. What does it say?"

She turned it around and read, "'The greatest danger could be your stupidity.'"

That made him laugh, made him look entirely too satisfied. "What did I tell you? Complete crap." Then he sobered slightly, grinned and asked, "What does yours say?"

"A chance happening will reveal your destiny." She stared at him through her lashes. "What do you think that means?"

A smile flickered in his eyes. "You know you look really good in my clothes."

She didn't try to drag him back to the subject he'd just leaped over. Instead she touched the soft cotton tee and smiled. "This old thing?"

"Hey, no digs about the clothes."

"Sorry."

"Seriously, those are my lucky sweats, and well, the T-shirt speaks for itself."

Nora glanced down at the writing across her ever-growing chest. Fire Down Below. "Yes," she said with a chuckle. "This needs no explanation."

"But even in sweats," he began, his eyes heavy lidded and predatory. "You look sexy."

She was determined not to blush. "Thank you."

He said with absolute gentility, "Come here, Nora."

Her stomach flipped as she looked at him, his expression no longer hard and impassive in his need for her. Every inch of her body screamed for his touch. For a moment, she struggled with her own weakness. She had sworn off Gabe London, promised herself she would never allow him access to her heart or body again, and here she was standing up, cautiously walking to him, hoping he would reach for her, grab her, haul her against him and make it impossible for her to think and react with anything but the desire flooding her.

Ashes jumped down from his lap and scampered away, into the kitchen for, no doubt, more food. Unchaperoned and unwilling to tell Gabe to go to hell, she let him pull her onto his lap, sucked air through her teeth when his hand slipped under her T-shirt, moaned as he grazed the underside of her breast, then wanted to weep when he retreated and cupped her belly.

He nuzzled her neck. "This is our destiny." His voice was weak and whiskey laced, and her heart squeezed.

"You sound like a fortune cookie," Nora uttered, the muscles between her legs flexing as he flicked his tongue over her earlobe.

"Then here's another prediction," he said as he stood

up, cradled her in his arms and headed for the stairs. "Change is happening in your life, Nora Wallace, so go with the flow."

CHAPTER NINE

GABE REVELED in the unsteady hitch of her breathing as he carried her upstairs and down the hall to his bedroom. The sound meant she was excited, on edge, as desperate for him as he was for her, and he couldn't wait to feel her hot skin against his own.

The mattress dipped with their weight, and Nora had her hands around his neck, her mouth parted and eager. Gabe felt a surge of desire in his groin so intense it was akin to pain. For months he'd lain in this bed, thinking about her, his hand helping him to find the only possible solace.

And here she was.

Head on his pillow, back to his sheets, eyes imploring him.

Poised over her, he bent his head and took her mouth, took her kiss with hard satisfaction. He wanted to consume her, lose his mind in her. And when he slipped his tongue into her mouth, Nora met him, angling her head, suckling his tongue deep, moaning and bucking her hips against his erection.

There was too much between them. Cotton and denim for starters. Gabe wanted her skin, her heat, the wetness between her legs as she thrust her hips against his thigh. He tugged down her sweats impatiently as she tore off her T-shirt. He felt her hands on his shirt, pulling the black fabric over his head until her fingers delved into the hair on his chest, her nails lightly passing over his nipples.

A growl escaped his throat as he covered her mouth again. She tasted like honey and salt and he wanted to taste further. He moved to her throat, suckled at the thin band of muscle, nibbled at her pulse, grazed his teeth over her collarbone.

He felt like a man possessed, a man who needed not only this woman's body, but her soul.

Nora arched her back, thrust her large breasts up, and Gabe devoured them. Gasping for air, she fisted his hair as he suckled her hard, dark pink nipples. He loved the way she responded to his touch, so open, no shyness about her body or the way it moved. She was so perfect for him, he thought as he circled the curve of her other breast with his finger. The way they fit together, their humor, their banter. If he could just let go of what had happened in the past.

But he'd never been any good at forgiving the past.

NORA FELT as though her mind was going to explode. Four months ago, their lovemaking had been hot and sweet, but tonight it was as though they needed to consume each other or perish.

Gabe had abandoned her breast for the moment and was staring down at her, his intense black eyes fixed on hers. She wondered if he was going to say something, because he looked almost pained for a moment, but then she drew in a breath. His middle finger had dipped between her legs and was slowly slipping down the seam until it reached the entrance to her body.

"This is where it all began," he whispered huskily.

"What?" she asked.

"Our past and our future. What the hell are we going to do?" he fairly growled as he captured her mouth hungrily.

His blatant need, his raw emotion fused with the electricity shooting through Nora's blood and she wrapped a leg around him, thrusting herself against his hand. Gabe responded by giving her what her body was asking for, plunging his finger deep into her.

"Gabe, please," she begged, her heart pounding, her body on the edge of orgasm. She tugged at his jeans. "Make love to me again, please."

"Nora…" he whispered against her mouth. "Is it okay?"

"Is what okay?"

"I don't want to hurt you or the baby."

"No, it's fine."

"You're sure. I couldn't bear it if—"

"It's perfect," she assured him. "Doctor-approved, even."

He chuckled huskily, withdrew his fingers from her, then fumbled with his button and fly. When he was naked, she stared at him, at the perfect, rock-hard length of him. She could almost feel him inside her, feel his long shaft thrust into her, then jut up against the softness of her womb.

She couldn't help herself. She fisted him, burrowed his erection between her legs. He entered her with one long, desperately hard stroke and she gasped.

"Too much?" he breathed.

"No. Never. More."

He didn't seem to need to hear anything else. Nora pulsed around him as he thrust into her, circled his hips, then held himself inside her, deep inside her as he nuzzled her neck, then her breasts.

She was on the verge of climax, so close she begged herself to stop.

Not yet, not yet.

But he was so deep, a part of her. Then his hand tunneled between them and his fingers danced over her in light, teasing strokes.

And she was lost.

She gripped the comforter and thrust her hips up. Gabe rose out of her, then slammed back in. Over and over, his thrusts hard and full. Nora moved her hips, felt his tongue lapping at her nipple.

"So tight. Oh, Nora. Yes!" Gabe took her nipple between his teeth as he came, his body pulsing.

Then Nora followed, crying out, waves of electric heat rippling through her as she bucked and convulsed.

Heart to heart, they stayed connected, still moaning, still thrusting as their pulses slowed and their bones turned to liquid.

It was only minutes before they both fell asleep.

MORNING DAWNED bright and sunny, and Nora felt a strong urge to jump out of bed and sing. But she felt way too lazy, so instead, she rolled onto her back and stretched.

"It's about time you woke up."

The husky male voice had her grinning, and she opened one eye. Sitting on the edge of the bed, fully dressed, was a freshly showered Gabe.

"You should be in here next to me," she chided. "Naked and wanting more."

"I've been wanting more since five this morning. But I wasn't going to wake you up." He shrugged and gave her a smile that had the muscles between her legs leaping to life in recollection.

"Five this morning?" she repeated, aghast. "What have you been doing since five?"

He held up a rectangular box with a sort of short, wide wand attached to it. "Borrowed this from a friend of mine at the hospital."

She recognized it immediately from her doctor's office. "A Doppler?"

He inched closer to her on the bed, his expression slightly anguished though hopeful. "Have you already heard the heartbeat?"

Smiling softly, she nodded.

"I want to hear it, too."

A wave of sadness moved through her. She should have told him. She should have marched right onto the base, torn him from that woman's arms and laid it on the line. Despite her jealousy and stupid pride, he deserved to know about his child. He deserved time with the baby, and she was going to make sure he got it. She couldn't make up for that stupid article—that was over and done with—but she could do this much.

"Did they give you any lotion?" she asked.

"Right here," he said, handing her the lavender tube.

Nora squeezed out a palmful of lotion, then coated her lower abdomen.

With a steady hand, Gabe laid the Doppler just above her pelvic bone and flipped the switch. A whooshing sound, like wind through the trees, echoed out of the small speakers. Gabe moved the wand to her left side, but neither of them heard anything. He looked at her and smiled, then shifted the wand to her right side. Suddenly, a sound very similar to feet stuck in mud could be heard. It was rhythmic and beautiful and it made them both grin like fools.

"That's the heartbeat, Gabe," Nora said, watching his expression intently.

He closed his eyes and sighed. "Strong and fast."

"It's perfect."

He opened his eyes again and looked at her with an expression close to love. "I want to be there for every appointment from now on."

Unease moved through Nora. She removed the wand from her belly and pulled the covers up. This was the future they were talking about. "You don't have to do that, Gabe. I want you to, and you're welcome to come with me anytime. But before you commit, maybe you should see how you feel later, when the time comes."

He shook his head and moved closer to her. "No. I don't want to see how I feel. I know how I feel. I had one parent, Nora. Sure, there were plenty of stand-ins for a mother, but nothing was permanent. And my father was so angry at my mother for leaving, he had no clue how to love me or anyone else. This child deserves the love of both parents, the attention and time of both parents, and I intend to make sure he or she gets it. From the very beginning."

She nodded, desperately glad to hear his resolute stand on the subject. But there was still anxiety in her heart. If they were going to talk about the future, maybe they needed to get it all out on the table. She released a breath. "And us? What about us?"

Gabe looked only slightly puzzled.

Her heart squeezing with pain, Nora pushed onward. "I'm a modern woman, Gabe. I can be an unmarried mother and work and go about my life, but that's not the ideal—not my ideal."

"What are you saying?"

"I want a relationship with someone. Something lasting."

All the tenderness that was in his eyes a moment ago dissolved in an instant.

She reached out and took his hand. "You need to forgive me, Gabe. Really forgive me. Our romance or affair or whatever you want to call this aside, we need to care about each other and be respectful of each other. For the baby."

He didn't speak for a moment, but when he did, his tone was soft, complicated. "I do forgive you. It's the forgetting part that's got me."

"A grudge is fruitless. Nothing good can come of it."

"That's a pretty good argument in theory, but the truth is, marriage is out of the question for me. Relationships are fine and easy, and this child will be the most wonderful thing I could hope for, but marriage doesn't work. I've seen too many failures to believe any good can come from it."

She nodded, hating that she had to accept his bitter views. "Well, I do believe in marriage. And you've got to know that someday that might happen for me."

"What?" He shook his head. "What are you talking about?"

Nora sighed, sat up. "I could meet someone and fall in love, and—"

"You have to date to fall in love," Gabe interrupted sourly.

"Yes."

"You're not going to date. Not while I'm around."

Nora remained calm as she digested what he said, then tried to find another road to take, one he could understand. "So, you're suggesting I remain an unmarried, lonely, man-deprived nun until your unfortunate demise."

"Something like that."

"While you remain a free-and-easy man able to date any free-and-easy lady that comes along?"

He cursed and looked away. "I know this is awkward, and I'm being unreasonable as hell, but—" The sound of his cell phone cut him off. He glanced at her, shrugged. "Sorry. London here." He listened to the caller for no more than ten seconds, and when he hung up, his expression had morphed into that of the serious, intense man she'd seen access a fire. "I've got to go. I have a jump in twenty minutes."

CHAPTER TEN

GABE AND HIS fellow smoke jumpers flew northwest above the mountains and into the national forest. Fires raged everywhere, creeping flames going unchecked, ugly, smoking pits where the fires had left their mark.

Sweating in full gear, Gabe leaned back against the plane's metal wall and wondered if he'd be going home, back to Nora anytime soon.

Odds weren't good.

"What's the holdup?" Marc Geller yelled to the spotter over the scream of the engines.

"Trying to decide which one to take first," the spotter shouted back.

Marc turned to Gabe, who was seated on his right, and rolled his eyes. "Just want to get down there, get the job done."

Marc was a good guy, a real family man, been with the Redding smoke jumpers for close to seven years. Even though he was younger than most, the bros looked up to him, wanted what he had—stability, something great to go home to.

A shot of envy ran through Gabe's gut. The feeling startled him. All his days on the job, he'd never thought of anything but the job ahead. Now his mind was on Nora and their baby, and if she'd skip out even though he'd asked her to stay until he returned.

"Hey man," Marc shouted over the din. "You okay?"

Gabe didn't know what made him start talking. He knew he was about to sound like a sap, like a real wimp, but he didn't give a damn. "Is Kathy happy?"

"What?" Marc looked totally confused.

"Being married to you. Is she happy?"

Marc shrugged. "You'd have to ask her. Wait, no, don't ask her." He grinned. "Truth is, I try every damn day to make her happy."

"And the kid?"

"My little girl," he shouted. "Ella. Best thing that ever happened to me, man."

"You feel lucky, huh?"

"It's no luck. I wanted them. I had nothing growing up, less than nothing, and they're everything." Marc's eyebrows drew together. "What's going on with you?"

"Nothing."

"Thinking of taking the plunge?" Marc asked with a wide grin. "That'd be something to see."

"Get serious," Gabe tossed back as the spotter finally found the first jump spot. "The only plunge I'm doing is right out that door."

WAITING IN AN UNFAMILIAR HOUSE was maddening.

Waiting for word from Gabe was torture.

But waiting for answers on the status of her cabin couldn't go on much longer.

Then again she'd promised him.

Nora pulled one of Gabe's gray sweatshirts over her head—he'd given her free rein in his closet, which was riddled with very manly clothes like jeans, T-shirts, underwear and socks—and sat down on the edge of the bed. She'd spent the evening curled up on the couch with Ashes, watching reality TV and stressing about Gabe's well-being.

She'd always been an independent girl, a free thinker who rarely gave in to demands. But she was over the moon for Gabe London, truly and irrevocably in love with him, and when he'd asked her to stay put until he returned, he hadn't had to push her very hard to agree.

She pulled on a pair of large white running socks. She was getting antsy. She'd had no word from Gabe, and her mind was tossing out addenda to Gabe's demand. She'd agreed to remain in Redding, and at his house, but that didn't mean she couldn't venture outside. After all, she was living on the point of desperation here. She had to know what had happened to her cabin, and like it or not, she thought bleakly, as Ashes jumped on the bed and curled up against her thigh, she had to try to find the dog's owners.

Standing up, she tightened the belt on Gabe's jeans to fit her growing belly, then went downstairs to call a taxi.

TWO DAYS TO ATTACK and bring down that blaze.

Not bad.

Still sporting a light dusting of smoke retardant, Gabe pulled up to the house in his borrowed truck. He'd never worked so hard in his life. He and Marc, Will and Ty had put out a hundred-fifty-percent effort to build that fire line.

He should've been exhausted. But as he climbed the front steps and stuck his key in the lock, all he wanted was a hot shower with the beautiful woman who just happened to be carrying his child. Then, over dinner, he had some things to say to her.

The thick sound of silence met him when he opened

the door. That shouldn't have worried him so quickly, but it did. When he didn't see or hear her in the next thirty seconds, fear moved through him like a tidal wave—unstoppable and frantic. He called out her name, then the dog's.

Nothing.

"Nora?" he shouted more intently this time. "Ashes?"

Nothing.

The effect of two days of hard-core labor dropped away in an instant. He flew up the stairs, checked every room, bathrooms, basement and backyard.

She wasn't there.

He paced beside the couch for ten minutes, waiting to see if she and Ashes would come back from a walk. Dread stabbed at him, running head-to-head with a sickening emotion that hadn't surfaced in twenty-five years or more, not since his mother had walked out on him.

Grief.

And guilt. A child's guilt for pushing the woman he loved out of his life. But he wasn't a child anymore. He was a grown man who had put up every roadblock he could to keep a good woman out of his life for fear she'd leave him, too.

He slammed a hand against the wall. He loved Nora. His heart ached with it.

He grabbed his keys from the kitchen table, then froze, his heart slamming against his ribs. There, staring up at him, was a note.

Dear Gabe,
I'm sorry, but I couldn't stay any longer...

He was out the door before he'd even glanced at her signature.

CHAPTER ELEVEN

NORA SAT CROSS-LEGGED on the scorched earth and stared up at what was left of her family's cabin. Memories flooded her senses like a thousand little drums against her brain. She saw her mother at the window, setting out blueberry pies to cool, yelling at little Nora and her friends that she'd be out in a minute to play touch football with them. Then there was her father lying on his bed reading the *Wall Street Journal,* combing the front page for just the right story to argue about over dinner.

Tears pricked her eyes. She missed them so much, and wished they could have seen her pregnant, been there to see their first grandchild born.

Nora heard the revving sound of a car's engine, and knew her cab was heading up her street. It was time to go back, back to Gabe's house, then back to L.A. She needed to find her life again. Gabe could be macho and possessive over her potential dating life—over something he didn't even want—but he'd come to terms with their future in time.

"Do you think our kid's going to have this stubborn streak?"

Nora jumped and turned around to find Gabe sitting in his borrowed truck. She shook her head and laughed. "Lord, I hope so."

He got out of the truck, walked over to her and sat down beside her on the charred ground. "I was just trying to keep you safe, Nora. That's all. Not trying to pull a power trip."

"I know. The firemen said it was okay to come back here now."

"Yeah, they mentioned that."

She stared at him, at the chalky dust that coated his hair, face and clothing. "You look odd."

"It's retardant."

"From the jump?"

"Yep."

She checked him over, said with concern she couldn't tame, "Are you okay?"

"Sure."

"You know, you didn't need to rush out here. I bet you're exhausted." She brushed some powder off his cheek. "Why didn't you take a hot shower first?"

He grasped her hand and held it firm. "I have no idea, Nora. All I know is I came home, you were gone, the dog was gone, your note…" He shook his head. "I've jumped out of airplanes, been sleep deprived to the point of delirium, dug trenches until my hands bled, wondered if I was going to break my neck landing in a tree, faced down a tidal wave of fire, but this—" he gestured to her and then back to himself "—this has my guts in a knot. You and me. My heart's pounding like a fist on a drum right now."

She went very still. "Why?"

At that moment, Ashes came bounding out of the woods toward him. He jumped on Gabe, lapped at his face and barked like a crazed beast.

Gabe chuckled, giving the mutt a good petting. "He's still here."

"He is."

"Your note said you were going to find his owners."

"Owner," Nora corrected, a deep sadness moving through her. "Ashes' owner was an elderly woman. She didn't get out of her home in time."

Gabe sighed. "Dammit."

"I know. I spoke with her daughter and offered my condolences. I offered to hold on to Ashes until she could come and get him, but—" Nora paused, shaking her head "—she didn't want him. She couldn't deal with seeing him."

Gabe put his arm around her and pulled her close. "I'm sorry you had to do that."

Nora burrowed into his chest for warmth, for support. "She asked me if I knew anyone who might want to adopt him. I told her I would."

"You mean, *we* would."

Her heart leaped into her throat and she looked up at Gabe. "I'm going back to L.A."

"Because you want to or because you feel you have to?"

"It's my home."

"You can do your work from anywhere."

"Well, sure, but—"

"Do it from here," he interrupted. His eyes were clear and accessible and he looked willing.

But she couldn't hope. "What are you saying?"

"I love you, Nora."

She stared at him, disbelieving. Yes, he was here, beside her, holding her, looking extraordinarily handsome in his dusty jeans and T-shirt. But was he real—was what he'd just said real?

He leaned down and kissed her. A soft, tender, probing kiss that sent coils of heat through her.

He nuzzled her mouth and said, "I know. I'm just as surprised as you are."

She laughed, tilted her chin up and kissed him.

"I didn't think it could happen," he said, brushing a thumb over her cheek. "I thought my heart was dead."

"But it's not?" she asked breathlessly.

He cupped her face and looked deeply into her eyes. "Not to you, and not to our baby."

She wilted just slightly. "If this is just about the baby, maybe—"

"No. God, no." His mouth covered hers, sank into hers.

Nora sighed and eased back, gazing up at him. "Gabe, I love you, but I don't want you to ever have to pretend—"

"Stop." He kissed her again, then he said, "You know, I jump out of planes, fight fires, throw myself in danger every day, but I realize that I haven't truly been a man until now."

His words went straight through, bandaged her doubts and bathed her fears. "I love you," she said, her heart fusing with his.

He held her tighter. "I'll admit that the idea of our child softened me. Allowed me to see you, your heart, and get over all mistakes of the past—yours and mine. The idea of our child made it okay for me to be real, be a man, be in love with the woman of my dreams." He paused for a moment and laughed softly. "Won't our child love to know that he or she brought its parents together, that through him or her, their father found his soul again?"

"And its mother stopped running and realized the true meaning of the word *love*."

Gabe gathered her in his arms, covered her mouth

with his and kissed her. "I love you, Nora, and I want to be with you always."

"I want that, too," she said breathlessly. "So much."

"Marry me?"

"Yes."

His hands were in her hair, his eyes, dark and loving rested on her face. "Be my wife and my friend. Butt heads with me across the breakfast table and lie naked with me at night. Tell me when I'm being an ass, but remind me when I'm doing good."

Tears welled in her eyes. "Gabe…"

"But most of all, let me give you everything—all of what's in my heart."

She smiled, and he smiled.

"That's one hell of an offer, London," she said, laughing through her tears.

He pulled her closer, laughed with her. "You really do have a way with words. Is that a yes?"

"That's an absolutely!"

A bird called out in the trees and, thinking it a sign, Nora tore her gaze from Gabe. But what she saw was only the horrible wreckage of her family's cabin.

"It's amazing what happens after a fire," Gabe said close to her ear. "The forest comes back, Nora, and quicker than you think. In a few weeks, you'll see plants sprouting. Everything begins to heal."

As they sat there, in front of her cabin, blackened by a raging fire that had consumed so much life, Gabe held on to Nora and kissed her with a passion he had never known existed. They had begun their life here, and like the forest surrounding them, they were starting over here, too, clinging to a life force in their hearts and the hope for a happy and contented future.

Everything you love about romance...
and more!

Please turn the page for
Bonus Features.

Dangerous Desires

BONUS
FEATURES
INSIDE

Author Interview:
A Conversation with
KATHIE DENOSKY

Tell us a bit about how you began your writing career.

My favorite classes in school were always literature
and English because I got to do the two things
that I love the most—reading and writing. While
my classmates grumbled and complained about
having to write a term paper or do a book report,
I was excited. And yes, the majority of them
looked at me like I'd sprouted another head.
They considered writing assignments cruel and
unusual punishment and just couldn't believe
that I actually wanted to spend my time doing
them. Unfortunately, we were only required to do
so many writing assignments a year, so while I
was waiting for the next one, I turned to my other
love—reading. I picked up my first Harlequin
Romance novel at the age of twelve or thirteen
and I've been hooked ever since. Years later, after
my children started school, I finally gave in to the

4

voices in my head and, combining my two loves, I wrote a romance. Once again, I was hooked. I sold my first book about eight years later and the rest, as they say, is history.

What's your writing routine?
In a word, *crazy*. My writing "day" usually starts around ten or eleven at night and goes until I drag myself to bed around four or five in the morning. After a few hours of sleep, I'm up by eight or nine to start my other career as a chauffeur, cook and housekeeper—aka wife and mother. I do take a late-afternoon nap for a couple of hours, then get up to spend the evening watching TV with my husband. And somewhere in between the naps, driving, cooking, cleaning and laundry (okay, I'll admit that the last three slide more times than I care to admit), I even get some reading done. Then it's time to start my "day" all over again. But as crazy as life gets sometimes, I wouldn't have it any other way. I get to be at home with my family and I get to work in my jammies. I don't have to pay for the latest hairstyle because I have a perpetual case of "bed head" (I'm sunk if the messy/spiked look ever goes out of style), and because I'm always working on a deadline, I have the perfect excuse not to cook, clean or do laundry. Color me happy.

How do you research your stories?

One of my favorite things about starting a new story is the research. I spend hours reading books, interviewing people about their careers and going online to find out all kinds of details that will make the story come alive. Another thing that I love is getting to visit the area where the book will be set. Let's see, traveling, talking to new people and learning new things. Is it any wonder that I love my job?

When you're not writing, what are your favorite activities?

Besides reading and catching up on sleep? Actually, I have so many things that I love to do, there isn't enough time to get them all done. Being a former folk art teacher, I still love to paint, weave baskets and do all kinds of needlework—usually while I'm watching TV with my husband. I also love to travel, go to rodeos and attend country music concerts. Does anyone have any suggestions how I can add a few more hours to each day?

Do you have a favorite book or film?

I have so many favorite books that my keeper shelves are filled to overflowing and so are my DVD shelves. But if I had to choose one book that has stuck with me for years and that I reread from time to time, it would have to be *Gone with the Wind.* I also have several favorite films, but the one that I've watched so many times I could probably recite parts of the dialogue would be *While You Were Sleeping.* It's humorous, romantic and at the end emotional—at least for me. It's classic romance with a happily-ever-after that never fails to make me smile.

Any last words to your readers?
It's my fervent hope that you enjoy reading my stories as much as I enjoy writing them. Nothing pleases me more than hearing that I've taken you on a satisfying journey to a happy ending. If, along the way, I bring a smile to your face, a tear to your eye and happiness to your heart, then I know I've done my job. And that's what makes me happy.

Author Interview:
A Conversation with
KRISTI GOLD

Tell us a bit about how you began your writing career.

I had an idea, told my sister about it and she said, "Don't talk about it, just write the thing." I said, "Okay." In other words, I jumped into writing totally ignorant and unarmed, operating solely on instinct. I finished that novel in two years and although it will never see the light of day, it was a fantastic learning experience.

What's your writing routine?
I'm definitely a late-night writer. I use the late-morning hours for tending to business or editing, designate 3:00 p.m. until 11:00 p.m. as nap and family time, then I tackle my current work in progress until the wee hours of the morning, or until my face hits the keyboard, whichever comes first.

How do you research your stories?

So much of that is dependent on the story itself. I utilize the Internet quite a bit and I like to discuss specifics with those who have expertise, if at all possible. For example, when it comes to any medical aspects in a book, my husband is a retired surgeon and a great resource. He's been my technical adviser in the past, and if it's not within his realm of expertise, he tells me so. But he also points me in the right direction. In the case of *Upsurge,* I went to straight to the source—hurricane survivors.

When you're not writing, what are your favorite activities?

Other than catching up on sleep, I love taking beach vacations and bringing books along to read. I'm also a baseball fanatic, and when the season arrives, you will find me in front of the TV watching my favorite team, or taking a weekend trip to the ballpark. I'm also addicted to several television shows and schedule them in during my breaks. *Law and Order SVU, Medium* and *Numbers* are among my current favorites.

Do you have a favorite book or film?

I have so many favorite books it would be difficult to narrow it down to just one, particularly when it comes to romance. Anything by Sandra Brown and Leigh Riker comes to mind. I've also been a huge Stephen King and Elizabeth Berg fan for years and love biographies. My recent favorite movie is *Phantom of the Opera*. Nothing quite like a gorgeous, tortured man, even if he is, uh, a bit misguided. And *While You Were Sleeping* will always remain a favorite because it has it all— comedy, emotion and a great love story. It's a classic romance.

Any last words to your readers?
I think it's important for readers to know that they're an author's greatest asset, and the motivation behind why I do what I do. Some of my most memorable moments have come from reader correspondence, and that serves to make the sometimes crazy schedule and deadlines all worthwhile. A heartfelt thanks to each and every one of you! I appreciate you more than you know.

Author Interview:
A Conversation with
LAURA WRIGHT

Tell us a bit about how you began your writing career.

Well, I've always been a massive fan of romance. I devoured three to four books a month while I taught ballroom and Latin dancing at Arthur Murray Dance Studio. But after teaching and competing for ten years, I knew that reading romance wasn't enough anymore. I said, "This is what I want more than anything! To write books where women feel empowered, loved, redeemed and sexy!" I enrolled in a romance-writing course at UCLA, met five amazing women who formed a critique group and worked my tail off every day (literally), and within five years I'd published my first book. A dream come true!

What's your writing routine?

It used to be every minute of every day. But now I have a two-year-old, so it's catch can! I have a very supportive husband though, and he's a great help. (He's standing over my shoulder, so I have to say this.)

How do you research your stories?
The Internet is amazing. Thank God we have it. But I have to say, one-on-one interviews are my favorite. I think this comes from my acting days—I have to see the person, their features, how they speak when they tell me their story.

When you're not writing, what are your favorite activities?
I *love* to cook! My hubby's Italian, so I feel that I am Italian by association, and I must cook all things tomato, pasta, olive and bread! I also adore painting, reading, playing with my three dogs and *anything* with my little girl!

Do you have a favorite book or film?
My favorite book would have to be *Demon Lover* by Victoria Holt. This is old-school romance, (ladies, you know what I mean) but it's the most wonderful story. I can read it over and over again, and wish for that one night with the Baron...! By the way, my husband's still standing over my shoulder—and he's laughing at me right now.

Any last words to your readers?
Read to escape. Read to breathe evenly. Read to remember those twenty-four-hour kisses. Read to feel happy, feel sad, feel magic, feel lust. Read to reconnect with yourself, your husband and your children. Read to know you're a woman.

Living in "The Alley"
by Kathie DeNosky

We asked Kathie DeNosky to tell us a bit more about tornadoes. Here Kathie discusses what it is like living in Tornado Alley.

Tornadoes have occurred all over the world, claimed thousands of lives and caused countless billions of dollars in damage. But there is one section on earth where the right mixture of atmospheric elements comes together with such explosive force that these devastating storms are not only more frequent, they are a way of life for some of us. Having lived my entire life in the eastern portion of the area meteorologists, storm chasers and weather watchers have nicknamed Tornado Alley, I can't count the number of times I've sat huddled with my family in a storm cellar, waiting for the threat of severe weather to pass by.

There are no official geographic boundaries for Tornado Alley. You won't find it marked on a road map or an atlas. But it's generally accepted that most of the central and east-central United States is included in this area, because this is where violent tornadoes are generated with the highest frequency in the world.

On average, 1,000 tornadoes are confirmed each year, with the majority of them occurring in the Alley. As one might expect, the "Hot Zone"—where some of the largest tornadoes have been sighted—includes west Texas, Oklahoma, Kansas and Nebraska. But it's the eastern side of Tornado Alley—where I live—that has the deadliest reputation for killer tornadoes.

In fact, on March 18, 1925, the most deadly tornado in history passed within six miles of where I live now. Known as the Tri-State Tornado, this vicious storm cut a mile-wide path of death and destruction from southeast Missouri, across the entire width of southern Illinois and into southwest Indiana. Staying on the ground an unheard of three and a half hours, the F5 tornado traveled 219 miles with estimated winds in excess of 300 miles per hour. By the time it finally dissipated, over 15,000 homes had been destroyed, entire towns had been wiped off the map and property damage totaled $16.5 million—a phenomenal amount of money back then. But it was the loss of 695 lives (600 in southern Illinois alone) and over 2,000 injuries that makes it the single worst tornado disaster in U.S. history.

Some might wonder why, since I live in an area with this kind of history for violent storms, that I chose to set "Whirlwind" in the Texas Panhandle, instead of my native southern Illinois. It's actually pretty simple. Most photographic and scientific storm chasers don't like venturing into the eastern region of the Alley. Visibility is key to observing and photographing these storms, and the lack of it in our region makes chasing extremely dangerous. Because of the dense foliage and hilly terrain, a tornado could be hidden by a line of trees or come over the top of a hill and overtake a chaser with little or no warning. I suspect this also accounts, in part, for our deadly history.

18

Another fact of life for anyone living in my part of Tornado Alley is that we have to watch out for tornadoes and severe storms throughout the year, not just in the spring or early summer months. In past years, we've even had tornadoes in December, January and February. Case in point—while I was writing "Whirlwind" we had our first tornado watch of the year—in January—and although we didn't see a tornado in my immediate area, two lives were lost in Arkansas to a tornado spawned from the same storm system that generated our tornado watch.

Fortunately, weather prediction and early detection of these killer storms have come a long way in the past eighty years. Due to the heroic efforts of meteorologists and storm chasers who put themselves in the line of these storms to collect atmospheric data, aided by the invention of radar and satellite imagery, there is a much better understanding of how tornadoes form and where the greatest danger lies. But as good as the warning systems are, we're all still at the mercy of Mother Nature's whims.

For safety tips on tornado preparedness, more information and pictures of the devastation from the Tri-State Tornado, please visit these Web sites: www.noaa.gov/pah/1925, www.noaa.gov/tornadoes.html, www.fema.gov/hazards/tornadoes.

Fujita Tornado Damage Scale

Developed in 1971 by Dr. Theodore Fujita of the University of Chicago.

F0 *Light damage* (40-72 mph): Some damage to chimneys; branches broken off trees; shallow-rooted trees pushed over.

F1 *Moderate damage* (73-112 mph): Surfaces peeled off roofs; mobile homes pushed off bases or overturned; moving autos pushed off the road.

20 **F2 *Considerable damage*** (113-157 mph): Roofs torn completely off frame houses; mobile homes demolished; boxcars pushed over; large trees snapped in two or uprooted; light objects become flying missiles; cars lifted off ground.

F3 *Severe damage* (158-206 mph): Roofs and some walls torn off well-constructed houses; trains overturned; most trees uprooted; heavy cars lifted off the ground and thrown.

F4 *Devastating damage* (207-260 mph): Well-constructed houses leveled; structures with weak foundations blown distances; cars thrown and large objects become flying missiles.

F5 Incredible damage (261-318 mph): Rare.
Strong frame houses lifted off foundations and
disintegrate; automobile-sized objects become
flying missiles and are hurled in excess of 100
yards at approximately 100 mph; trees debarked.

Percentage of All Tornadoes
F0-F1 Weak 74%
F2-F3 Strong 25%
F4-F5 Violent 1%

A Day in the Life of a Rookie Smoke Jumper in Training

Several smoke jumpers from the Redding, California, and Missoula, Montana, bases contributed wonderful information on the rookie training process. Smoke jumper training officer Robert Bente spoke to Laura Wright about a typical day in the life of a rookie.

0600: Wake up. (Didn't have much sleep last night thinking of all I did wrong the day before.)

0700: Show up early for PT (physical training) and put on issued gear. Really hot today—not used to this kind of weather.

0800: Base manager (a no-nonsense, all-work kind of fella) has us on The Mutilator—which works on PLFs (Parachute Landing Falls)—the tower, which works on exits, and the letdown station, where you learn how to rappel out of trees. My execution is off—think the trainers want me to quit.

0900: On to the O-course, which consists of a gravel pit, PLF ramps, exit ramps, rope climb and monkey bars. I'm hot as hell in the suit. Trainer yells, *"Hit it!"* We all freeze, try to look wise and shout back, "Jump-thousand, look-thousand, reach-thousand, wait-thousand, pull-thousand, check your canopy, check your airspace, check your three-rings, disconnect your Stevens, start steering."

1200: Five-mile run. Feel hot, dizzy and disoriented. Like most days. Again I consider throwing in the towel, but my rookie bros won't let me.

1400: Drink my weight in water and feel more hydrated. This afternoon we have class on parachute manipulation and turns on the simulator. Feels like learning to drive, awkward and punchy. I ask the instructor if this is like the real thing. He smiles and says, "Doesn't matter. When you jump out of an airplane, you'll have the strength born out of desperation."

1600: Exhausted, but starving. Head out for dinner with the rookie bros, and over stuffed shells we talk about our first jump tomorrow. It's starting to sink in for all of us that we're doing the one thing we've always dreamed of doing—that no matter what trash is talked about jumpers, to us this is the pinnacle, where we've always wanted to be.

Wilderness
Survival Tips
by Laura Wright

SUMMER

1. In the woods—pine sap, which is easily gathered from tree wounds, makes a wilderness glue and sealant that is hard to beat.

2. To keep deerflies and mosquitoes away while in the woods, pick a sassafras leaf, roll it between your hands and put it behind your ear. The smell will keep them away, and is pleasing to humans.

3. The Little Orange Survival Whistle—it is an item that can contain matches, line and fishhooks, iodine tabs and other medication, money, etc. Its value is doubled with the addition of a small mirror, compass and whistle.

4. Do not throw away that dryer lint! It is a great fire starter. Save it in Ziploc bags and flatten them, or pack it into a small plastic vitamin jar for your survival kit. Dampen the lint with lighter fluid, and you have a "surefire tinder."

5. Water can be found in virtually any outdoor environment. If you dig deep enough and in the right place, you can find the water table. In deciding where to dig, use common sense. Shaded areas, muddy ground, low spots and vegetation-rich areas are more likely to contain water than dried-out high spots with little or no plant life. But MAKE SURE you purify it first, either by boiling or with iodine tablets.

SPRING

1. Balsam fir resin makes an excellent wilderness antiseptic for treating cuts and abrasions. To obtain it quickly, simply pierce the resin bubbles that appear on the bark surface.
2. Wear the lightest footwear possible. It is cooler and less fatiguing on long hikes, dries faster and doesn't interfere with feeling the trail, especially at night.
3. For backcountry wear, choose wool clothing, because it maintains its loft and insulates even when wet.
4. Cattails are one of the most abundant and best-tasting plants out there. They have six edible parts and numerous other utilitarian uses.
5. A pull-string garbage bag makes a GREAT rain poncho. Just cut, rip or tear a hole in the bottom and one on each side. Your head goes

through the bottom one and your arms
through the side ones.

EXTRA: FOR THE KIDS

1. Stay together, DO NOT separate—if with a
   friend or pet.
2. Stay in one place or area. DO NOT WANDER!
3. Put out something bright.
4. Look bigger for searchers.
5. Do not lie on the bare ground.
6. Do not eat anything you are not sure of.

THE ROYAL HOUSE OF NIROLI

...International affairs, seduction and passion guaranteed

Volume 1 – July 2007
The Future King's Pregnant Mistress by Penny Jordan

Volume 2 – August 2007
Surgeon Prince, Ordinary Wife by Melanie Milburne

Volume 3 – September 2007
Bought by the Billionaire Prince by Carol Marinelli

Volume 4 – October 2007
The Tycoon's Princess Bride by Natasha Oakley

8 volumes in all to collect!

THE ROYAL HOUSE OF NIROLI

...International affairs, seduction and passion guaranteed

VOLUME ONE

The Future King's Pregnant Mistress by Penny Jordan

As the King ails and calls for his heir, it's time for playboy prince Marco to claim his rightful place...on the throne of Niroli!

Marco Fierezza: Niroli's playboy prince, he's used to everyone obeying his every command... especially the women he beds!

Emily Woodford loves Marco, but she knows she's not marriage material for a future king. It's devastating when Marco summons her to Niroli as his mistress to continue their discreet affair.

But what will this king-in-waiting do when he discovers his mistress is pregnant...?

Available 6th July 2007

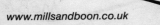

Queens of Romance

The Australian Outback breeds men who are tough to resist and dangerous to marry!

Master of Maramba

Catrina Russell jumped at the chance of a job as governess
on a North Queensland cattle station. But while his young
daughter and Carrie really got on, Royce McQuillan
wondered if beautiful Carrie could be content living an
isolated life with the master of Maramba.

Strategy for Marriage

Tough, eligible and determined cattle baron Ashe McKinnon
took one look at Christy Parker and swept her off her feet.
Ashe was impossible to resist, but he made it clear that any
marriage to him would be on a business basis only. Why
then was Christy fast falling for him?

Available 15th June 2007

Collect all 4 superb books in the collection!

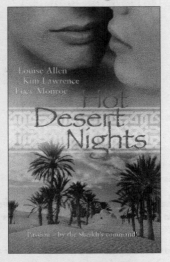

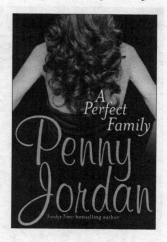

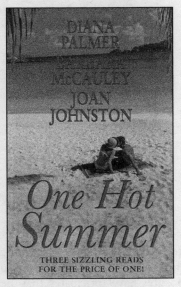

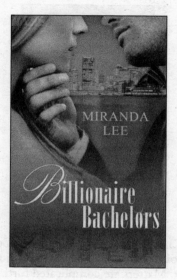

MILLS & BOON

MODERN™

On sale 6th July 2007

MILLS & BOON
Romance

On sale 6th July 2007

Get ready for some summer romance from gorgeous Greece to the crystal clear waters of Cape Cod, the swirling mists of Irish Valentia and the silent majesty of the Outback...

THE FORBIDDEN BROTHER *by Barbara McMahon*

Laura is in a dilemma when she falls in love with her ex-fiancé's twin brother! Is it him she loves, or the mirror-image of a man she was once engaged to?

THE LAZARIDIS MARRIAGE *by Rebecca Winters*

This award-winning author brings you a brooding Greek billionaire you won't forget in a hurry as he battles with his attraction to international it-girl Tracey.

BRIDE OF THE EMERALD ISLE *by Trish Wylie*

Meet cynical Garrett who's about to encounter the woman who will open his heart again...and give him hope for the future.

HER OUTBACK KNIGHT *by Melissa James*

Take an Outback road trip with Danni and Jim as they begin a quest for the truth which might just turn this journey into one of the heart...